SHOOTING ELVIS

DCI Charlie Priest and his team are presented with a bizarre murder that leads to the discovery of low-tech industrial espionage, but is selling your employer's confidential records enough to warrant this particularly sadistic murder? Appearances deceive, and it transpires that the victim may have attracted the murderer because of his facial resemblance to a local serial killer known as the Midnight Strangler. The next victim is murdered in even stranger circumstances, and with old enmities surfacing within his team, Charlie begins to wonder if he himself is the catalyst that motivates the killer...

SHOOTING ELVIS

SHOOTING ELVIS

by

Stuart Pawson

Magna Large Print Books
Long Preston, North Yorkshire,
BD23 4ND, England.

British Library Cataloguing in Publication Data.

Pawson, Stuart
    Shooting Elvis.

    A catalogue record of this book is
    available from the British Library

    ISBN   0-7505-2577-0
    ISBN   978-0-7505-2577-0

First published in Great Britain in 2006 by Allison & Busby Ltd.

Copyright © 2006 by Stuart Pawson

Cover illustration © Old Tin Dog

The moral right of the author has been asserted

Published in Large Print 2006 by arrangement with
Allison & Busby Ltd.

Magna Large Print is an imprint of Library Magna Books Ltd.

Printed and bound in Great Britain by
T.J. (International) Ltd., Cornwall, PL28 8RW

To Doreen

As always, thanks to the following
for their unfailing help:
Dennis Marshall, John Crawford,
Dave Mason, Clive Kingswood,
Dave Balfour.

Special thanks to DCI Peter Ramsay and the staff of the North East RART, who are pioneering new techniques in the fight against crime, and to Karl Floyd, who uses more traditional methods. Apologies to them for my departures from police procedure, but the story takes precedence.

Chapter One

'Don't touch him!' Dave ordered, alarm giving his words a sharp edge. 'He might still be alive.'

I looked at the eyes rolled back in their sockets like one of El Greco's saints, at the silver streak of dried dribble from the toothless cavern of his mouth and at the flies homing in on the corpse, attracted by the smell of corruption that was as inviting to them as freshly baked bread is to hungry coppers.

'Pardon?' I said.

'I don't mean living and breathing alive,' he explained. 'I mean electricity alive.'

I withdrew the hand I'd extended towards the man's neck in the hope of making a snap judgement on the time of death – nothing precise: this morning or last week would have done – and straightened up.

'Right,' I said. 'I see what you mean.'

I'm Charlie Priest of Heckley CID, and Dave is big Dave 'Sparky' Sparkington, one of my detective constables. We work together most of the time and over the years Dave has stopped me making a prat of myself on numerous occasions, plus saving me from stabbings, shootings, various custard pies,

9

and now, electrocution. The body was sprawled in an easy chair with the man's arms resting on his knees, the palms turned upwards as if in supplication. An orange electric cable like the one for my vacuum cleaner snaked away from him and terminated at a wall socket. At this end the wires were bared and wrapped round his thumbs – the brown wire around his left, the blue around the right. A whisky glass was wedged between the man's leg and the chair arm, together with a set of lower dentures, and an empty Bell's bottle lay on the floor. The upper dentures sat in his lap.

I followed the cable to the wall socket. It was plugged into a timer that looked to me as if we were now in an *off* part of the cycle but I wasn't taking any chances. I switched the socket off, using the end of my thumbnail, and Dave wrote the details of the timer in his notebook.

'So did he jump or was he pushed?' he asked, clicking the top back on his pen.

'It's a good way to murder someone,' I said, 'if you can get them to stay still long enough.'

'That's what the whisky's for.'

'And not a bad way to commit suicide.'

'God, you'd have to be desperate. There'd be no going back.'

We'd both seen enough suicides to know that the person usually changes his or her

10

mind when it's too late. The water closes over them, paralysingly cold, and they make a desperate attempt to swim to the side. Or they kick the chair away and as the cord bites into their neck they try to climb the wall. We'd both seen the arcs of skid marks that trainers have left on cell walls, testament to a change of heart.

'What do you think?' Dave asked.

The deceased's home help, who came once a week to clean for him, had found the body and sent for an ambulance. The ambulance men had sent for us. My job was to decide on the degree of police involvement. It was a suspicious death but that didn't mean anything criminal had taken place. An old man – he looked about seventy – had topped himself. That's all. He'd grown tired of life, perhaps he had some medical history, and he'd decided to get out while he could. It happened all the time and I had a certain sympathy for that point of view. Sitting gaga in a nursing home staring at a wall or, worse, daytime television, had little appeal to me.

A suicide would be tidy. We were overworked and over budget, and needed another murder enquiry like giant pandas need contraception. I looked at the old man and the shiny orange cable that connected him to the national grid as if he were a Christmas tree. We were in a depressing room in the downstairs flat of what are known as maisonettes in this part of the world. They are blocks of four flats, each with its own outside door, which have now been taken over as sheltered housing for older citizens. Some are carefully looked after by sprightly ladies and gentlemen, and some have fallen into neglect, inhabited by folks too tired to care, worn out but defiantly clinging on to their independence.

This one was in the latter stages of decay, but in a week or two it would be cleaned out, given a fresh lick of paint and a new tenant would move in. It's a natural progression and it's strictly one way. I looked around the room, trying to read the signs that would tell me about the dead man.

There wasn't much. Three days' worth of tabloids – the raunchier ones with bare breasts and crutch shots *(Danielle has a degree in accountancy, she can massage our figures anytime!!!)* – and an assortment of beer cans, all empty. The stale air in the room stank of tobacco smoke, the mantelpiece and a small table by his chair were fringed by a pattern of cigarette burns and there was a piled-up pub ashtray down by his feet. So he liked a drink and he smoked. They pay me for deductions like that.

The furniture was shoddy and the curtains were dingy. He'd probably inherited them with the flat. I couldn't imagine anybody bringing and installing stuff like that, but he

12

may have lived there a long time. He owned a couple of cheap candle holders, complete with half-burned candles, and a decorative plate celebrating the centenary of Oldfield brass band. The pendulum of a clock in a glass dome swung dispassionately to and fro, to and fro, measuring the passage of time, as if we could forget it. The television was off, plugged into an adaptor it shared with a table lamp and a convector heater. The plastic adaptor, discoloured brown with overheating, lay on the floor under the fateful socket.

I walked over to look at the clock. A little plate screwed to its base bore the inscription: *To Alfred, from his mates at Ellis and Newbolds, April 1996.* Fifty years service and they buy you a clock. How thoughtful. The home help had told us that he was called Alfred Armitage.

'Have you been in one of these flats before?' I asked.

'Mmm,' Dave replied.

'Where would you keep the vacuum cleaner?'

'There's a cupboard under the stairs.'

We moved out of the room into the hallway and Dave pulled open a wooden door with a sloping top. The cupboard was piled high with the normal household junk, but the front item was an ancient upright Hoover, complete with coiled cable.

13

'It might be faulty,' Dave said, so I lifted the cleaner out of the cupboard and carried it into the tiny kitchen. He plugged it in, I pressed the button and the Hoover roared into life.

'Not much wrong with that,' I declared, after it had whined to a standstill.

'So why'd he buy a new length of flex just to top himself?'

'Good question.'

'Ring the pathologist?'

'Yeah, we'd better. And the rest.' I glanced towards the door into the room where the old man lay. The superintendent would not be pleased. 'All is not what it seems,' I said. 'It's a bit late, now, but let's see if we can give the poor old sod some attention. He probably deserves it.'

'Tell me again,' the superintendent, Gilbert Wood, said, glancing at the clock on the wall behind me. We were in his office on the top floor of Heckley nick.

'He looks a good candidate for suicide,' I told him, 'but a few things don't add up. Wiring your thumbs to the mains and then drinking yourself into oblivion might seem a good way to go out, but it does require a certain amount of technical aptitude.'

Gilbert said, 'There was a case somewhere a few months ago where a fellow erected this complicated guillotine and went to

14

sleep under it. When he was well away the blade dropped and decapitated him.'

'I remember it. But I've no doubt he had some mechanical know-how, not to mention imagination. Poor old Alfred Armitage had worked at a company called Ellis and Newbolds all his life, as a storeman. They made brass castings for plumbing access-ories until they went bust. I suspect his electrical skills were about the same as mine – nil, and his imagination didn't extend beyond whipping the knickers off the bimbos in *Sunday Sport*. There was no knife lying around for baring the wires, there was no note and he bought bread, bacon and beer at Morrison's two days ago.'

'Sounds like a good diet.'

'It does, doesn't it?'

'So where are you with it now?'

'PM scheduled for five o'clock. Jeff Caton's on his way there. The rest of the troops are knocking on doors and talking to the neighbours, looking into his back-ground, anything that might help. Ellis and Newbolds closed down in 1998, so we'll have problems finding anybody who worked with him.'

'Big meeting in the morning?'

'I think so. When we know a bit more about the man and his background we'll be in a better position to make a judgement. Who knows? He may have connections with

Colombian drug cartels.'

'Or he might be a harmless old codger who reached the end of his tether.'

'You could be right.'

'Either way, tomorrow could be a long day, so I suggest you get off home while you can.'

'I'll drink to that.'

Back downstairs the troops were filtering in. I asked them all if there was anything earth-shattering and they all shook their heads. 'Then save it for the meeting in the morning,' I told them. In my own office I rang High Adventure, an indoor-outdoor pursuits resort over in Oldfield, and asked to speak to the assistant manager.

'It's Charlie,' I said, when Sonia Thornton answered the phone. Sonia was an inter-national athlete until a car accident smashed her knee two days before she was due to fly out to the Atlanta Olympics. I met her six months ago, after her ex-boyfriend was mur-dered, and we've been seeing a lot of each other since.

'Hi Charlie!' she said, brightly. 'What sort of a day have you had?'

'Busy, as usual. We have a suspicious death on our hands.'

'Oh! Does that mean you'll be late home? The casserole in the slow cooker should be OK for a while. You can leave stuff in them

16

for days and they never dry out. Well, maybe not days, but a long time. Should I have mine or wait for you? Or I could make you...'

'Sonia!'

'What?'

'Shut up. No I won't be late home. Remember what you promised?'

'Um, I'm not so sure...'

'It's tonight or never.'

'Do we have to?'

'Yes. You promised.'

'It's been a long time.'

'I know, and it's not easy for you, but you'll be OK.'

'Right, if you say so.'

'I do. And you want to, don't you?'

'I think so, but I'm a bit scared.'

'Uncle Charlie will look after you.'

'Then I've nothing to worry about, have I?'

'No. What are you wearing?'

'My office clothes. I'll change at your place.'

'Don't be late.'.

'Or you.'

On the way home I called in B&Q and bought ten metres of flex like the stuff that lit up Alfred Armitage. Sonia had run the fastest 5,000 metres in the world in 1996 and was a serious contender for a gold medal. She was unknown outside Yorkshire until the Olympic trials, when she strode home an easy winner and Britain had a new golden girl. After a race in France the press there dubbed her *La Gazelle* and the name stuck. A lot was expected of her.

But a car accident destroyed the dream. Her right knee was shattered and her confidence torn to shreds. Surgery and rest repaired the knee, but when she tried to train again it let her down. When I met her she hadn't run for six years.

You've got to learn to walk before you can run. She'd done some rock climbing as a teenager but wasn't as familiar with the hills as I was. I took her to the Dales, the Lakes and down into Derbyshire. We tramped all over Wensleydale, Swaledale, the North York Moors and the Peak District. If the weather was bad we stayed nearer home, trudging up onto Saddleworth and Withens Clough in our waterproofs, grinning at each other's discomfort as the occasional trickle of rain found its way down our necks.

But before all that I took her to see John Wesley Williamson, better known as Dr Bones. The Doc is physiotherapist to the stars, and his hands have restored the flagging careers of more football and rugby players than Grecian 2000 and Viagra. I don't know what his written qualifications are, if he has any, but his hands work magic. They say he was a major league basketball

18

player in the Caribbean until a brain tumour robbed him of his sight.

I hadn't told Sonia that he was blind when I persuaded her to see him. She said she'd had the best medical advice available, paid for by the AAA, but it hadn't worked. I said she hadn't seen Dr Bones. He rose to greet us when we entered his consulting room and extended a hand. I felt Sonia hesitate as I made the introductions. She shook his hand and we sat down.

'First of all, how are you, Mr Priest?' he asked.

'Fine, Doc. I'm fine.'

'Still got the pellets in your back?'

'Yes, they're still there.'

'But no trouble?'

'Nothing.'

'Well, after all this time I doubt if they will be.' He paused for a beat, before saying, 'I won't charge you for that,' and throwing his head back in laughter. 'And now,' he went on, 'let's have a look at Miss Thornton.'

Sonia was wearing her running shorts and a baggy T-shirt. He walked around his desk, trailing a finger along its edge, and Sonia reached for his extended arm, telling him where she was. 'I'm here.' He took her hand and he asked her to turn round and stand up straight. He put his hands on her neck, massaging it, feeling for knots in the muscles, abnormalities in the bones. Slowly he worked over her shoulders and down her spine, hips and legs. 'Could you lie on the couch, please?' Sonia did as she was told and now he concentrated on her knees: first the left one and then the right.

'Does this hurt?'

'No.'

'Any discomfort?'

'No.'

He flexed her legs, holding each ankle with one hand, the knee with the other, his face pointing away, as if something on the wall was demanding his attention.

He said, 'Your patella was shattered?'

'Yes.'

'Did they clean it up?'

'They took some bits of bone out, I believe.'

'Any other fractures?'

'The top of my tibia.'

'That's a typical dashboard injury.'

I'd carried my chair off to one side slightly, out of the way. I watched the Doc stretch Sonia's legs out and rest them on the couch before feeling his way back behind his desk. 'Come and sit down, please, Miss Thornton,' he said. She swung off the couch and took her seat facing him across the desk.

'Did you play games at school?' he asked.

'No.'

'No sports at all?'

'None. It was a convent school. They didn't

consider it proper for girls to do sports.'

I sat up and smiled. I'd never realised she was a convent girl. I'd heard about convent girls.

'And you believe that your knee problem is due to injury to your cruciate ligament?' he said.

'Yes.'

'Is that what they told you?'

'Mmm.'

'The anterior cruciate ligament?'

'Yes, I believe so.'

'It's an easy diagnosis to make, probably owing more to statistical probability than clinical judgement. Female athletes are more prone to injuries to the anterior cruciate ligament than men, partly because they do not strengthen the supporting muscles by playing games when young, and partly because of the wider hips, although that's obviously not a problem in your case. But your injury is not a strain, caused by strenuous activity. It was traumatic damage, caused by a motor accident. The injury is to your posterior ligament, not the anterior. In other words, the one at the back of your knee. Generally speaking, this is a stronger ligament, much bigger, and does not usually fail. It's the weaker, front one that goes. Does that make sense?'

'Yes.'

'And that we can deal with.'

'We can?'

21

'No problem.'

Rest and then exercise was the solution. She'd had the rest, so now it was a strict regime of exercises to strengthen up the supporting muscles around the knee. Running hammered the joint, but it did little to strengthen it. When the Doc learned that Sonia had access to a million pound gymnasium, you'd have thought he'd won the lottery.

'You're a remarkable young woman,' he told her. 'God has given you a perfect physique and a remarkable talent. You can conquer this. OK, so you probably won't ever run at the Olympics, but you can beat the injury and run again. Maybe even win races. Do you hear what I'm saying?'

Sonia nodded, then said, 'I think so, Dr Williamson.'

'Give me your hands,' he said, and she reached across the table towards his outstretched ones. He took hers and held them gently.

'I remember your accident,' he told her. 'Your not going to the Olympics was a disappointment for all of us. We shared it with you. Look at me.'

Sonia looked at him.

'What do you see?'

She hesitated, then said, 'I see a very kind man. And a wise one.'

He smiled, big teeth flashing in his dark

face. 'I can be really mean at times, my wife tells me. And foolish, too. But if there is one thing I know about, it's disappointment. It takes time, but you have to move on from it. Do the work, Miss Thornton, and I'll listen out for The Gazelle on the sports channel.'

It's an old army trick, spitting on your shoes when you polish them. *Spit and polish*, that's what they call it. At first it dulls whatever shine you've achieved, but then, as you buff the leather, it begins to reflect its surroundings back at you with increased intensity, taking on their colours until the blackness is defined by its absence. Newton declared that the colour black was caused by the total absorption of light, but he never considered an old soldier's boots. Or maybe he chose to ignore this contradiction to his theory. The man gave the shoe a final rub with the yellow duster, held it up for inspection for a moment and placed it on the floor tiles, next to its glowing partner. He pulled on his leather slippers, looked at his watch, and went into the parlour, where the television stood.

He'd listened to local radio throughout the day, when he had the opportunity, but there had been nothing about the strange and untimely death of Alfred Armitage, just the usual gossip about sport. TV news was, hopefully, more comprehensive. After the montage of activities that the people of the area ceaselessly indulge in – fell running, hot air ballooning, white water canoeing – the familiar, slightly embarrassed, face of *Look North* came onto the screen. The presenter gave his nervous smile, swung round to the next camera and launched into his script. A woman had been stabbed in Harrogate; a terrier was trapped down a badger sett near Selby; police were hunting a hit-and-run driver in Bradford. No old men had been found electrocuted.

The man stroked his chin and wondered why the news hadn't broken. Alfred's home help came on Monday mornings and should have found the body, which left plenty of time for the story to leak out. Perhaps the police were withholding the news deliberately while they pursued their lines of enquiry. He smiled at that thought. If that was the case, they were wasting time. It was possible, of course, that the home help never arrived – everybody knew how unreliable social services were – and Alfred was still sitting there, undiscovered. He wondered about making a phone call to speed things up, then decided against it. Patience was the word; he'd give it another twenty-four hours. He killed the BBC and switched to a video he'd made of *Top Gear*.

Sonia had done the work, spending hours after her shift ended on the cycling machine and all the other contraptions that look as if they were modern-day equivalents of Inquisition instruments of torture, until her knees were strong enough to kick over a JCB. Apparently the exercises were designed to develop her slow-twitch muscle fibres. It's the fast-twitch ones that bodybuilders are fond of, so Sonia's legs didn't change shape, for which I was grateful. We'd done the Three Peaks and I'd had her on the Mosedale round in the Lakes, over Pillar, Scoat Fell and Yewbarrow. The descent from Yewbarrow is a real knee killer. When we arrived back at Wasdale Head our knees were throbbing like cobblers' thumbs, but the pain came in matched pairs, hers and mine, so that was OK.

And tonight we were going running for the first time.

Sonia had checked the casserole in the slow cooker and declared it still edible, and was already changed into her kit when I arrived home.

'It's just over three miles,' I told her. 'At a slow pace. In running circles I'm known as the Mr Toad. We'll park in the golf club car park and do a circuit through the woods. That's good fun. Then we'll skirt the golf course until we come out on Rhododendron Drive, which is a straight blast back to the clubhouse. Tonight you are learning the route, that's all. Then you'll be able to come and run it at your own speed, all by yourself.

Do you understand?'

Sonia was tying the lace of her trainer. I put my hand on her head and said, 'Are you listening?'

'Yessir!' she exclaimed, standing up. 'I've got to keep my place behind you. Now come on, let's go.'

It really is fun, running through the woods. Frankly, it's rare that you can describe anything about running as fun, but in the woods you are more concerned about keeping upright than travelling fast. The path is narrow, snaking in and out, up and down, between the trees. Fallen branches have to be skipped over, twigs scratch your legs and brambles tug at your clothes. The sunlight slanting down through the branches flickers across your face and if there's been rain lately, and there usually has, the air smells of leaf mould and wild garlic.

'Log!' I shouted over my shoulder as I adjusted my stride to step over it.

'Got it!' Sonia called back to me.

We burst out of the shadows of the trees onto the rolling fairway of the golf course and she moved alongside me. The sun was low, casting long shadows, and three golfers making their way towards the next hole gave us a wave.

I tried to glance at her without moving my head, so she couldn't see that I was watching her. Sonia's style of running is unusual. Her head pecks back and forward with each stride, like a chicken, as if she's urging herself on. She holds her hands in front of her rather than by her sides, and lifts her knees higher than necessary. Sonia Thornton doesn't run puffing and blowing, head rolling, face contorted with effort. She prances, like a fancy pony in an equestrian show.

'Are you allowed to tell me all about the suspicious death?' she asked, as casually as if we were sitting down for our evening meal.

'It's ... an old man,' I replied, between breaths.

'What happened?'

'It looks ... as if he ... electrocuted ... himself.'

'Poor man. So why is it suspicious?'

'Do you ... mind if I ... tell you ... about it ... later?' I gasped.

We dropped off the grass onto Rhododendron Drive. This is about half a mile long, the first bit slightly downhill before it levels out and becomes a climb. We speeded up slightly on the firmer ground, my big feet going *slap-slap-slap* as they pounded the surface, her smaller ones making a soft *tch-tch-tch* as they skimmed over it. I was feeling tired now, the chest hurting and the legs wobbly. As the slope turned against me Sonia edged away and the gap between us widened. I thought of an elegant yacht leaving the quayside, and I was the hapless fool who had cast her loose, left behind on dry land.

I was over a hundred yards behind when she reached the car. There were about six vehicles parked near the clubhouse and another four at the other side, near the trees. Three of these belonged to dog walkers and the other was mine. I padded up to it and rested my head on my folded arms on the car roof, sucking in air like a black hole. After a few seconds her arm fell across my shoulders and I turned to her, our faces barely an inch apart. Perspiration was glistening on the side of her nose and she smelled of perfume and something else. Something that I thought I liked.

'Are you OK, love?' she said.

'Yeah,' I managed to mumble. 'I'm OK. I'm very OK.'

After we'd showered and eaten I cut the orange wire into four equal lengths and bared the conductors on one of them, just like I'd seen earlier in the day. I asked Sonia to sit in an easy chair and gave her the ends of the wire.

'Right,' I said. 'The cat has choked to death after eating the goldfish, the milkman has left you pasteurised instead of full cream and that new dress you'd ordered from Grattan's catalogue for the company Christmas party is the wrong colour, so you've decided to end it all. By electrocution. I want you to wrap the wires around your thumbs, nice and tight, please.'

She took hold of the cable. 'Like this?'

'Um, no. The copper bit. Round the thumb first, then twist it. And we'll do it like he did, for the sake of accuracy: put the blue around your right and the brown around your left. That's the way.'

Sonia held her hands up. 'Are you going to turn me on?'

'Ah! Any other time, yes, but tonight your luck has changed. Your last payment to the electricity people was lost in the post and they've cut off your supply. You live to fight another day. Let me just make a sketch of the way you've done it.'

I noted the way she'd wrapped the wire around each thumb and then the direction she'd twisted it to make it secure.

'Can I take it off now?' she asked as I closed my notebook.

'Yes, thank you. That was a big help.'

'Did I do it the same as him?'

'Not quite.'

'Oh. So what does that prove?'

'It proves that Sonia Thornton is unique, but I already knew that.' I placed my hand on the back of her neck, letting her short hair run through my fingers, and moved my face closer to hers. 'What did you think of the run?' I asked.

She smiled at me, resting her forehead

29

against mine, and something churned in my stomach. Sonia smiles like a spring morning, when the daffodils are in full bloom, and when it's just for me I wonder what I've done to deserve such riches. 'It was good,' she said. 'I felt ... I don't know, I haven't the vocabulary, but running does something to me. I feel as if I'm flying, as if I could take off and soar. Thanks, Charlie. I'd forgotten the joy of it, but tonight I felt it again. You made it possible, brought it back to me.'

'It's been a long day,' I whispered. 'I think we should have an early...' But by then the room was falling end over end, and I never got to tell her what we should have an early one of.

Alfred Armitage was a bit of a nuisance, I learned next morning when we gathered in the classroom at the nick. His wife had died in 1997, less than a year after he retired, and since then he'd turned to alcohol for solace and gone into a slow decline. Four landlords in the vicinity of his home told how he would come into their pubs early in the evening and slowly get drunk. Then he'd start berating customers about anything that he'd read in the papers – asylum seekers, lenient penalties for murderers, hospital waiting lists – all the usual right-wing scaremongering that the tabloids indulge in. Most of the customers agreed with him, the landlords said, but they came out of the house to get away from it, not have it rammed down their throats night after night. Two of them had asked him to either moderate his opinions or find somewhere else to drink.

'So had he enemies?' I asked.

Apparently not. He was regarded as harmless, they assured me, and some of his drinking companions took delight in winding him up. He was good for a laugh, at his own expense.

'Do we know a cause of death, yet, boss?' somebody wondered.

'Yes,' I replied. 'Sorry, haven't you got it? The PM results say he died of heart failure, probably caused by electric shock. He was discovered at ten-thirty yesterday morning and had been dead for ten to fifteen hours, so the time of death was sometime between seven-thirty and half-past midnight. What did the door-to-doors find?'

'Not much, boss. He was well liked when his wife was alive but he'd driven most of their friends away. One or two seem ripe for a good gossip about him once they get over the shock, so we'll call on them again when we've finished here.'

'That's the way. And let's see if we can find someone from Ellis and Newbolds who knew him. Right, now I want four volunteers. You four will do.' I pointed to four DCs on the front row. 'And you can help with this,' I said, looking at Dave Sparkington.

I pulled the four lengths of orange cable out of my briefcase and handed one to each of the DCs. The wires were already bared for them. 'Here's what I want you to do.'

Five minutes later they were sitting there like the Three Wise Monkeys, plus a friend, with their thumbs wired together. 'Right,' I said. 'Let's see if we can find a winner. You keep the score, Dave.' I examined the wires on the first DC's hands. 'Number one,' I announced. 'Left hand, over the thumb, twisted clockwise. Right hand, over the thumb...'

'Wait a minute,' Dave protested. 'Did you say clockwise?'

I was holding a new stick of chalk. I broke it in two and offered him half. 'Do it on the board,' I told him. 'Make a chart. You know what we're looking for.'

When he was ready we started again. 'Left hand, over the thumb, clockwise.'

Dave wrote it on the board. When he'd finished I said, 'Right hand, over the thumb, anti-clockwise. Number two. Left hand, under the thumb, clockwise. Right hand...'

When it was done we all looked at the chart for several minutes, not sure if it made any sense. No fingerprints were found on the cable or the timer, so we had to assess whatever we could.

'What does it show?' I asked.

Jeff Caton raised a finger.

'Go on, Jeff,' I invited.

'Well, two of them put the wire over their thumbs and two of them put it under, which is not a big help. But they all twisted the wires similarly: clockwise on the left thumb; anti-clockwise on the right.'

Jeff had seen the report we'd done of our first findings, knew what I was getting at, but the Wise Monkeys hadn't.

'How was it done on the body?' one of them asked.

I thought about it, long and hard. Everything pointed at a suicide. There was nothing to suggest that he'd been murdered. He hadn't been robbed; it would be a particularly sadistic way to kill someone; he didn't fit any profile of murder victims.

Except... How many times had I said that?

'On the body,' I began, 'both wires were twisted the same way. Clockwise. So where does that leave us?'

'Clockwise is the way all the wires were twisted by the right hand,' Jeff informed us. 'I presume our volunteers are all right-handed.' They nodded and mumbled their agreement. 'So it looks as if each wire on the body was fixed by a right hand.'

'Which means what?'

'He was ambidextrous,' someone suggested.

'There's always a clever sod,' I responded, flicking my piece of chalk at the offender.

'Which means he had some assistance,' Jeff said.

'Exactly. In other words, boys and girls, this is looking like a murder enquiry. So let's go to it.'

'Can we take these off now?' one of the monkeys asked, proffering his hands.

'Not yet,' I told him. 'For the next part of the experiment I need one of you to volunteer to be plugged in...'

The man with shiny shoes washed his hands after buffing the shoes to a brilliant glow and went upstairs, to the spare bedroom-cum-office where he kept his mementos. His patience had been rewarded. Tuesday morning Radio Leeds had reported the death of an unnamed man by electrocution in Heckley and it made the local TV news in the evening. Wednesday, the *Heckley Gazette* made it their front-page feature and a couple of tabloids gave it a mention. The man with shiny shoes bought all the papers and read them as eagerly as a wannabee pop star.

He reached up to a shelf above his desk and lifted a scrapbook off a pile of similar volumes. He opened the book at the first blank page and placed the carefully prepared newspaper cuttings on it, moving them around until they fit nicely. As the story had spread to page 2 of the *Heckley Gazette* he'd had to buy two papers. The nationals had covered the story briefly and flippantly, more for the curiosity value of the modus operandi than for any possible criminal content or feelings for the victim. When he was satisfied with the layout he tacked the flimsy sheets down with a Pritt Stick and then secured them more permanently with Scotch magic tape, running the back of his thumbnail over the tape to make it invisible. The untimely death of Alfred Armitage had now taken its place amongst his collection of newspaper cuttings of murders and rapes that stretched back over twenty years. Alfred was an impostor, not worthy of appearing alongside such exalted company, but the man with shiny shoes smiled as he closed the book: it was early days, yet.

He finished his breakfast of Kellogg's Fruit'n Fibre, wholewheat toast and marmalade and coffee, and rinsed his plate, bowl, cup, knife and spoon under the hot tap. They could be left to dry naturally. He drove fifteen miles in the early morning traffic to the motorway services and dialled a number that he had written on an old pay-and-display ticket. Just as he thought the answering machine might chime in a breathless male voice said, 'Hello.'

'Have you seen the papers?'

'Yes.'

'You owe me £500.'

'I know.'

'Here's what you do.'

When he'd delivered the message he found his car again, did a u-turn at the next junction and drove the fifteen miles back to town, back to work.

Chapter Two

'Assisted suicide,' Mr Wood stated, placing a copy of the *Heckley Gazette* in front of me. 'That's what they're saying it could be, and my money's on it.'

'I know, Gilbert,' I replied. 'We're considering it, but as he appears to have been in good health and relatively sound of mind, if it was assisted suicide it's almost as good as murder or unlawful killing. The enquiry is the same.'

'What about contacting the organisations that help with these things?'

'Maggie's on with it, but they're hardly likely to hold up their hands. They work outside the law. There's a professor at Leeds University who's a founder member of Die-When-You-Like, or whatever they're called. The Euthanasia Society, that's it. He wouldn't disclose if Armitage had been in contact with them, but he said that electrocution was not one of their recommended methods.'

While Alfred had been on the dissecting table, waiting for his appointment with the pathologist's bone saw, the undertaker had done some work on his face, strictly under the pathologist's supervision. He'd replaced the dentures, applied a tasteful touch of Max Factor where necessary and closed the eyes. Our photographer had taken a series of mug shots and I had an envelope full of them on my desk. Sometimes we ask a police artist to do a drawing from them of the victim's face, for showing to witnesses, and sometimes I do it myself. It's more respectful than using an actual photo, doesn't upset any relatives. I'd intended doing a drawing of Alfred, but hadn't had the time. I pulled a photo from the envelope and studied it.

Alfred had a comedian's face. It was long, with a long jaw and a long nose. His ears were long, stretching down the sides of his face like wardrobe doors. In a different career it could have made him a fortune. As it was, it probably caused him a lifetime of piss-taking and embarrassment. His hair didn't help. He'd kept it all, but even that was an unkind cut. It was as wiry as pan scrubbers, piled up on top of his head in a tangled, lopsided mass, accentuating his head's longness. I felt sorry for him.

'So what's your next move?' Gilbert asked.

'We're locating the people who used the same pubs as him and asking about his acquaintances, movements, anything that might be relevant. Robert has traced some names from Ellis and Newbolds. One of them lives down on Rastrick Road, so I've arranged to see him at ten. He's still unemployed.'

'Good. Good. Keep me informed. So how's the jogging going. I've heard all about it.'

I laughed. 'Who from?'

'Never you mind. Is this the real thing?'

'Your golfing friends. You should stick to fishing, Gilbert. There's less opportunity for gossip.'

'You've been seen out twice this week. It must be love.'

'I'm just her coach, that's all.'

'And I'm the Duchess of York. You're a lucky devil, Charlie. A lucky devil.'

'Call me Simon,' he said, after he'd unplugged the lawn mower I'd caught him using. I admired the striped square of grass in front of his semi and wondered what I was doing wrong. We shook hands and he said, 'Inside or out?'

'Let's sit outside,' I suggested. There was a garden seat under a window, his borders were a blaze of colour and the sun was shining. A blackbird landed on the newly cut lawn, hoping to find a freshly chopped worm, saw us and flew off, protesting loudly. The only discordant note was the family of painted gnomes gathered around a tiny pond.

'Want to buy one?' he asked with a laugh when he realised I was staring at them.

'Um, not if you don't mind,' I replied.

'Awful, aren't they? They're another of my get-rich initiatives that didn't take off. Concrete gnomes. I took them to a few car boot sales, but when I did the figures I was losing about 50p per gnome. And that didn't include my time.'

I took in the neatly edged grass, the carefully banked flowers and the low stone wall with tiny alpine plants growing along its top. It had all been carefully planned. 'The garden's brilliant,' I said. 'Can't you find something in that line?'

'Nothing permanent, and I've said that I wouldn't work for anyone else again. But it's difficult going self-employed. If you earn a bit of money you have to sign off and lose your benefits. Then, if the work dries up, you have to sign on again. You lose a fortnight's benefits every time. There's no encouragement to make the effort.'

'Does your wife work?'

'School dinners. That's all.'

'It's a shame, Simon, and I don't know what to suggest. Now, what can you tell me about Alfred Armitage?'

Simon, I discovered, had started work at Ellis and Newbold straight from school in 1990, which made him about thirty now.

Alfred was the storekeeper, and as part of his training Simon had spent a month in the stores, working with him.

'He was a queer bloke,' Simon said. 'I didn't like him. He was moody, and seemed to resent me being there. And he was always eating. He used to sit at his desk in the corner, his back to the office, nibbling at a sandwich and sipping tea from a flask. All I did was sweep up. I'd have thought he'd have me stocktaking or something, but he never did.'

'Was he particularly friendly with anyone at the factory?' I asked, but Simon shook his head.

'Did he have any enemies?'

'He didn't have any anything,' he replied. 'He came to work, did his job and went home. The stores were open from ten till two-thirty and if you didn't have a note signed by the foreman you couldn't have anything out. The rest of the day he spent on paperwork and stocktaking. He was a stickler for procedure. Nobody had a good word for him, but reluctantly agreed he was doing his job, protecting Mr Newbold's assets.'

'Did Mr Newbold still work there?'

'No. Not after about, oh, 1993 or 4, something like that. He went to live in Spain and we didn't see much of him after that. He still owned the company, I think, but his son managed it for him. If you can call it managing. That's when it started going downhill.'

'What happened to the son?'

'He wasn't interested. He had a degree in biology or something and went to work in California. DNA and all that stuff. Do you reckon Alf was murdered, then? The paper made it sound like suicide.'

'I don't know. The coroner will have to decide that; I'm just the gatherer of evidence. Can you make me a list of everybody you remember from Ellis and Newbold, please?'

'What, now?' he replied, somewhat disconcerted. He'd been looking forward to cleaning the gutters, not racking his brain and making lists.

'Oh, tomorrow will do. But you can give me a head start. Off the top of your head, who would you recommend I see first?'

He thought about it, long and hard, then said, 'Eric Smallwood. He was the secretary-stroke-accountant-stroke-wages-clerk. He just about ran the company towards the end. Mr Smallwood was the only other person who had free reign to enter Alf's little empire.'

'How'd it go, sunshine?' I asked Sparky later that afternoon when we were in my office. Maggie Madison joined us, carrying three mugs of tea.

Sparky took a long sip. 'Ah, that's good,' he said, adding, 'I know we're not supposed

41

to say these things, but you've got to admit that women make better tea than men do.'

'It's years of practice,' Maggie told him. 'The famous glass ceiling that's holding us down has a lot to answer for.'

'But Maggie,' Dave countered, 'if you got through the glass ceiling you'd only complain that we were looking up your skirts.'

'That's why I wear trousers.'

'Does anybody know anything about this suspicious death we're supposed to be investigating?' I asked.

'Sorry, boss,' Dave replied. 'I've turned up a couple of things in the pubs. Apparently Alfred had made a new friend recently. None of the regulars bothered much with him, but suddenly this chap appeared on the scene and they were like old buddies. The new bloke did all the paying, apparently, so they thought that Alf was just sponging off him. I have a description. Also a strange white van was seen in a couple of the car parks, which may have belonged to him. They don't get much motorised trade in these estate pubs.'

'A Transit type?'

'No, a small one. Five hundredweight.'

'Wasn't a small white van seen in the road outside his house on the day he died?'

'One report of it, that's all.'

'One's enough.'

'Have you found anything?'

I told them about my meeting with green-fingered Simon. 'Tomorrow I'm seeing this Eric Smallwood,' I said. 'Which of you fancies working a Saturday morning?'

They both volunteered but I gave Dave the job. Maggie's husband can be a bit touchy about the hours she works, and Dave would be more amenable for a lunchtime drink. Then I remembered that I was down for a training spin with Sonia in the afternoon, so the drink was out.

'How's the family?' I asked Dave as we drove out of the nick car park. His daughter, Sophie, was the first member of the family to go to university – Cambridge – which earned her hoggings of Brownie points in her father's eyes. Then, in her final year, she became the first member of the family to get pregnant out of wedlock, which redressed the balance somewhat. She's my goddaughter, so I have always taken a godfatherly interest in her welfare. All part of my duty, of course, and nothing to do with her being a real stunner.

'They're all fine,' he replied. 'Sophie sends her love, as always.'

'And how's young Splodge?'

I felt the warmth of Dave's grin without having to turn my head. Sophie was living with her boyfriend, whose family owned half of Shropshire or Shrewsbury or some-where, and had redeemed herself by making

43

Dave granddad to a healthy bouncing boy.

'He's brilliant,' he told me. 'Just brilliant.'

'Have you bought him his first football boots, yet?'

'No, not yet.'

'I'll get him some, then.'

'It's a bit early, at eight weeks.'

'Is it?'

'So I'm told.'

'Right. What's the address again?'

The man with shiny shoes glanced at the computer display on the dashboard as he turned into the multi-storey car park. He'd covered 78 miles in 95 minutes, giving him an average speed of 49.3 miles per hour. Not bad for that journey. He took a ticket from the machine, the barrier lifted and he followed the arrows up the ramps, all the way to the top floor.

There were only five cars there, out in the open, and three of them had been parked all night, by the look of the condensation on the windows. None of them was a blue Rover 75. He drove back down a floor and manoeuvred into a spot where he could see the *Up* ramp. He was early but that was OK. He'd leave as soon as the job was done and have an all-day breakfast at the Truckstop café, back in Heckley.

Brian Bousfield followed the instructions he'd been given to the letter. It was only a fifteen-minute drive for him, and he swung into the car park at one minute before nine. He parked on the top floor near the stairs, checked for the tenth time that the package was safe in the glovebox and swung his legs out onto the concrete floor.

It was chilly up at this height and he wasn't wearing a coat, just his normal T-shirt and shell suit bottoms. The elderly Rover had central locking but not remote control. He locked the car doors with the key then unlocked them again. He tried a door to confirm it was unlocked and turned his back on the vehicle, heading downstairs.

The man with shiny shoes saw him arrive. When another five minutes had passed he pulled a Burberry tartan baseball cap low onto his head, turned up his coat collar and headed for the staircase. As always, it stunk of Friday night's piss and vomit in there. He almost puked with disgust as he strode up one floor and gratefully found himself out in the open, in the fresh air. The Rover was right where he expected it to be. Keeping his head down so as not to present a full facial to any handy CCTV camera he slipped into the driver's seat, reached across to the glovebox and extricated the manila envelope. A rare smile flickered across his face as he weighed the package in his hand. He didn't bother opening it. He'd asked for £500, that's all, and had no reason to believe he'd be short-changed. Three minutes later he handed his ticket and a pound coin to the attendant, the barrier lifted and he turned into the traffic, heading home. Before he reached the motorway he stopped in a lay-by and counted the money. It was all there, the notes were used and their numbers random. He wound down his window, flung the Burberry cap into the ditch and continued on his journey. All in all, it had been a good morning's work. For both of us, he thought.

Brian Bousfield had left the car park and walked to the shopping mall, as instructed. There had been an awkward moment when he ordered a coffee and the schoolgirl behind the counter had asked him what sort. He'd blustered something about white and the girl, taking in the bulging biceps with their obligatory tattoos, gave him a regular latte. He drank it slowly and thought about things.

In February 1992 he'd jumped to his feet in a Court of Law and sworn to kill a man. 'You're dead!' he'd screamed, his voice echoing between the panelled walls and over the polished rails and upturned faces. 'You're dead. You're dead meat. I swear it. I'll kill you if it's the last thing I ever do.'

He was twenty-two years old at the time, and seventeen months earlier he'd been to a disco at a local pub which had acquired a reputation for good music, cheap drinks and easy availability of drugs, for those who wanted them. Brian's sister Julie, three years his junior, had begged to be allowed to go with him.

It had been a good night. The weather was warm and the pub had opened its french windows so the party could spill out into the beer garden. They'd danced in a crowd, the drinks flowed freely and there was no trouble. At fifteen minutes past eleven the DJ started to wind things down and the dancers split into couples, holding each other close, stroking, nibbling and kissing. 'Baby I'm A Want You', by Bread was playing, he remembered, followed by the Hollies' 'All I Need Is the Air That I Breathe'.

He was dancing – although that was hardly the word for what they were doing – with a girl called Bernadette who worked at the local egg-packing factory. She had the biggest tits in the village and, according to her reputation, only did it with friends. Although, his workmates were quick to assure him, she had no enemies. He felt her pressing her loins against his, rotating them to the music, and looked around for his sister. Julie was dancing, not too closely, with an older man he'd seen before but didn't know. They were talking, not smooching, and she looked happy. He gratefully turned away and explored Bernadette's ear with his tongue.

Thirty minutes later he was having sex with her in the shadow of the cemetery wall.

The grass was dry, the moon was high and Bernadette was a willing, enthusiastic partner. What he learned much later was that 150 yards away his sister, Julie, was having reluctant sex with the older man. Next morning he learned that he'd strangled her and the next day the tabloids proclaimed that the Midnight Strangler had claimed his third victim.

Terence Paul Hutchinson was arrested and charged within days. He pleaded Not Guilty and the trial lasted two weeks, during which he claimed that his victims were willing sexual partners with reputations for being good-time girls. The evidence against him was overwhelming and he was sentenced to life imprisonment with a thirty-year tariff, but that wasn't good enough for Brian Bousfield. Their father had been diagnosed with terminal cancer shortly before Julie's murder, and he didn't live to see the trial. Along with the death of his sister, Brian blamed Hutchinson for his father's rapid decline and death, too. When Hutchinson had grinned and waved at the jury as he was being led away, like the main attraction at the end of a concert, Brian had been unable to hold back his feelings.

It was bravado, of course, but for twelve years he'd thought of Julie every day. Ten times a day. Some of it was hatred of the man who killed her, some of it despair at a legal system that allowed murderers to live in luxury until they were released, and some of it sorrow for the way his own life had been blighted since then. Not once did he feel any guilt, or recognise that his own driving force that night had not been too dissimilar to that of the man he hated.

And then the telephone call came. Hutchinson was out of jail, it told him, and living under an assumed name at a secret address in Heckley, Yorkshire.

'What about the thirty-year tariff?' he'd asked.

'Good behaviour,' he'd been told, 'or perhaps he'd appealed to the Home Secretary. He may even have been deemed "cured". Nobody serves full term these days.'

The man on the phone wouldn't say who he was, but he had reasons of his own for wanting Hutchinson dead. He was related to one of the other victims. He perfectly understood if Brian didn't want to be involved with the actual execution, but he himself would be going ahead with it. He knew people who did this sort of thing, and £500 would help towards their expenses.

Brian pondered on what he'd been told, and thought of things that people had said to him about closure and getting on with his own life. Julie's death had ruined every relationship he'd had. Maybe they were right. Maybe, with Terence Paul Hutchinson dead, he'd be able to move on.

'Five hundred?' he'd queried.

'Yeah, that's all. Payable after the deed's done.'

'How will I know you've done it?'

'It will be in the papers,' he was told.

'We don't get the Yorkshire papers.'

'Then I'll have to make sure it gets reported in the nationals, won't I?'

The man with shiny shoes parked his car on the drive in front of his detached house and checked the computer. He'd averaged 41.2 miles per hour at an average fuel consumption of 34.5 miles per gallon. Slightly worse than usual, he thought. Perhaps the car needed a service. He belched and tasted the egg and sausage he'd eaten a few minutes earlier. Up in the spare bedroom-cum-office he found the scrapbook dated 1990–1994 and leafed through the pages until the long, asinine face of Terence Paul Hutchinson was staring at him. He held a picture of Alfred Armitage next to it and began to laugh. Allowing for the age difference, the passage of time and the ravages of prison life, the similarity between the two men was remarkable.

'Sorted,' he said, triumphantly, and closed the book.

Eric Smallwood lived in a neat Sixties-style

bungalow with long views across the Calder valley. Its main feature was the external chimney built in random stone, acting like a buttress for the rest of the building. The garden was neat and a six-foot lapboard fence isolated the neighbours on each side. One of the neighbour's gardens boasted a For Sale sign, with the name of a local estate agent.

'Just a sec,' Dave said as I parked the car in the road, across the front of Smallwood's drive. He tapped a number into his mobile and I listened to his half of the conversation.

'Oh, hello. You're acting for a bungalow that's for sale on the Hebden Bridge road, just outside Heckley. How much is it please?' He pulled a face and asked how many bedrooms it had. 'OK, thanks a lot. No, I'll call into your office for the details. Thanks. Bye.'

He switched the phone off, saying, '£349,995 for a quick sale. Cheap at half the price, I'd say.'

'And vital information. C'mon, let's see what the man has to say.'

The drive was block-paved with no weeds or moss growing in the cracks. I wondered how he managed it. Block paving is not as labour saving as I'd hoped it would be. The garage door was closed and no car stood on the drive. Dave pressed the button on the white PVC doorframe and within seconds the front door opened. Even his bell worked.

51

This man was too good to be true.

Mr Smallwood was wearing a tweed jacket, with shirt and tie, and cavalry twill trousers, with turn-ups. He was tall and slightly stooped, and on his head was a black and silver helmet, as worn by cyclists.

'Mr Smallwood?' Dave asked.

'Er, yes.' He sounded furtive and stepped across the threshold, pulling the door half-closed behind him. 'Who are you? I was just going out.'

'DS Sparkington and DI Priest, from Heckley CID. Could we have a word, please?'

'Well, um, it's very inconvenient. What's it about?'

'We're making enquiries into the background of Alfred Armitage. You may have read that he was found dead a few days ago. We understand you used to work with Mr Armitage at Ellis and Newbolds.'

'Yes, that's right, but I don't see how I can help.'

'You probably can't, sir, but we have to follow every avenue. You were chief accountant there, I believe. For how long did you know Alfred?'

'Actually I was company secretary. The accounts were just a part of my remit. How long did I know Alf for? I'm not sure. I worked there from July 1969 until we closed in October 1998. Twenty-nine years. Alf started before me and retired about 1996, I

52

think, so I must have known him for, what, twenty-seven years?'

I took his word for it. All those dates were making my head buzz. I glanced down at his feet and noticed that he wasn't wearing bicycle clips. Very suspicious.

'Can we sit down somewhere, please?' Dave asked. 'We still have a few more questions to ask.'

Smallwood looked uncomfortable and pulled the door closed. 'Um, yes,' he replied. 'We can sit round there.'

He led us round the corner to where a hardwood table and two chairs stood on a small patio. He took one chair, me the other, and Dave perched on the corner of a low wall that enclosed a rockery. The sun was shining and a peacock butterfly settled on a sedum plant, flicking its wings closed then slowly lowering them in some ritual designed to repel predators. A glass of lager would have gone down well, but Smallwood wasn't offering. His helmet was one of those streamlined ones that project at the back. It said *JetPro* on the side, and was fastened with a clasp under his chin.

'Did Mr Armitage have any special friends at Ellis and Newbolds?' Dave was asking. A bluetit landed on the fence, looked at us and flew off in a huff. Someone nearby was cooking bacon.

Alfred, it appeared, was an insular sod

who never spoke to anybody if he could help it.

'So why did Ellis and Newbold close after all those years?'

Smallwood shuffled in his seat. 'Various reasons,' he replied. 'Cheap imports from the Far East. To start with they were counterfeiting our products, right down to the packaging. Mr Newbold tried to take action: spoke with the Department of Trade; various politicians; but to no avail. Then they started to undercut us on the open market. There's not much you can do about that.'

'Was there ever any suspicion of any irregularities at the factory?' Dave asked.

'Irregularities? What do you mean: irregularities?'

'You tell me. I'm not an accountant, but it occurs to me that Mr Newbold could have been siphoning off excess profits, or Alfred could have been diverting valuable non-ferrous metal to friends in the scrap trade. In your position as chief accountant did you ever suspect anything like that?'

Negative. The firm had gone into steady decline, caused by unfair competition, and, in spite of attempts to diversify, the writing had been on the wall for the final few years. Say it, Dave, I thought. Ask him if he had his neatly manicured fingers in the till. Instead he asked for the names of other workers at the factory, and Smallwood offered to make a comprehensive list over the weekend.

'Anything to add, Chas?' he asked, turning to me.

'No,' I replied in my best bedside voice. 'I think you covered everything. Thanks for your cooperation, Mr Smallwood, and we apologise for disturbing you.' I rose to my feet and they did the same, Dave brushing a hand across the seat of his pants.

As we walked round to the front I said, 'I take it you're a keen cyclist, Mr Smallwood.'

He shook his head and looked puzzled. 'A cyclist? No. What made you think that?'

'Oh, sorry. The helmet. I assumed you were about to go for a ride. It's a lovely day for one.'

He reached up and touched the helmet. 'Oh, this. No, I wear it for medical reasons.'

'Medical reasons?' I echoed, instantly regretting the incredulity in my voice.

'Yes. The hospital suggested I wear one. I had a scan a few years ago and they discovered that my skull is paper-thin. Thinner than an egg shell. Any simple knock could prove fatal.'

I hoped I wasn't smiling as I asked, 'And they suggested you wear it all the time?'

'Well, actually, I asked if it would be a good idea and they said it would.'

I wanted to know more but couldn't trust myself. Dave does deadpan better than me. I heard him say, 'What do you do at night?

If you fell out of bed it could be nasty, but you couldn't sleep in that thing. You'd never get comfortable.'

'You're right,' Smallwood replied. 'I have another for in bed. One without the streamlined back.'

'A good idea. Well, thanks for your time, Mr Smallwood.' Dave probably offered a handshake but I was facing the other way, heading down the drive back to the car, so Smallwood couldn't see the tears trickling down my cheeks. I held on to my composure as we drove off, but seconds later I pulled into the side and we both lost it completely.

The troops were massed in the office when I came down from my Monday morning meeting with the super. I was in a good mood. The force was in the process of creating dedicated teams for investigating murders, and, trying to keep ahead of the game, the ACC wanted me to head a pilot scheme in East Pennine. It doesn't exist if it hasn't an acronym, so I was now surrogate chief honcho of the local Homicide and Major Enquiry Team, known as HMET. I had no illusions – they wanted me to catch the flak and do the dirty work of splitting up a winning team until someone with a higher rank could take over – but I didn't mind: they were offering me Acting DCI, and I'd only be doing what I was already doing, so I pretended to be surprised and grateful and said 'Thank you' like a good little boy.

There'd been the usual quota of drunks, thefts and assaults over the weekend, but apart from two burglaries there was nothing to interfere with the silky-smooth running of the CID. Jeff Caton, one of my sergeants, had sat in on the meeting with Mr Wood and he would oversee the everyday stuff while I concentrated on the Alfred Armitage job.

Another of my sergeants, Eddie Carmichael, was holding court, some of the younger DCs grinning widely at his comments. 'That's right, guv, isn't it?' I heard him say as I approached.

'What?' I asked.

'I was just saying: the only problem with an inflatable woman is that she can't help you change the duvet cover.'

'Leave me out of it,' I replied.

'But that's only twice a year,' someone said.

'OK, listen up,' I told them. 'Jeff is doing the everyday stuff. Pick your team, Jeff. Meanwhile, anybody who's never done a murder enquiry but would like to, raise your hand.'

A couple of hands went up. 'I thought it was a suspicious death,' one of the owners asked.

'It is, but we treat it like a murder enquiry until we are convinced otherwise. OK, we want follow-up interviews with people we've already seen, we have a list of drinking acquaintances to talk to, and later this morning we should have a list of just about everybody who worked at Ellis and Newbolds. A Mr Smallwood is preparing that for us. Could you collect it, please, Eddie, and you might like to do a follow-up while you're there. I think you'll find him an interesting character. See Dave's report for further details.'

Dave stirred as I mentioned his name but didn't speak.

'Anybody anything to add?' I asked.

'Yes,' John Rose replied. 'Alfred died sometime on Sunday, but the landlords in the two pubs he called his locals say they hadn't seen him for several days, which was unusual. I was wondering about widening the search, seeing if he'd found a new watering hole and maybe a new audience.'

'Yep, do it,' I said. Maggie Madison was staying silent, so I brought her into the discussion. 'Maggie. I'd like you to talk to his neighbours again, but first see if you can track down the owners of the company. Apparently Mr Newbold lived in Spain, but I don't know if he's still alive.'

People were standing up, scraping chairs, pulling jackets on. 'One last thing,' I shouted above the noise. 'And I'm disappointed to have to say this.' All faces turned to me. 'Last week a photograph of poor Alfred Armitage appeared in some of the tabloids. It was of his death mask, taken by our own photographic department for use in the investigation. At least a hundred people have access to that picture, and one of them leaked it to the press. It's not the sort of behaviour expected of professionals, and whoever leaked it will be out on his neck if we find out who it was. That's all.'

Off they went, every one of them hurt by my comments. Except for the one who took the pieces of silver. We'd had a good run at Heckley, with the best team in the business, but time was catching up with us. Some of my top officers had moved on, and I hadn't always had a say in their replacements. I held no truck with prejudices of any kind, but political correctness, carried to its extremes, was just as damaging. Policemen – and women – were individuals, with different strengths, priorities and abilities. If you were backs to the wall in a city pub with a bunch of yobbos facing you down, you didn't want to be with the fast-track graduate with the Bachelor of Law degree, unless he was also a black belt in tai kwando, or whatever. In a good team you need a spread of talents and you deploy them appropriately. That had been my strength, and it worked. We had the best clear-up rate in the division.

Dave Sparkington followed me to my office and sat in the spare chair, slumped forward, elbows on knees. I pinned the jobs priority chart on the board, tore Saturday and Sunday off my calendar and read the day's homily out loud: *'It is a curious subject of observation and enquiry, whether hatred and love be not the same thing at bottom'.*

'Who said that?' he asked, without looking up.

'Erm, let me see ... Nathaniel Hawthorne.'

'Who's he?'

'He was a biologist, I think. They named a bush after him.'

'Did they? I wish I'd gone to grammar school. We never learned useful stuff like that at the sec. mod.'

'You'd have looked silly in the cap.'

'I know. God, how we pitied you lot having to wear one of those.'

'So what's bothering you?'

'Nothing. Did you go jogging over the weekend?'

'No, we went running. We're runners, not joggers. You were invited, you could have joined us.'

'What, with you and Gazelle? No, you've left me behind, I'm afraid. So why was he sent to us?'

'Who?' As if I didn't know.

'Eddie the Lip.'

'You mean DS Carmichael. Career development, I'm told.'

'Uh! He needs career development like I

need breast implants.'

'What's he done now?'

'Oh, nothing. He was sounding off about unmarried mothers, that's all. He has strong feelings on the subject.'

'I don't think Sophie comes into that category, Dave. They'll get married, as soon as the studying's over.'

'It was all for my benefit, no doubt about it.'

'Well, keep your hands off him.'

'I'll try, but listen – I've been thinking about Ellis and Newbolds and I reckon someone was ripping them off. They made things out of brass, and brass is valuable. Alfred was probably in a position to augment his wages by siphoning off some of it to the friendly neighbourhood scrap dealer. On the other hand, Smallwood could have been cooking the books. Or, third alternative, they could have been in it together.'

'So what do you suggest?'

'I'm not sure. I wouldn't mind talking to the local scrappies, looking at their books, but it's been a long time. What did you think of Smallwood?'

'Ah!' I grinned at the memory. 'He's weird, that's for sure, but I think we were probably unkind to him. If he has a paper-thin skull, wearing a helmet is a sensible precaution.'

'*If* he has one.'

'Mmm. OK, you talk to the scrappies. I'm

61

having a couple of hours on reports and paperwork. Maybe we can get out somewhere later.'

Dave went off and I wondered about what he'd said. He was right about one thing: DS Carmichael had been foisted on me by HQ. Every month I'd report that I was short-handed, and every month nothing would happen, until last month when Eddie was seconded to me. I got straight on to the chief superintendent and asked what it was about. CID sergeants are not moved sideways for nothing.

Eddie had had a chequered career. He'd started in East Pennine and made it to sergeant, then made the big jump to the Met to get into plain clothes. Unfortunately a fracas with a suspect saw him busted back to uniform and he eventually came back north. At HQ a female in the case building unit had accused him of harassment after she'd spurned his overtures, which had led to him being moved to Heckley under a 'leave it with me' agreement.

'You can sort him out, Charlie,' the chief had told me. 'He has some old-fashioned ideas, that's all. Nothing you can't deal with.'

His record didn't bother me. If he was a good copper I could forgive him the odd transgression, but I wasn't happy about Dave's attitude towards him. We weren't bobbies anymore, we were a human resource, trained to salivate when required, to run and fetch on demand, and to turn the other cheek when some thieving little rat-fink with the IQ of a sausage gave us two fingers as he walked free. Clear-up figures were the Holy Grail; putting bodies in front of judges and convicting them counted for little. The old order was changing, and it hurt, but there was nothing we could do about it. Sometimes, I thought, we needed more officers with old-fashioned ideas.

I'd met him before, I remembered. It had been bugging me but suddenly it all came back. The Old Mother Twanky case, we called it. Edith Tweddle lived all alone in sheltered housing, never bothering a soul, until one evening she became over-excited while watching an old Cary Grant film and spontaneously combusted. I was duty inspector for the first time in my burgeoning career, and the green-eared PC who called me out was the one and only Eddie Carmichael.

The postman had smelled smoke and sent for the police and fire brigade. All we found of Mrs Tweddle and the easy chair she'd been sitting in was a pile of ash, a right foot and a left hand. She was identified by her wedding ring.

It made the nationals as another example of the mysterious phenomenon known as spontaneous human combustion. The papers were full of it, and the more lurid ones showed pictures of the poor woman's remains. Eddie and his sergeant were interviewed by the press and credited with extravagant descriptions of the scene. They made great capital out of relating that one foot, one hand and the rest of the room were completely untouched by the conflagration, as if that were proof of strange forces at work.

I had a word with the fire chief and learned differently. In every recorded case of supposed spontaneous human combustion there has been a possible source of ignition close to the body – usually a cigarette or an electric fire. Mrs Tweddle was a smoker, *and* there was a three-kilowatt electric fire blazing away eighteen inches from her remains.

And, the fire chief told me, we are composed largely of fat. Particularly elderly women. Once ignited, we burn like a candle. Light a fire, he said, and let it burn out – doesn't matter if it's a bonfire or a campfire – when it is dead there will be the unburned ends of pieces of wood surrounding the ashes, just like Mrs Tweddle's hand and foot. I made a statement at a press conference, expounding my newly found knowledge and pooh-poohing the spontaneous combustionists, and it was shown on *Look North.*

I found an Argos catalogue in Jeff's drawer and looked at the price of mountain bikes. They were cheaper than I expected. Sonia was in a different league to me when we went out jogging. Sunday morning we'd driven to the park and I'd accompanied her on one three-mile circuit; then she'd done another one, much faster, while I waited in the car. Afterwards she'd suggested that in future she might even run the two miles back home. She'd bought a ledger and started entering her times and distances in it. Maybe a mountain bike would give me an edge, I thought.

John Rose and Dave came in together just as I finished the reports. We always appoint a report reader to scrutinise them and extract possible pertinent details, but I like to go through them myself, when I have a chance. We call it gatekeeping. They brought chicken and stuffing sandwiches in with them, and we had a picnic in the big office.

'Find anything?' I asked Dave after he'd supplied me with a mug of tea.

'Not much. Jeb Smith and Son is now run by the son, Jeb junior, who just happens to have a degree in physics. And it's a recycling centre not a scrap yard. He'd just started working for his dad back in the early Nineties, and he couldn't be sure but he suspects that they were taking stuff from Ellis and Newbolds. He certainly remembers the company, but no names. He admits that things were a bit shady in those days. Unfortunately his father is dead, so we can't ask him, but it did mean that young Jeb

65

spoke more freely.'

'Fair enough. It was worth a try. Have another word with him when he's had time to think about it. What have you found, John?'

'I'm not sure. The landlord at the Coiners, up on the tops, thinks Alfred and another man may have been in once or twice a couple of weeks ago. They sat in a side room, so the landlord couldn't see him clearly, but a couple of his regulars may have. Unfortunately I was a bit early. He said they don't come in until about two, and I didn't think you'd want me hanging about in licensed premises for another couple of hours.'

'No, we couldn't have that. Are you happy if Dave and I have a ride up there and talk to the regulars? I need some fresh air.'

'No problem. I've plenty to do.'

I looked at my watch and then at Dave. 'Fifteen minutes, Booboo. OK?'

He tipped me a wink. 'Ready when you are, Yogi.'

There was a note on my desk from Eddie Carmichael saying that he'd arranged to go to the indoor shooting range to keep his firearms authorisation up to date. About half of us are authorised firearms users, but I'm not one of them. I threw the note in the bin and rang High Adventure. Sonia was staying in her own house through the week, because my hours were uncertain. We chatted for a while and I said I'd drive over that evening if I didn't finish too late. She told me she was doing some speed work on the track at Huddersfield after she finished, but she'd be home by seven. Earlier in the day she'd climbed the ice wall at the centre, one of the girls in the office was pregnant, some celebrity from local TV had been practising her snowboarding all morning and did I want a new fleece from Tog 24 because they were having a sale?

'Wait! Wait!' I interrupted when she paused for breath. 'I've work to do. Tell me all about it when I see you.' I put the phone down feeling ridiculously happy, like I always do after I've spoken to her.

We drove to the Coiners in my car. The pub is a relic from the days when stagecoaches and packhorses roamed the hills, carrying wool and cotton and finished goods from town to mill and mill to town. Not much has changed since then, including the plumbing. I glanced round, taking in the obligatory sales rep on his way between the two counties; and the middle manager out with one of the typists, somewhere off the beaten track. I ordered two halves of Black Sheep and explained to the landlord who we were.

Tom and Francis were two brothers who lived in a farmhouse a few hundred yards from the pub. Every lunchtime they drove there in an old van, taking turns behind the wheel so one of them could overindulge, and had the landlady's special. In the evening they came again and played cribbage for pennies. I didn't dwell on what they might do for the rest of the time.

'Aye, that's 'im,' Tom assured us, after Dave showed him the photo of Armitage's dead face. We'd explained who we were and asked them about any strangers they'd seen in the place two or three weeks earlier. Two interlopers into their snug little back room, with its tobacco-stained walls, flypapers and beer-ringed tables was quite an event. They remembered them well. One was tall, they said, with a long, unhappy face and bushy hair; the other one, unfortunately, was more ordinary.

'Aye, that's the one,' Francis confirmed, when Tom passed him the photo.

'But what about the other one?' Dave asked. 'What did he look like?'

'Sort of ... ordinary,' we were told.

'How tall?'

'Not very. Well, not as tall as you. A bit stocky, you might say.'

'How old?'

They looked at each other. 'Forty-ish?' one of them suggested.

'Aye, forty-ish.'

'Or mebbe a bit older. Not as old as us. Or you.'

'Thanks. What was he wearing?'

Chapter Three

'And he was wearing one of these cycling helmets; the type with the long tail at the back for streamlining. Sitting there as large as life, having his dinner with this thing on his head.' Eddie Carmichael turned when he realised we'd walked into the room. 'Hi, guv,' he said in his offhand way. 'I'm just telling them about Eric Smallwood. Boy, did you set me up with him. If he's OK in the head I know where there's a big house full.'

Everybody calls me Charlie. I encourage it. Except when somebody of a more senior rank is present, of course. But we're a team, and I know that every one of them would risk his or her neck for me, and I for them. Except Eddie. He rarely uses my name, which is his problem, but there was something about the way he said 'Hi, guv' that I didn't like, as if being on first names was a step too far for him, like prostitutes never kissing their clients. Besides, 'guv' is a Met expression; we don't use it up here.

'How did the shooting go?' I asked, making a gun shape with my hand.

'No problems,' Eddie replied. 'The King can safely be laid to rest.'

'The King?' I queried.

'Elvis,' he explained, and smiles were exchanged around me.

'Right,' I said, not having a clue what he was talking about. There were some things in the department that I wasn't party to. 'I take it you passed,' I added.

'With flying colours.'

'Good. I'm sure we'll all sleep more soundly in our beds for knowing that. Did Smallwood give you a list?'

'Right here.' He handed me a foolscap sheet with a list of names in minute handwriting covering the top three inches. 'What a fucking tosspot,' he went on, now addressing his audience again. 'And he has this big Scalextric track in his front room. Biggest you've ever seen. He sits there all day, with his helmet on, pretending he's Michael Schumacher. What a fucking tosspot.'

Dave said, 'What difference does it make what he does in his own home? He's not hurting anybody. Maybe he does have a thin skull.'

Eddie spun towards him, eyes wide, hackles crackling with static. 'Who rattled your cage?' he demanded.

'I joined the police to protect people like him from bullies and bigots,' Dave stated. 'Maybe he is a bit weird, but that's not against the law.'

'Who are you calling a bully and a bigot,

70

constable?' Eddie replied, easing himself off his chair. John Rose started to whistle and looked towards the window. Somebody else coughed and said, 'More tea, vicar?'

'If the boots fit...' Dave responded, pulling his legs under him.

'Hold it! Hold it!' I interrupted, extending an arm between them. 'That's enough.' I pointed at Eddie, saying, 'My office, now.'

I heard the scrape of his chair as he stood up and felt him follow me towards my little enclave in the corner. He closed the door and sat down.

'Rule one,' I told him. 'When that outer door is closed there are no ranks in this team. Everybody has an equal contribution to make. OK?'

'I'll not take crap from him or anyone else,' he replied.

'You'll have to. It's the way we do business. Dave's a good cop and a blunt speaker. Sometimes that's what we need. You're a bit like that yourself, so let's try to rub along, hey? We don't have time or room for personal animosities.'

'If you say so.'

'I do.'

'Will you be telling him the same?'

'I certainly will.' I stood up and opened the door for him. As he walked away I shouted, 'Dave. In here. Now.'

He came lumbering through the door and

sat down. I spent a few seconds looking at a letter from a local councillor alerting me to the underage drinkers in one of the town centre hostelries, and a note from HQ about a collection for a memorial seat for some old superintendent who'd died at the age of ninety-nine. I did a quick calculation. If he retired at sixty then he'd drawn his pension for longer than he'd made contributions. That's the way to do it. I placed the notes side by side and turned to Sparky.

'Did you know about this giant Scalextric?' I asked him.

'Never saw it,' he replied.

'What are we going to do about it?'

'I think we'd better check it out, don't you?'

'Mmm, first excuse we get.' I handed him the notes. 'Stick these on the board, please; any contributions to me. Now look suitably chastised and keep out of Eddie the Lip's way.'

Maggie's team of door-knockers had come up with something. Alfred's next door neighbour, an elderly curtain-twitcher with a penchant for *Songs of Praise* on television, had heard Alfred's front gate creak just as the choir was breaking in to 'Oh Lord We Heard Thy Trump On High'. She'd leapt to her feet as fast as her arthritic knees would allow but had failed to see the visitor. He'd knocked briskly on the door and Alf had answered and quickly allowed the visitor in. *Songs of Praise* started on BBC1 at five-forty. The neighbour had heard a vehicle drive slowly by a few minutes earlier and park briefly in the street before almost immediately driving off. It was, she said, a small white van. Now Maggie had found residents two streets away who had seen a strange white van left there for an hour or so, Sunday teatime. Nobody saw the driver.

'He's our man,' I told her. 'No doubt about it. He drove by to see if Alf was in, or to simply check the address, then left his van where it would be away from the scene of the crime and attract less attention. Are there grass verges near where he was parked?'

''Fraid not, boss,' Maggie replied. 'The verges have been made over with green tarmac.'

'Damn. We won't get anything from them. OK. So go back, get the names of everybody in the street from the electoral roll and interview every man, woman and child. In fact, borrow a white van and park it in the spot. It might jog someone's memory. Pick your team and get on to it first thing. Anything else?'

'Mmm,' she replied. 'I've tracked down Mrs Newbold.'

'Of Ellis and Newbold fame?'

'That's right. Ellis was only part of the company for a couple of years, when it first

73

started, just before the First World War. Alvery Newbold bought him out and the company eventually came to his son, Percival. Percy died in 2000, two years after the company closed. His wife is called Josephine and she lives in Leyburn.'

'Leyburn,' I exclaimed. 'I thought they lived in Spain.'

'She came back. Apparently their daughter is a GP in Leyburn.'

'Blimey, I bet she finds it bleak up there after the Costas. You've done brilliant, Maggie, just brilliant. I'll have to talk to her. Do you want to come with me or are you happy door-knocking?'

She winked at me and pulled the door open. 'I'd only cramp your style,' she said.

As soon as she went out Eddie jumped up and came in. I was reading Maggie's notes and transferring Josephine Newbold's address and phone number into the murder log book. I gestured for him to sit down. When I'd finished I said, 'Maggie can put a white van in the next street at teatime on the Sunday in question. It looks like our man's. And she's tracked down Mrs Newbold, wife of the proprietor of the company.'

'Great,' he replied. 'I always said that stills have their uses. They're good at that sort of thing.'

I threw my pen on the desk, exasperated, saying, 'Do you do it deliberately, Eddie, just to annoy me?'

'What, guv?'

'You know what, and cut out this guv business.'

'Sorry, guv. I mean, boss. It's just that I haven't time for this political correctness stuff.'

'It's not political correctness, it's common courtesy. We have two female officers and as far as I'm concerned they are bloody good officers. Now what have you got?'

It's another of his Met habits. They used to refer to women police officers as splits, until there was a furore about it and threats of severe disciplinary action. So the wags in the locker room started calling them stills, because they were still...

He passed me a copy of the list of names Eric Smallwood had given him. 'I've been checking these off against the PNC. They're all clean except one.' He pointed with his finger. 'Him there. Done for attempted bank robbery in 1999. Took an eight, served four, currently unemployed. I think we should pay him a visit.'

'Donovan Bender,' I read. 'I remember him well. It was Christmas Eve and he daren't go home because he'd lost all the Christmas money on the ponies or peed it against a wall. He's a resourceful lad, decided to hold up the National Westminster, using a carrot inside a paper bag. He was arrested outside with

£2,000 in his pocket, waiting for the taxi he'd ordered. When the judge asked him why he'd used a carrot inside a paper bag he said that he couldn't afford a cucumber. Poor old Donovan is the stuff of legend.'

'I still think we should go see him.'

'I agree. It's as good a place to start as any. First thing in the morning.'

May is my favourite month. The days are stretching out, the birds are bonking on the windowsill and then singing it to the world, and optimism starts to creep through the veins like a mug of hot chocolate. May is the month of rebirth, of blossom on the trees and office girls in summer dresses. The cricket season starts then, too, but you can't have everything.

Except tonight it was raining. Sonia had planned to do a fast training spin and then train lightly and rest for the remainder of the week because Sunday was her big day. She'd entered the Oldfield 10K road race and this would be her official comeback. It was always a big field – a couple of thousand in the men's race and three hundred or so in the women's – but not what you would call a high class one. Sonia had a definite chance of doing well.

'It'll be muddy in the woods,' I warned her as we drove to the golf club. 'Could be tricky underfoot.'

76

'Mmm,' she agreed, pensively.

'Want to go round on the road?'

'No,' she decided. 'I want to do it against the clock; see what time I can do. It's only a short stretch in the wood, and the rain might not have got through to the ground yet. We haven't got a standard time for going round by the road. We'll do the woods. It'll be OK.'

We reckoned the circuit was slightly under three miles and the routine was that she did two laps of it while I slogged round just the once. Our speed difference meant that I was back at the car about eight minutes before she came steaming up Rhododendron Drive at the end of her second lap.

Sonia was doing her stretching exercises while I took my tracksuit bottoms off, when one of the dog-walkers approached us. She was a middle-aged lady with a West Highland terrier on a lead.

'Excuse me,' she said, 'but are you Sonia Thornton?'

I saw the colour flood into Sonia's cheeks as she admitted that she was.

'I saw you win a race at Roundhay Park one Bank Holiday Monday,' the lady said. 'You were wonderful, only about seventeen. I thought you'd retired.'

'No,' Sonia said, still blushing, and the lady wished her good luck and went on her way, the dog leaping up at her, wanting to be released. I was amazed how awkward

Sonia had been, almost embarrassed. She was shy and tongue-tied, but when she was with people she knew you couldn't stop her talking. I nodded to her, she nodded back, I clicked the watch and she went plunging off into the woods. I put the stopwatch in the car, locked the doors and plodded after her.

The man with shiny shoes opened his scrapbook for 1998 and read about a hit-and-run case where the underage, over-the-limit driver had killed an elderly couple and escaped with a six-month sentence and a two-year driving ban. There were, the court was told, mitigating circumstances. The couple were wearing dark clothing as they crossed a busy road only fifty yards downwind of a zebra crossing. Very irresponsible. This had contributed in no small way to their unfortunate deaths. The youth was driving the car as a favour to a friend, not realising he was over the limit from a previous drinking session, and his overwillingness to help a friend in need had led to his downfall. Driving away from the scene was a moment of madness brought on by panic.

The man with shiny shoes noted the names and turned to his computer. He slid a CD of the whole country's electoral roll (*'44,000,000 names and addresses at your fingertips'*) and clicked the icon on the screen. In seconds he was scrolling through names and addresses that could have belonged to the drink-driving youth.

'Let's have a look at what we've got,' I said to the murder team, Wednesday morning. I wiped the whiteboard clean and tried a blue pen in the corner of it. It worked.

'Are we convinced it's murder?' someone asked.

'Yes.'

'Right, in that case it was premeditated.'

'Good.' I wrote the word near the top of the board.

'Organised,' someone else added. That's the buzzword. Killers are either organised or disorganised. It covers a lot of ground. Some murderers are opportunists, some plan to the most minute detail. *Organised* went on the board.

'How old is he?' I asked.

'Alfred was in his seventies, and his killer appears to have befriended him.'

'So he's probably not in the normal age range, twenty to thirty-something?'

'No, he's middle-aged.' That went on the board.

'Alf was a racist, so his friend would be a white man.' I wrote it up.

'What does he do for a living?'

'He's an electrician,' John Rose suggested. 'Murderers use what knowledge they have. Doctors use poison ... um, that sort of thing.'

'What sort of thing?' Sparky asked, sensing John had backed himself into a corner.

'You know what I mean.'

'No I don't.'

'Mad axe men use axes,' someone else suggested.

'Exactly,' John agreed.

'OK,' I interrupted, before the meeting degenerated. 'Let's just say he had a knowledge of electricity. He may be a plumber or similar.'

'An artisan.'

'That'll do.' I wrote *artisan* on the board. 'What else.'

'He's police aware.'

'Why?'

'The white van. It's not on any CCTV cameras. He left no prints. He had the sense to park some distance away.'

'I'm convinced, but he could have picked that up from watching *Crime Scene* on TV.' I wrote it on the board. 'What about his education?'

'Above average intelligence,' someone said and everybody nodded. We like to think we're up against master criminals. Up it went.

'Marital status?' I asked.

'Divorced, with twin boys and another on the way.'

'Keep it serious, please.'

'Sorry, boss, but we're getting into conjecture.'

'I know, but let's try.'

'A sad loner,' I was told.

'No, they're usually married to a devoted wife who thinks the moon and stars rise out of their backsides,' someone argued.

'OK, we'll leave that one. Anything else?'

We kicked ideas around for another hour. Our murderer didn't take risks, probably had a criminal record and lived not too far away. None of the normal motives fit. He was a sociopath, incapable of recognising another person's feelings, and he'd done what he did for the hell of it. He was a sadist and would probably kill again.

'So what was the purpose of the killing?' I asked.

'He did it for fun,' I was told. 'Or just to feel what it was like. He'd probably fantasised about it for years.'

'And how did he pick his victim?'

'He looked for a lonely old man that nobody would miss.'

'So it wasn't personal?'

'No.'

'Perhaps the killer's a gerontophile,' one of the young guns suggested, showing off.

'In that case, wouldn't there have been some form of sexual interference?' I responded.

'Um, yeah, probably, boss.'

'That's it, then,' I told them. 'Remember, this is not evidence. Hopefully it's given us an insight into the type of person we are looking for, but in itself it's not worth a hill of beans.' God, I wished I'd said that.

Eddie Carmichael hung back after the meeting, waiting for me. 'Are we going to see this plonker bank robber?' he asked.

'Right now,' I said, pulling my jacket on. I asked one of the DCs to make a note of what was on the board and headed for the door.

'I need to collect a gun,' Eddie said as we passed through the foyer.

'A gun? What for?'

'Because he's a convicted armed robber.'

'He was using a carrot in a paper bag.'

'Only because he didn't have a gun. He'd have used it if he'd had one.'

'He'd have used a cucumber, if he'd had one,' I argued.

'With respect, guv, you're relying on your memory of the case. The file has him as an armed robber, so I want to be armed, just in case.'

'Have you got authorisation?'

'Right here.' He waved it under my nose. 'I saw Mr Wood, first thing.'

The armoury is what was intended as number eight cell, hastily converted when the Yardies started shooting each other, with a counter inside, racks for the few guns we have and shelves for the ammo. There are Heckler and Kochs, Glocks, a sniper rifle that will shoot off a gnat's left testicle at half a mile, and a sawn down shotgun for firing lead powder-filled cartridges that can blow a door off its hinges. The H & K machine gun is the standard weapon, with a Glock pistol as standby for when the Heckler jams, but in this case Eddie would just take the Glock.

It's fairly routine. If there's a faint chance that a suspect or witness may have a gun we might carry one concealed in a belt holster, just in case, although I've never bothered and neither has Dave. I killed a man, once, but that was on a raid. He fired at me and I fired back, three times. I didn't know his gun was empty, but I don't lie awake at night wondering about it. Not too often.

The desk sergeant led the way with Eddie hard on his heels, me loitering. He unlocked the thick door and let himself behind the counter.

'One nine-millimetre Glock 17 semi-automatic,' he said, as he placed the weapon in front of Eddie. 'You want a holster for it?'

'Yes please.'

''Spect you'll want a bullet, too.'

'A bullet! A full magazine, if you don't mind.'

'You can have fifteen. They cost money, y'know.'

'How many does it hold?' I asked. I'd never used a Glock. In my days it was all Smith and Wesson revolvers. I picked it up, felt the weight of it and how it fit my hand.

'The mag holds seventeen,' the sergeant told me, 'but we only put fifteen in to avoid compressing the spring too far. It helps prevent jams, not that they jam too often. You don't want one, do you, Charlie?'

Eddie strapped the belt round his waist, put the gun in the holster, checked the hang of his jacket. I swear he looked round for a mirror.

'No,' I replied. 'A carrot in a brown paper bag is all I ever use.'

'How do you like the Mondeo?' Eddie asked as he settled into the passenger seat.

'Love it,' I replied.

He ran his finger over the console with the delicacy of a devotee, checking the numbers, the quality and God knows what else. 'Two litres?'

'Yes.' I started the engine and steered us out onto the road.

'Hmm. It feels nice. What do you get to the gallon?'

'Thirty ... something.' I told him.

'Press the button on the end of the stalk.'

I did as I was told.

'Thirty-six point five,' he read from the digital display. 'Not bad. Press it again.'

I pressed it.

'At an average of 38.4 miles per hour.'

That kept him happy for the rest of the

journey. Donovan Bender lived in one of the project blocks at the bottom end of the Sylvan Fields estate. Bottom end geographically and socially. The lift stank of the usual, the car parking area held the standard array of shopping trolleys and wheel-less vehicles, and if a window cleaner had ever ventured into the flats he'd have found a sanding machine more useful than a wash leather.

'Police,' Eddie shouted through the door in response to Donovan's 'Who is it?'.

He let us in and asked us to sit down. His wife was at work, behind the desk at a local filling station, and he was preparing vegetables for when the kids came home from school. The TV was showing cartoons but he switched it off. The room was surprisingly neat and tidy.

'What am I supposed to 'ave done now?' he asked, wiping his hands on his jeans and sitting down.

'We don't know. What have you done?' Eddie responded.

'Noffing. Noffing at all.'

'Where were you on Sunday the ninth? That's a week last Sunday.'

'Nowhere. I never go anywhere, do I? Down to the pub on a Saturday, watching cricket or football at the rec. in the afternoon, and that's it. Can't afford to go anywhere, not wiv two growing kids. If I do go anywhere it's wiv them, innit?'

'When did you last see Alfred Armitage?'

'Huh! So that's worrits about, is it. Loopy old Alf. I thought it was 'im when I saw it in the paper, but I wasn't sure.'

'You haven't answered the question.'

'When did I last see Alfie Armitage?'

'That's right.'

'Dunno. Probably the day Ellis and Newbolds closed down. I've certainly never seen 'im since.'

'What did you do at Ellis and Newbolds, Donovan?' I asked.

'I was just a labourer and van driver, wasn't I?'

Eddie quizzed him some more, gave him a hard time, suggested he might prefer to come down to the station to make a statement, but he had nothing to offer us. Donovan remembered Eric Smallwood, said he was weird, and that the two men hardly spoke to each other, but it never came to violence. He couldn't think of anybody at the factory who might want Alfred dead. Nobody cared that much about him.

'How are the daughters, Donovan?' I asked. 'Have they forgiven you for ruining their Christmas?'

'Yeah,' he replied, blushing and looking sheepish. 'It was a long time ago. We 'ave a laugh about it, now and again. I'd been on the Carlsberg Special. She's forgiven me, except...'

'Except what?'

'Oh nowt. Just the job thing. It ain't right, the wife working an' me at home, is it? But there's noffing for me. Not now. Not wiv my record.'

I stood up and Eddie did the same. 'If you think of anything else, give us a ring.'

He followed us to the door, his brow furrowed as if he were working at some imponderable puzzle. 'There is somefing,' he said as we stood at the door.

'What?' I asked.

'I'm not sure. It's just that Smallwood 'ad a name for Alfie. Called 'im it behind 'is back.'

'A name. What sort of name?'

'I'm trying to fink. Midnight, or somefing like that. Yeah, that was it: Midnight. 'E called 'im Midnight.'

'Midnight?' we replied in unison.

'Yeah. I'm sure of it. Midnight.'

Four of them were stooped over Jeff Caton's desk, looking businesslike, when we arrived back. I wandered over to see what they were doing.

'Anything I should know about?'

Jeff looked up, grinning. 'Hi, Chas,' he greeted me. 'There's been another memo about this memorial seat for the old codger who's died. Can we suggest a suitable location for it?'

'Right. Well, no doubt the collective brains

87

of the CID can come up with something suitable.'

'We've a few ideas. If it was for you, where would you like it to be?'

'What? If the seat was for me? Do you mean for me to sit on or in memory of me?'

'In memory of you. The Charlie Priest Memorial Seat.'

'No idea.'

'C'mon, Chas, there must be somewhere where you've spent many a happy hour, just enjoying the view?'

'Um, I suppose so,' I agreed.

'Where, then?'

'Oh, let me see... How about... Yes, I'd like my seat to be overlooking Heckley Girls Grammar School netball courts.'

They smiled and chuckled and straightened their backs. Jeff said, 'Right, then. That's two for Robin Hood's Bay, one for somewhere in Nidderdale, one for Fountains Abbey and one for overlooking Heckley Girls Grammar School netball courts.'

When I was safe in my own office I rang High Adventure and asked to speak to Sonia. 'What's the chances of having an afternoon off tomorrow?' I asked.

'Sorry, Charlie. Can't do. We've some corporate people coming to use the ice wall and they expect the boss to be available. They're from the motor trade. Sales people from one of the big outlets. *Cars U Like,* or something equally naff. It's all about bonding. They share the dangers, or what they perceive as dangers, and become closer to each other as a result. And trust. They learn about trust. Trust in each other, trust in the equipment and trust in themselves. The sales people bond with other sales people, the managers bond with the typists, that sort of thing. They pay good money and expect value for it. And they all go away with a photograph to put on the office wall. They have a whale of a time and...'

'Sonia!'

'Sorry?'

'I'll take that as a negative, shall I?'

'I'm afraid so, Charlie. What had you in mind?'

'Oh, nothing special. I need to go up to Leyburn and it would have been nice to have some company.'

'Can't you take Dave?'

'Not really. It's a bit of a wild goose chase. And you're handsomer than he is. I don't get the same wobbly feeling when he's sitting next to me.'

'You say the nicest things.'

'What time tonight?'

'Seven.'

'Don't be late.'

I put the phone down and sat looking at it. A couple of months earlier there had been this article in the paper about a youth who'd had this tattoo put on his upper arm at great pain and expense. He'd asked for the Chinese symbols for Loyalty, Respect and Courage, assuming, presumably, that the tattooist was fluent in Mandarin. The irony of being a convicted thief and girlfriend-beater never occurred to him. Afterwards, he'd taken to wandering the streets wearing a singlet, even though it was February, showing off his newly acquired status symbol. Until, one night in his local takeaway, the chef, who was educated at Leeds University but had a smattering of his parents' native language, told him that having *Best before the year of the rat* tattooed on his arm was very amusing, very droll, very English. He loved the English sense of humour. The youth went straight round to his tattooist and broke the man's jaw.

It appears that not many tattoo artists are familiar with Chinese script, so when somebody comes in and asks for a Chinese cipher to be emblazoned across their torso, they turn to whatever they have handy in an attempt to oblige. This means that there are thousands of young men, and a few women, wandering around with memorable legends such as *Do not exceed the stated dose* and even *Warning! This product may contain peanuts* etched into their skin.

The youth's defence was that the tattoo had made him look like a twat. The prosecution argued that *all* tattoos make you look like a twat. Cops don't like tattoos. Correction: cops don't have tattoos. On other people, we love them. Usually. There's nothing we like more than looking at a grainy CCTV frame and picking out the letters LUFC on the scally's forehead but, generally, we don't like them.

We were lying in bed, last Christmas, just as dawn broke. It was warm in the room because we'd left the heating on all night and the duvet had worked its way halfway down the bed. Sonia was breathing rhythmically and occasionally mumbling something that I couldn't make out. Probably nonsense. I was wide awake but content to lie there, close up behind her, our bodies moulded together like two spoons.

I traced my finger down her spine, marvelling at this miracle of a woman – *La Gazelle* – who at one time could outrun almost any other female on the planet; at my good fortune in being the man here with her; the one she chose to be with. I kissed her neck lightly, to say thank you, and she snuffled and turned on to her stomach. My fingertips continued their journey until they reached the top of her bum. I pushed the duvet further down, and that's when I saw the tattoo.

It was only a rose, a red rose, but dismay engulfed me like snow falling off a roof. For a few seconds it felt as if a big gaping chasm had opened between us and was widening by the second. I'd seen lots of tattoos on women, often wondered why they did it, what they were for, and never come anywhere near understanding. The feeling of disappointment only lasted a few seconds but its power took me by surprise, hit me like a blow. I pulled the duvet up over our shoulders and settled back down beside her, trying to put things in perspective. She was with me, and that was all that mattered. I said a silent prayer of gratitude to whatever gods might be listening, added an apology for being so juvenile and tried to go back to sleep. But I couldn't sleep. I wondered if she'd had the tattoo done for *him,* tried to push the thought out of my head. It's a terrible thing, jealousy, when it overtakes you in the wee small hours.

There was a tentative tap at the window of my door and I looked up to see Maggie standing there with a steaming mug in her hand. I gestured for her to come in.

'Am I disturbing you, Charlie?' she asked. 'You looked miles away.'

'No,' I replied. 'I was just thinking about the usual: Love; Life and the Universe.'

'So how's it going?'

'The universe? Plodding on, much as before.'

'And the love life?'

Maggie's an old pal, tends to mother me,

or big sister me, and we've cried on each other's shoulders once or twice. That is, she's cried on mine once, I've cried on hers too many to mention. 'Oh, so-so,' I told her.

'That's not what I hear. How's the jogging going?'

'We're runners now, not joggers. It's going OK. Brilliant. Sonia's entered the Oldfield 10K race on Sunday. It's her comeback.'

'Great. Have you entered?'

'No way. I'm not good enough.'

'She's a super girl, Charlie. Why don't you make an honest woman of her?'

'We'll see.'

'What's the problem?'

'Twenty years age difference, Maggie. That's the problem. Twenty years.'

Dave and I went to see Eric Smallwood again, mainly to check out his Scalextric. Daniel, Dave's son, had an early model when he was a kid, but we never really mastered it. Perhaps the modern cars stayed on the track better. We went in mine, with Dave driving.

'Tell you what,' I said as we turned out of the nick yard. 'Let's go see Simon first. Head out on Batley Road.'

Halfway there Dave said, 'Ooh! Folic acid,' out of the blue.

I glanced across at him. 'What about it?'

'Can we stop at a health food store for some on the way back, please?'

'For folic acid?'

'Hmm. I've been reading about it. There's been a big survey and they've discovered that it delays the onset of memory loss and Alzheimer's. It's got B vitamins in it.'

'Does it? I'd better have some, then.' We were both at an age when we worry about these things.

'It sounded pukka gen. All done scientifically.'

'Where was this?'

'In the *Sunday Times*. The trials were in Finland.'

'Why is it always Finland?' I wondered. 'Did you know that Finnish children can read and write better than any other children in the world?'

'What? Read and write English?'

'No, read and write Finnish.'

'Well, they should be able to, shouldn't they?'

'Um, well, when you put it like that, I suppose they should.'

We were rapidly approaching Five Lane Ends with its abundance of direction signs. 'Where are we going?' Dave demanded.

'God knows,' I replied.

Simon was painting his garage door when we arrived. He wrapped the brush in cling film so it wouldn't dry out and invited us into the kitchen.

'Have you got anyone, yet?' he asked.

'For killing Alfred? No, not yet.'

'So how can I help you?'

Before I could answer his telephone rang. 'Excuse me,' he said as he lifted the receiver. We heard the usual half of the conversation. 'Um, yes it is. Um, yes. It's a bit awkward at the moment. Can I ring you back? What's your number, please?' At a guess somebody wanted some gardening done. Simon was working in the black economy, but it wasn't our business.

'Eric Smallwood,' I said when he was back with us. 'We had a word with him, as you suggested, and he told us some more names. Do you remember Donovan Bender?'

'Bendy? Sure I remember him. He was alright. Drove the van sometimes. He got done for robbing a bank after he left. It was in all the papers. Can't see him being a murderer, though.'

'Someone is,' I replied. 'Was there ever any conflict between Donovan and Alfred that you know of? Might, for instance, Donovan have been stealing the odd item of scrap and Alf warned him about it?'

Simon shook his head. We questioned him some more, mainly about security, or lack of it, but it was a waste of time. As we stood up to leave Dave said, 'Does the name Midnight mean anything to you?'

Simon looked puzzled for a second, before saying, 'Yeah. It does. One of them used to

95

call the other it. Don't know why.'

'One of whom?'

'Smallwood and Alf. That's right. Midnight. Smallwood used to call Alf it, and Alf got really annoyed. It really wound him up. Then, all of a sudden, he stopped, but it was never the same between them again. Someone said that Alf had sent him a solicitor's letter, but I don't know if it's true.'

'Do we still have solicitor's letters?' Dave wondered as we drove away.

'I suppose so,' I replied. 'Although I haven't heard of one for years. These days people are more likely to dive straight in with litigation. A solicitor's letter was like a shot across the bows to warn someone that you were thinking of taking action against them.'

'Stop it or I'll sue.'

'That's it. A *letter before action*. I think that's the proper name for one.'

'It'll be interesting to hear what Mr Smallwood has to say about it.'

'It will, won't it?'

But first we wanted to see his Scalextric. We used the standard ploy to get into the house – we'd like a statement, and perhaps he'd prefer to come down to the station to make it – and were admitted into his surgically clean habitation.

'One of your officers came to see me yesterday,' he protested, his tone suggesting that we were wasting public money, which we probably were. He was wearing his cycling helmet and I had great difficulty not looking at it. Every few seconds my eyes flicked towards it as if it might light up or start doing tricks.

'That would be DC Carmichael, sir,' Dave said. 'Unfortunately he's gone off work with shingles and taken his notebook with him, so we're trying to catch up.'

I winced at the explanation, but heaved a small sigh of relief that he hadn't said that Eddie had been killed in a car crash and his notebook destroyed in the resulting conflagration.

'Very painful, shingles,' Smallwood told us.

The room he took us in was furnished in dark wood and leather, with everything looking expensive and well looked after. The chesterfield gleamed and smelt of leather polish, the windows sparkled and he'd taken his Christmas cards down. Well, it was May. A glass-fronted fire with artificial flames flickered in the hearth and above it was a print of elephants, signed by the artist.

'When DS Carmichael rang in he said you had a big Scalextric set,' Dave was saying as I studied the print. It was a David Shepherd. The big bull elephant in the middle was looking extremely stroppy.

'Yes,' Smallwood replied. 'He looked

through all the windows before he knocked on the door, but I didn't let him in.'

'Quite right, sir. Sometimes he is a bit over-enthusiastic, gets carried away with the job. I'm thinking of buying a set for my son. Nothing too elaborate, unless he really takes to it. Is there any possibility of seeing yours, and I'd be very grateful for any advice you have to offer?'

So, for the next half hour the overburdened taxpayer sponsored Dave to play at racing cars and me to watch. Smallwood had designed the track so that one car went round as fast as possible all by itself. He explained how every segment of its track was on a separate supply of which he could control the voltage by a bank of transistors. That car would fly down the straights and slow for the corners according to how he'd set things up. The other car he controlled manually. It was like playing chess against a computer, except that playing chess is a useful skill that you can convert into other things, such as friendships. Racing toy cars his way was a lonely occupation, like playing with yourself in a darkened room. Lots of fun but difficult to share with others. I felt sorry for him.

'C'mon,' I said. 'There's work to be done.'

'You were really getting the hang of it,' he told Dave as he led us back into the other room.

'I was, wasn't I?'

'Mr Smallwood,' I began, 'does the name Midnight mean anything to you.'

'M-Midnight?' he echoed, his manner answering my question.

'Yes, Midnight.'

'No, I don't think so.'

'I think it does.'

'I can't remember.'

'I'm told by one of the Ellis and Newbold employees that you used to call Alfred Armitage Midnight. Did you?'

'I don't remember. I may have done.'

'I'm also told that there was talk of a solicitor's letter being sent. Do you know anything about that? It will be relatively easy for us to contact local solicitors.'

'It was just a joke, that's all. I used to tease him. For a laugh, but he couldn't take it and sent me the letter.'

'Do you think that Mr Armitage may have been stealing from the company?'

'No. I'd have known about it if he was.'

'Were you?'

'No.'

'Did they pay well?'

'Well enough.'

'But perhaps not as much as you thought you were worth.'

'I wasn't stealing from the company.'

'So who was Midnight?'

'I don't know.'

He'd clammed up on me, but the thought

of this helmet-clad, tweed-jacketed nerd taking the mickey out of anybody – of being the heart and soul of the company – was hard to swallow. 'Well thanks for your cooperation, Mr Smallwood,' I said, 'and if you think of anything else, however trivial it might appear, we'd be grateful for your help. This is a murder enquiry, after all.'

At the door Dave said, 'Thanks for the drive, Mr Smallwood.'

Smallwood opened his mouth to speak, then thought better of it.

'Was there something?' I asked.

'No, except...'

'Except what?'

He turned to Dave. 'I was going to say ... if you'd like to bring your son round for a drive, I don't mind.'

'Thanks,' Dave replied. 'I'll ask him.'

'Give me a ring, first.'

'I will.'

In the car I said, 'Will you?'

'Will I what?'

'Will you take Dan round for a drive?'

After a long pause he said, 'No, I don't think I will.'

Chapter Four

Leyburn is a super place. I could live there anytime. It's in the most northern tip of North Yorkshire and is the jumping off point for Swaledale, most desolate of all the dales. I leapt at the excuse for a trip up there.

And Mrs Newbold is a doll. Everybody should have a grandmother like her. She is attractive, well-groomed, and bakes the best scones this side of Giggleswick. I'd rung ahead and she'd made a trayful in preparation. We tucked into them sitting in an airy conservatory attached to the side of the converted barn that her daughter and son-in-law lived in. They were both out attending to the village's sick and lame.

'I could have asked the local police to talk to you,' I said as she leaned forward to pour me another cup, 'or I could have sent one of the team, but I decided on the personal touch and I'm glad I did. Perks of the job, and all that. This is a very pleasant way to spend an afternoon.' The sun was in my eyes and I twisted my head to find some shade.

'Ooh, that looks weak,' she exclaimed, as she saw the colour of the tea. 'I'll just show it the pictures.' She raised the teapot and waved it around, pointing the spout at the glass windows.

'*Show it the pictures,*' I said. 'I haven't heard that one before.'

'No? It's one of my mother's sayings. It gave her an excuse to agitate the pot if the brew looked weak.'

'Ah! My mother used to say things like: "Don't *tomorrow* me," or "I'll give you *in the morning.*"I never did know what she meant.'

'Oh, yes, I remember all those. Have another scone, inspector. My daughter said you wanted to talk to me about Ellis and Newbolds.'

I dragged what passes for my brain back from wherever it was wandering and remembered why I was there. 'Yes, that's right. Do you remember an employee called Alfred Armitage?'

She did, and had read about his death in the newspaper. Sadly, it wasn't his death that aroused the interest of the tabloids and broadsheets, but the manner of his dying. Alfred's five minutes of incandescence came too late for him to enjoy.

'I wasn't sure if it was the same Alfred,' she told me, 'but he was the right age, and lived in Heckley, so I imagined it was.'

She didn't know him very well, but sometimes took on secretarial duties when the usual woman took leave, so she had met most of the employees. Alfred had always been respectful and considerate, even if he was dull and unimaginative. Eric Smallwood was regarded as a faithful servant who kept a strict hold on the company's finances and other affairs, even if he was, she said, 'a little strange'.

'What do you mean by strange?' I asked.

'Oh, nothing tangible. He was just quiet, kept himself to himself, never socialised. My husband called him "still waters".'

'I see. Did you hear of any other nicknames for either of them, such as Midnight?'

She looked bemused. 'Midnight?' she repeated. 'No, not at all. What's that all about?'

'I was hoping you might tell me.' I leaned forward. 'Mrs Newbold, do you think either Alfred or Eric were stealing from Ellis and Newbolds? Either directly or via some sort of fraud?'

She looked awkward and fiddled with the hem of her cardigan. When she reached for the teapot again I shook my head and waited for an answer.

'I don't know,' she replied, eventually. 'Things went downhill quite rapidly. Percy – Mr Newbold – didn't say much but he became very depressed. He regarded the workforce almost like family. He paid them the top rate for the job, when he could afford to, and gave them benefits far ahead of his time. He couldn't believe that any of them would cheat him, but that was the conclusion he came to. A very painful conclusion. He felt betrayed.'

'Did he investigate it, or contemplate taking any action?'

'No. He hated unpleasantness of any kind. Our nearest competitor, a company called AJK, made him an offer and he accepted. He was glad to get out. He tried to protect the jobs of the men but after a suitable period AJK closed the factory down. He never really got over it. Judging a man was something he'd always thought he was good at, but the thought that Alfred and Eric were robbing him had really undermined his self esteem. He always believed them to be so conscientious. Why, they never took any holidays, neither of them. Just the occasional day, perhaps. They never took a whole week off.'

I asked her about Spain and the move back to England. It had been a happy interlude for a while, until Percy became ill, but she was glad to be back home, even if the winters were cold. I resisted a third scone, thanked her for a pleasant visit and climbed back in the car.

There wasn't time to have a quick look into Arkengarthdale but I stopped in the village centre to use the loo and buy a Wensleydale cheese. Then it was a hard thrash down the motorways back to Heckley.

Mrs Newbold had spoken about the feeling

of betrayal, about her husband's disappointment that two men he trusted could be so disloyal. Evidence of their apparent dependability was the fact that they worked such long hours and didn't take any leave. I pressed the button for the CD player and clicked through the discs until it found Thomas Tallis. Not taking leave is also a hallmark of the serious fraudster. He dare not have any time off in case the person who does his job while he's not at his desk rumbles the fraud. The Newbolds were nice people, and nice people believe the best for everybody else. I'm a cop, and cops take the opposite view.

It was after hours when I arrived back at the office and only Jeff Caton was in. We exchanged quick greetings and he reported that nothing was spoiling, which is how I like it. I dumped my briefcase and checked my desk for messages. There were two. Superintendent Stanwick wanted a word with me and so did the inspector in charge of the economic crime unit, or, as we all facetiously called it, the department formerly known as the fraud squad. I looked at my watch. Stanwick had left his mobile number, so presumably he didn't mind what time I rang him. I tapped it into my desk phone.

I don't know Mark Stanwick very well, which is unusual. I've been around a long time, wiped a lot of runny noses in the accumulated years that have made me the longest-serving inspector in East Pennine. Most of my senior officers are younger than me, but I don't mind: they've all passed through the Charlie Priest training college at some time in their careers, and if I need a favour it's usually there for me. Nothing important or against the rules, but if I need something quick, I usually get it.

But Stanwick had moved down to the Met early in his climb to dizzy heights. He was a desk cop, more interested in running the behemoth that is Her Majesty's police force than in catching villains, and had slipped out of sight for many years. I thought no worse of him for that. Somebody's got to do it. He'd returned north about six months earlier, as head of East Pennine career development. Maybe he wanted to know how we were getting on with Eddie Carmichael.

I was about to abandon the call when he answered. 'Mr Stanwick,' he said.

It's a bad opening line. A curt 'Stanwick' would have been appropriate. 'Superintendent Stanwick' would have given me two free pieces of information. But 'Mr Stanwick'? I registered it as a sign of insecurity.

'Hello, Mr Stanwick,' I replied. 'It's Charlie Priest here. You left a message.'

A dog barked in the background and I heard a door close, cutting the noise off. He was at home. 'Oh, hello Charlie,' he responded. 'Thanks for ringing. It's just a couple of things, nothing important. But before that, congratulations on the appointment. It's been long overdue.'

'You mean the acting DCI? It's only temporary.'

'Oh, I'm sure it will be consolidated.'

Yeah, I thought, providing I make all the right noises, learn the Newspeak, buy a suit and fall in with whatever he's about to ask. 'We'll see. What else was there?'

'Right, well, first of all, how is Eddie Carmichael fitting in?'

'Eddie's OK,' I told him. It wasn't totally true, but if I was going to assassinate the man I'd do it my way, not through snitching to the boss.

'Oh, that's good to hear. He can be a bit difficult, I believe.'

'Not really. He still has one or two bad habits he picked up in the Met, but he'll soon lose them. Who knows, perhaps he can teach us a few things, too.'

'That's the spirit, Charlie. I'm glad to hear it.'

'No problem, except, you seem to be taking an extraordinary personal interest in him. Is there something I should know about?'

'No, not really, Charlie. It's just that Eddie and I go back a long way. We both came down to the Met in the same intake and helped each other through those first difficult weeks. You know the sort of thing. Actually, we went back even earlier than that. We were both in the army for a while, which gave us something else in common. I wasn't as streetwise as Eddie. He helped me a lot, kept me out of trouble until I found my feet. I felt I owed him one, so when his file landed on my desk and I read about his spot of bother with the civilian girl I decided to try to help him, had him transferred to you. I thought if anybody could sort him out, it was Charlie Priest.'

'I'm flattered.' By 'finding his feet' Stanwick meant that he came in from the cold, abandoned being a street copper for the comforts of an office. Maybe I should have done the same. If I had it might have saved my marriage. In which case, I wouldn't have met... No, I was content with my lot. 'You said there were a couple of things...'

'That's right. I've been given the job of finding a media liaison officer. I straightaway thought of you. What do you think?'

I didn't have to think. 'Sorry, Mr Stanwick, but I'm not interested.'

'I didn't think you would be, but there's something else. We need a spokesman for talking to the public via the media. One or two recent examples haven't quite been public relations disasters, but they've come close. On the other hand, you've done several press conferences in front of the cameras and they've been superb. I've watched the tapes.'

'They got results, if that's what you mean.'

'Not just results, Charlie. They showed the force in a good light. You come across well. The public like you and trust you. You could become a star.'

It was results that mattered to me. I wasn't too bothered about being liked and trusted by the public, and stars come to fiery ends. 'I hate doing it,' I told him. 'I do it because nobody else will. We'll probably do one next week and I'll ask for volunteers, but I know I'll have to do it myself.' And, I thought, I'm supposed to be a detective – a plain clothes detective.

'I respect your feelings, Charlie. Once a thief-taker, always a thief-taker, eh?'

'I suppose so.'

'But you'll think about it?'

'Yeah, I'll think about it.' If it makes him happy.

'If we needed someone to face the cameras, anytime, would you do it if asked?'

'If asked, I'd probably have to do it, wouldn't I?'

'Attaboy, Charlie. Attaboy. Thanks for ringing.'

I replaced the receiver, wondering what it was all about. If asked to front an appeal for witnesses to a crime I'd do it because I believed it might produce results. I'd be sitting next to someone who'd been raped, or lost a child, or been badly beaten. I wouldn't be too bothered if my nose was reflecting the arc lights or if I dropped an occasional aitch. I went home. Fraud squad could wait.

The Oldfield 10K race started at ten a.m. Sunday morning, in front of the town hall. The course was dumbbell shaped and finished back where it started. I drove Sonia there and we arrived about an hour early. She was already wearing her kit, under two tracksuits. I'd suggested that she wear one of her GB vests, but she declined.

'The people would like to see you in one,' I argued, 'and the other competitors would be dead chuffed to compete against you.'

'I'm not representing GB,' she protested.

'But you used to. And the organisers would like it. It would raise the profile of the race.'

'And I might flop.'

'You're too modest.'

'Perhaps.'

For once she wasn't talking non-stop. It was nerves. Hers and mine. I didn't care where she finished, as long as it wasn't limping along with a damaged knee. The thought was never mentioned between us: as far as we were concerned, the knee problem didn't exist.

Hundreds of athletes of all standards congregated in front of the town hall, some already stripped down to singlets and shorts even though it was a cool morning. Ages ranged from teenage to much older than me and I briefly wished that I was part of it all, but the feeling didn't last long. There must have been about a million pounds' worth of kit on show. Nike and Adidas were the major players, with plenty of Diadora, Reebok and HiTech. Macmillan nurses were on prominent display, with ActionAid and lots of local charities well supported. The serious athletes looked grim and jogged back and forth as the big hand on the town hail clock edged towards the vertical. One or two shook hands as they acknowledged a rival. Sonia did her stretching exercises and bounced up and down, keeping loose. She rotated her shoulders and then her neck muscles: six times clockwise and then six times widder-shins. For races of this length you didn't warm up – you'd be warm enough after a kilometre or so. Nobody recognised her.

'Five minutes, love,' I said.

She nodded and began to peel off the layers until she was down to running vest and shorts. Some of the women wore what looked like bikini bottoms, but Sonia preferred the more traditional style. I stuffed her tracksuits into a bin liner and swung it over my shoulder.

'Laces tight?' I asked, and she squatted

down to check them.

Runners were making their way to the start line. The women started at ten o'clock, with the men fifteen minutes later. There were a lot of them, and it was important to be on the front row. I gave her a kiss on the cheek, told her to kill them all, told her that she was the Gazelle, and watched her push her way to the front, her head visible above almost all the others as she muscled her way through. I smiled to myself – she'd switched into competitor mode.

'Hello, Charlie, you OK?' I should have known the force would be well represented. Halifax had entered a whole team and they'd found me.

'Yeah,' I said, blinking and shielding my eyes. The morning sun was making them sting. 'I'd have brought my kit if I'd known you lot were entering.'

The gun sounded and the women were sent on their way. I watched a choppy sea of heads randomly bobbing up and down as they slowly moved off, and in seconds they were gone and the men were moving forward to fill the space they'd left. I thought I saw Sonia, near the front, but I couldn't be sure.

'Good luck, chaps,' I told the team, and started to follow a gaggle of spectators across the course to a vantage point at the halfway mark. That's when I remembered that I hadn't clicked the stopwatch.

I was in big trouble. I looked up at the town hall clock, waited until the hand hesitantly moved over the minute mark and started the watch. Phew! If I added a minute to her time – providing I remembered to *stop* the watch – that would be near enough.

Oldfield is an old cotton town, now cleaned up, bypassed and redeveloped like all the others. Once per year the centre is closed for the race and the whole town turns out to watch. It started as a half marathon during the first burst of enthusiasm for jogging, back in the Eighties, and is one of the few that have survived, albeit over the more sensible distance of ten kilometres. 10K is just over six miles. It's a hilly course, one of the toughest, and fast times are not expected. I found a vantage point just as the gun sounded for the start of the men's race.

Five minutes later a ripple of applause could be heard as the runners approached. It gradually grew louder and we craned our necks to see who would be first to loom into view. It was a black girl, all on her own apart from two motorcycle outriders, wearing the vest and green shorts that I believed were Kenya's national strip. There was something moving about seeing this little figure powering her way along, escorted by the two big riders on their BMWs. There was at least one class runner in the race poor Sonia had decided to make her comeback.

I started counting as a group came round the bend. At seven there was another gap, and then – I couldn't believe my eyes – it was Sonia. Her style was unmistakeable, completely different to all the others, high and courtly, as if she were an Egyptian princess surrounded by commoners.

The other spectators recognised it, too, and the applause intensified as she passed. Her fists were clenched and her cheeks flushed with exertion as she dipped her head and pushed forward to try to close the gap.

'C'mon Gazelle!' I yelled, and everybody turned to look at me.

As soon as she'd gone I nipped back to the town hall. Workmen were erecting a funnel of railings and stretching a ribbon across the finishing line. The clock read ten twenty-eight and the crowd was growing as spectators and helpers found their way back and waited for their charges. I found a spot ten yards after the finish and felt for the stop-watch in my pocket.

We had a good long view of the finishing straight and the sun was shining. It was a superb day for a race and if Sonia held her position, and I was sure she would, she'd be delighted.

That's what I thought, but I didn't know much about her determination. The motor-cycle outriders came into view and we all craned to spot the leader. Applause like distant gunfire came and went on the breeze and I stood on tiptoe.

There were two of them, side by side. One small and dark, wearing red and green and driving forward; the other tall and elegant, apparently skimming across the ground like a hovercraft. The tall girl pulled ahead and, fifty yards from the finish, the black girl threw her head back in a gesture that said she was beaten. Seven seconds later Sonia broke the tape.

The man with shiny shoes waited impatiently until the girl in the booth had told her friend on the other end all about the latest boyfriend. He supported Man U, drove a Ford Fiesta with wide wheels and liked to do things to her that would have stretched the ingenuity of a submariner on shore leave in Saigon. Of course, the man with shiny shoes didn't hear any of this, and wouldn't have waited with any more patience if he had.

Eventually, when she was content that her friend had reached a certain stage of sexual arousal and she herself had run out of coins, she hung up and left.

'Buy a mobile!' the man with shiny shoes exhorted as he watched her bulging backside waddle away, not realizing that she had one but had never understood the need to recharge the battery. He climbed out of the car and entered the booth. The receiver was soaked with the girl's perspiration and he flinched with distaste as he wiped it on a tissue before putting it to his ear. The phone he called was picked up after the third ring.

'Oh, good morning. I apologise for disturbing you but I've something I'd like to discuss with you.'

'I'm sorry, who are you?' the woman who answered the phone replied.

'My name is Smith, Martin Smith,' he told her, 'and I'm a probation officer. I've been dealing with several of what we refer to as cold cases, and the one concerning your late parents has been brought to my attention. If it's not too distressing I'd like to talk to you about it.'

'My parents, did you say?'

'Yes.'

'They're both dead.'

'I know. That's what I want to talk about.'

'It was a long time ago.'

'Six years. That's not very long when you are talking about life and death.'

'I don't suppose so. How can I help you?'

'Well, I hope it's me that can help you. We're having a new initiative in the probation service, talking to relatives of victims of murders and similar serious offences. At long last the government has realised that victims and their relatives should have an active part in the justice system. The courts are far too heavily loaded in favour of the offender.'

'Yes, I would agree with that.'

'Your parents were young at heart and quite active, I believe.'

'Yes. They led a full life.'

'Which was snatched away from them by a tearaway in an uninsured vehicle he wasn't qualified to drive.'

'I suppose so.'

'What did you feel about the sentence he received?'

'I thought it was derisory.'

'He laughed as he left the court.'

'I read that in the paper.'

'Did you know that he hasn't changed his ways? That he has had a string of convictions since then, all to do with vehicles? Did you know that he's been involved in another fatal accident but he's still free to roam the streets and put other lives at risk? How does that make you feel?'

'I ... I don't know.'

'You'd like him to be put away for a long time, wouldn't you?'

'I ... I suppose so.'

'That's too good for the likes of him. Three good meals a day, a colour TV, DVD; you name it, they'd give it to him. Jail's too good for vermin like him.'

'Well...' She tried to interrupt him, ask who he was again, but the man with shiny shoes was well into his spiel.

'I've been less than honest with you,' he

confessed. 'I'm not with the probation service. I'm like you: I lost a loved one to this scumbag. A little girl, six years old.' What is it about six-year-old girls that tug at the heartstrings, he wondered? 'She was the apple of my eye, and her mother's, until this ... bastard took her from us.'

'I'm sorry...'

'And what did the court give him? A slap on the wrist again, that's what. "She ran out in front of me", he said. "I had no chance to avoid her", and the court believed him. They weren't told of his previous record.'

'I don't know what to say...'

'Hanging's too good for people like him. I'm going to put a stop to him, once and for all. Would you like to help me?'

'Help you?' The woman's voice was shrill with alarm.

'Yes. Not physically. I can handle that. Just, you know, encouragement. Tell me that you support what I'm doing. I know we'll both feel better when it's done. It'll be closure on a sad episode in our lives. We'll be able to move on.'

'I have moved on.' She wanted to slam the phone down, was convinced that she was talking to a madman, a nutcase, but she couldn't.

'I lost my job,' he went on, ignoring her comment. 'Times are hard, and I'll incur some expenses. I already have done, but I know where he lives. When it's over, you might feel that you'd want to help me a little, cover my expenses. Just a couple of hundred, something like that, as a gesture of goodwill.'

'When it's over? When what's over? What exactly do you have in mind?'

'What do you think?'

'Are you talking about *killing* him? About *murder?*'

'I prefer to think of it as execution.'

'You need help. Whoever you are, you need help. I don't know where you'll get it, but you should talk to someone.'

'I'm talking to you.' He could sense that he was losing her. 'Please help me. Avenging my daughter is the only way out for me. I've spoken to therapists and analysts until I'm blue in the face. I thought you at least would understand how I feel.'

'I'm sorry,' she said, firmly. 'I'm terribly sorry about your daughter, but what you are suggesting won't help. I'm putting the phone down, now, and I recommend that you have a word with your GP.' The line went dead.

'Fuck!' he hissed, and kicked the wall at the foot of the booth with his immaculately polished brogue. 'Fuck!' He kicked again, but it didn't help.

First thing Monday morning I rang our press officer. 'It's Charlie Priest,' I told him.

'I have a little story for you.' He expected a juicy murder, but I told him all about *La Gazelle* and her triumphant comeback. He promised to do what he could.

I watched the troops drift in, some carrying their jackets, others with tabloids tucked under their arms and sandwich boxes in their hands. Cups of coffee were brewed and distributed. A new week was starting. When they were all present I joined them.

'Listen up,' I shouted above the hubbub. 'Put your comics away and be quiet. First of all, a message from Mr Wood. He has a few tickets left for the Rotary spring ball this weekend and would like to see as many of you there as possible.'

'How much?' someone asked.

'A mere twenty pounds,' I told him, 'including finger buffet.'

'For two?'

'Each.'

'Grrr! No chance.'

'Don't say you weren't invited. And now for something else. There's been a great deal in the papers and on the radio lately about the decline of standards in written English, particularly in the overuse of clichés, and I'm glad to see that some of you have taken this on board when writing your reports. It is highly commendable. However, I would like to make an observation.'

'You mean – you read them?' someone

asked, incredulous.

'Oh, yes, I read them all. As I was saying, I'd like to make a couple of observations.'

'You said *an* observation, boss.'

'Shut up and listen. As I have said before, reports catch crooks. What do reports do?'

'Catch crooks,' they mumbled in reply. Sometimes I can wrap them round my little finger.

'However,' I continued, 'it should be noted that your reports are legal documents, heaven help us, and can be used in a court of law as evidence. It follows that the language used should be clear and to the point. In these cases, colourful language or an original turn of phrase is not necessary. Courts like clichés. They know where they stand with all the usual clichés.' I sought a face amongst the ones turned towards me. 'Robert,' I said. 'You are an offender. The youth who didn't pay at the Texaco station could have been described as driving off at high speed, not "He left like shit off a shovel".'

'Sorry, boss.'

'That's OK. And you, Gerry. When you described the woman who walked out of the mini-mart with the bottle of whisky under her coat, it would have been perfectly appropriate to describe her as having sharp features, not "a face like a bag of spanners".'

'Sorry, boss. It won't happen again.'

'I should think not. That's it for now. Let's

split into our two teams.'

As I led the murder team down the stairs to the incident room Sparky loomed up alongside me. 'How did the race go?' he asked.

'She won,' I replied.

'She won? Gazelle? That's brilliant! Brilliant! Did you think she was in with a chance?'

'Not really. I thought she'd do well, but not win. I was chuffed to bits.'

'I bet you were. Tell her congrats from me, please.'

'I can't tempt you with the spring ball?'

'Sorry, Chas. We'll let you represent the department. You do it so well.'

I studied the pictures on the walls, the charts and the lists of names. Nothing had changed since Saturday morning. 'Has anyone anything to report in the hunt for the killer of Alfred Armitage?' I asked, when they were all congregated.

Nobody had.

'No great breakthroughs? No burning lines of enquiry that have opened up?'

Head shakes all round.

'The trail is going cold,' I told them. 'Another week and questions will be asked. I spoke to Mrs Newbold last Friday and came away convinced that Alfred and Eric Smallwood were stealing from Ellis and Newbold. Whether it was both of them or just one, I don't know. Fraud squad aren't interested.

One of the suspects is dead, Mrs Newbold hasn't made a complaint, and pursuing Smallwood would be unlikely to produce a result and therefore not in the public's interest, so that's the end of that avenue.'

'It was a long shot, right from the start,' John Rose declared.

'You're right, John,' I agreed, 'but it had to be followed. It's looking like Alf was murdered by one of the great unwashed, so, unless he kills again, our chances of finding him are about as good as Brendan's chances of pulling Julia Roberts.'

Brendan, one of my younger DCs, blushed. He keeps a photo of Ms Roberts behind his locker door.

'If it is one of the great unwashed, we could be in trouble,' John said. 'I'm thinking Dennis Neilson. He befriended and killed lonely, gay men. It'd be more convenient for Smallwood to have done it.'

'Was Armitage gay?' someone wondered.

'Not that we know of.'

'So is Smallwood still in the frame?'

'He's all we have. One thing we haven't looked at is the Midnight connection.'

Some of them looked quizzical. They don't all read each other's reports, so it's my job, when I have the chance, to share relevant information amongst them. 'Apparently,' I told them, 'Smallwood used to call Alfred Midnight, for some reason or another. This really riled Alf and he had a solicitor's letter sent to Smallwood, which put an end to it, but it didn't do much to improve relations between them.'

'Midnight, did you say?'

'That's right.'

'Sounds like a racehorse. Maybe they had shares in a racehorse.'

'Good point. Will you look into it, please?'

'Will do, boss.'

'And you, Brendan. Could you have a word with local solicitors and see if you can find who Alfred used to send the solicitor's letter? They'll plead client confidentiality, but use your Gaelic charm and if that's not enough tell them that client confidentiality doesn't extend to protecting murderers.'

As they drifted away I caught John Rose's attention and gestured for him to see me upstairs in my office when he'd finished deploying his DCs. Somebody had brought sachets of hot chocolate in, so I made one for myself and sipped it with my feet on the desk. I'd nearly finished it when John tapped on my window and came in.

'There's one thing we haven't tried,' I told him, after he'd refused a drink.

'What's that?'

'The Serious Crime Analysis Section.'

'At Bramshill? It hasn't been long enough for them to take an interest, has it?'

'It hasn't been twenty-eight days, but the

motive is unknown and it's a rather bizarre MO, so it qualifies on both those counts. Have a word with our nearest contact officer, please, and see if they have ever come across anything similar. It's a long shot, but we're grasping at shadows with this one.'

Everybody knows Bramshill to be our training college, but it is also the head-quarters of various initiatives using high-tech methods to solve crime. Amongst these is a database of violent crime going back nearly fifty years, storing details, both gruesome and mundane, that have enabled them to find obscure patterns of behaviour in hundreds of apparently unconnected offences and put the perpetrators behind bars. They also have links with similar databases all over the world. Crime really is a mug's game, these days. If there was a mad electrocutionist on the loose we'd soon know about it.

I'd told Dave that I was delighted, over the moon, when Sonia won the race, but that was a bit like saying that Moses was fairly pleased when the waters parted. My heart had stopped and I couldn't breath. It was as if I was in a different orbit, looking into the rings of Saturn, or swinging between Jupiter's moons, and I couldn't take in the wonder of it. I was as chuffed as a million rabbits in a carrot park.

I stood back as she shook hands with the

second girl and an official placed a medal around her neck. Photos were taken and people fussed around her, grabbing her hand, touching her arm, wanting to be part of the action. I stepped forward and gave her a towel. She flashed me a grin and hugged me, her body still heaving with the effort, her heart going like a machine gun. 'Well done,' was all I could say, so I said it again, 'Well done.'

A couple of minutes later the first man arrived. Sonia changed her shoes and put one of the tracksuits on. There was a presentation at half-past eleven in the town hall, with the lord mayor presenting the prizes. He bumbled his way through it, buzzes of electronic noise deafening the audience as he demonstrated his lack of microphone skills, and mispronounced several names, including the sponsor's. We get the politicians we deserve, but what the citizens of Oldfield had done to deserve this buffoon escaped me. He probably was big in potted meat, or something like that.

The winners were on the stage, and the third home in the men's race was paying Sonia a great deal of attention. He had the gaunt face of a runner, now scrubbed clean and pink with oxygen as his cardiovascular system adjusted to the change in its duties. His spiky hair was brushed back and edged with blond highlights. He put his arm across her shoulders as they shared a joke. Sonia shrugged it off.

A few minutes later she introduced him to me. He was kingpin at the local athletic club, knocking at the door of international honours but never quite making it. 'You need some speed work,' he told her as we said our goodbyes. 'Perhaps we'll see you at the track more often.'

'Perhaps,' Sonia replied, and we went home. On the way she rang Dr Bones and told him of her success. I heard his squeals of delight over the noise of the car.

'Ask him if they'd like to come out for dinner tonight,' I whispered. We'd already decided that we'd have a celebration, win or lose, and had booked a table at the Wool Exchange, a posh restaurant in Heckley. She asked, but they were expecting a visit from family, so had to decline.

I was down in the incident room, completing the log, when Brendan rang. 'We might have a bit of a breakthrough, boss,' he said.

'Tell me about it.' I like breakthroughs. Sometimes it's something really useful, like a fingerprint or bloodstain; other times it may be merely a rumour about the victim's relationships. Oh, yes, I love breakthroughs.

'I've just been to Ross and Ross's,' he replied. 'They were quite helpful. Alfred Armitage is on their files and they sent the solicitor's letter to Eric Smallwood. I've seen a copy and it specifically mentions the name Midnight and says that Smallwood must cease to use it or any other name intended as demeaning when addressing Alfred.'

'That's interesting,' I said, feeling slightly deflated. It wasn't what I'd call a breakthrough.

'There's more,' Brendan told me. 'There were some old newspaper articles in the file, that Alfred had brought in to explain his case. They were about the trial and conviction of one Terence Paul Hutchinson, aka the Midnight Strangler, who allegedly murdered three girls back in '91. He was given a thirty-year tariff.'

'The Midnight Strangler? Hey, that *is* interesting,' I said, with a little more enthusiasm than I'd shown earlier.

'It is, isn't it?' Brendan replied, 'but wait until you see his photograph.'

Chapter Five

'If he was given thirty years back in '91 he still has ... ooh, a long time to do,' Dave told us after Brendan arrived back at the station with copies of the files.

'He'll be out in 2021,' I said, after doing

the maths.

'That's seventeen years left,' Brendan added.

'Crikey. I'd top myself.'

'Check with HMP, Brendan,' I suggested. 'See if they still have Hutchinson. They might look similar but they are obviously not the same person. Alfred Armitage worked at Ellis and Newbolds since about 1951, man and boy. I think somebody would have told us if he'd broken his service for a murder trial and a long spell in the slammer.'

'Mistaken identity?' Brendan wondered.

'It's a strong possibility.' I turned to Dave. 'Tomorrow, Dave,' I said, 'will you please have a look at the files for the three murders. To start with just see if anything jumps out at you. Then get copies of the relevant stuff.'

Eric Smallwood, it appeared, had christened Alfred Armitage Midnight because he had seen the photos of Hutchinson – the Midnight Strangler – in the papers and noticed their facial similarities. Alfred wasn't too pleased by this and found himself a solicitor. This, in turn, displeased Smallwood, who regarded the whole thing as a bit of a hoot. It was probably the only humorous creativity he'd ever managed in his whole life, and it wasn't appreciated, but that was hardly a motive for murder. Perhaps somebody else had noticed the resemblance and come to the wrong conclusion. Somebody with stronger reasons for wanting the Strangler dead.

The man with shiny shoes decided to go ahead anyway. The daughter of the dead couple said she didn't want any involvement with retribution against the youth who had run down her parents, but he was convinced that she'd feel a little glow of satisfaction when she read of his death. His untimely and violent death. She was a middle-aged lady herself, conditioned by years of believing and doing the right thing. She was law abiding and liberal, and when put to the test had resisted the urge for revenge and accepted the way of the law. Highly commendable, but he knew, he knew, that when she saw it splashed across the papers that the man who murdered her parents had died, she would sleep easier in her bed at night. She would move on.

It was a thirty-mile drive to the town where the driver's namesake lived, but it was rush hour and the man with shiny shoes averaged only 27 miles per hour, at a fuel consumption of 31 miles per gallon. He checked his A to Z a couple of times and soon found the street he wanted. There was a good chance that it was the wrong man, but that didn't matter. Not too much. Those who knew the case would assume it was the right person. They'd *will* it to be him, and deep inside they would find a contentment that they hadn't known for years. And if it was the wrong person... Well, none of us is without sin, are we?

'God moves in mysterious ways,' he mumbled to himself, 'but sometimes he appreciates a little help.'

He parked in the next street, shrugged his arms into a poplin jacket and pulled an old cheese-cutter flat cap onto his head. He sat gathering his senses for a few minutes, watching the occasional pedestrian go by, looking for curtains twitching. Nobody was paying him any attention. He pulled the forged ID card from the glovebox, pushed it into his pocket and opened the car door.

The houses were in long terraces with little front gardens, most of which were tidy and starting to blossom with the new season's blooms. A man clipping his tiny lawn with shears didn't pause in his labours as the man with shiny shoes walked by, and a woman and little boy passing in the opposite direction didn't lift their heads to look at him. He rounded the corner into the street he wanted and started reading the house numbers.

The photos in his scrapbook weren't a big help in one way, but they were in another. The offender was always carefully concealed, either under a police blanket or by the hood of his sweatshirt. All you could see was his hand, pulling the hood tight across his mouth. Otherwise, he had been the typical profile for that sort of offence: white, teenage and undernourished. The man with shiny shoes would not be able to tell for certain if this was the right person, but neither would anybody else. Neither would the victim's daughter. But the name would be the same: William John Hardcastle. It was not a rare name, but not a common one, either. He chuckled to himself: vengeance was not a precise science.

He pulled the ID card from his pocket, checked it was the right one, and entered the little garden. This one was overgrown and the gate stood open, hanging on one hinge. Just what he expected. He knocked and heard footsteps on bare floorboards, reinforcing his feelings that this was a worthy victim. Then the door opened.

The man with shiny shoes craned his neck backwards to look up into the face of the man who stood before him. For a few seconds he was speechless.

'Can I help you,' the man said, eventually.

'Oh, er, yes, you may be able to.' He waved the phoney ID and the words came tumbling out as he struggled to regain his composure. 'Um, I'm Detective Inspector Smith. I'm looking for William John Hardcastle. Does he live here?'

'You found him, man. How can I help you?'

'You? You're William Hardcastle?'

'The one and only. What's the problem?'

'Oh, I'm sorry. I think there's been a mistake. The person I'm looking for is ... well, he's smaller than you. And he's, um...'

'White? Are you telling me that I'm not the one because I'm black?'

'Er, yes, it looks like that.'

'Hey man, that's a first. That ought to go in the papers. I never heard anything like that before.'

The man with shiny shoes said, 'I'm sorry to have troubled you,' and turned to leave.

'Any time, man. Any time at all,' the black giant called after him.

He averaged 47 miles per hour on the journey home, but didn't know because he forgot to check. He warmed up the lasagne that had been left for him but only picked at it and steered it around the plate, his appetite destroyed by disappointment. It hadn't been like this the last time. He'd come home ravenous after the last time, and wolfed his dinner down. That was surely a sign that what he was doing was right. He felt so comfortable with it; so ... *justified*. He went upstairs to study his files. There was still plenty of work left undone.

Angie's ex-boyfriend struck again during the night. Angie is a hairdresser in town, on the part of the main street that is slowly being taken over by charity shops since the new mall opened. She's a typical twenty-something-year-old Heckley girl: long frizzy two-tone hair; midriff bulging over the waistband of her low-cut Farahs; nose ring and some obscure design tattooed on the small of her back. Most of the local totty sport what is known as the Heckley face-lift. They pull their hair savagely back and secure it with rubber bands, thus achieving the dual roles of making it look reasonably tidy and ironing out most of their facial wrinkles. Angie has her work cut out persuading them to park their baby buggies outside and come in for a proper hairstyle.

When they can afford it they like to club – that's Newspeak for getting rat-arsed over the weekend, which starts on Thursday – including Angie. Especially Angie, as she has a source of income that doesn't involve queuing at the post office or DSS once a fortnight. Angie likes to enjoy herself. One boyfriend, she decided, wasn't enough for a business lady on the up.

The regular boyfriend she ditched wasn't too pleased, so he took action. One morning about a year ago, as we came to work, some of us noticed that Angies' Unisex Salon had suddenly become Angies' sex Salon. Angie wasn't pleased, either, and came to us, sobbing and calling him names that made the desk sergeant blush to his socks. We gave the ex-boyfriend a caution and reported her to the apostrophe police.

Now he'd struck for the fourth time and according to the sign painted on her window she was offering a cut and blow job for a fiver. It wasn't funny anymore. Well, it was, but we tried to keep it serious. I wondered if his behaviour was becoming obsessive so we fetched him in.

Dave rang me, late in the day, from Lincoln, where he was trawling the records for information on the Midnight Strangler's career.

'We could be onto something, Charlie,' he said. 'The third case was a girl called Julie Bousfield that he raped and murdered. Her brother jumped up in court after sentence was passed and swore to kill Hutchinson. He's called Brian Bousfield. The other two cases are just as bad, though. It could be family from any of them.'

'Have you had chance to run a PNC on him?'

'Not yet.'

'Fair enough. How do you fancy staying down there overnight and I'll come down in the morning?'

'No problem. I'll ring Shirl and tell her. There's a Travel Inn just off the M1. Shall I see you at the nick?'

We talked about it and decided that he'd let

me know where he was staying and I'd pick him up there, early. I rang my opposite number in Nottingham to let him know we were operating on his patch. He sounded keen to be involved and asked me to keep him informed. The murders had left some wounds in the local community that still hadn't healed.

Later, I drove Sonia to the golf club and we went for a run. I did my one lap and she did two. The 10K race had been a crucial test for her but she'd come through it well. Not because she won, but because the knee took all the pounding that the hard road surface could give it. She'd trained on the soft, undulating ground through the woods and over the golf course, where the varying surface gives the legs a good workout without hammering any particular part of them. On the road, it's *bam-bam-bam*, bashing away at the same point, twice per second, for mile after mile. She'd put the knee on the rack, and it had survived.

The bees were gorging themselves on the new blossom, long shadows stretched across the fairways and the golfers were out in force. We stick to the edges of the course and they don't mind the distraction, most of them giving us a friendly wave. At least, we assume it's friendly, although they are often brandishing a number three iron at the time. Heckley is hardly St Andrews, and most of the members are just recreational golfers, not fanatics. I towelled the sweat on Sonia's neck and shoulders for a few moments then handed her the towel.

'Your name was in the *Daily Express* this morning,' I told her.

'Really!' she said, looking up from changing her trainers. 'What did it say?'

'It said, "Women: S. Thornton".'

She gave one of her little giggles. 'Gosh, fame at last.'

'It's a start,' I said. Our press man had done his bit, and the local paper, the *Heckley Gazette*, was promising quite a spread about the race, but I didn't tell her that. I nodded over towards the golf clubhouse. 'Don't forget that we're coming here on Saturday.'

'Is it this week?'

'Yes.'

'Will Sparky and all your detectives be there?'

'No, just me and the boss, and don't let Sparky hear you call him Sparky.'

'Right. I'd better start looking for a dress.'

As we buckled our seatbelts I said, 'How about a pint of lager shandy on the way home?'

'Mmm, that sounds nice,' she agreed. I put the car in gear and reversed out from the line of cars at the dog-walkers' end of the car park. All the regulars were there, and at least one stranger, but it didn't register. When I'm with Sonia my powers of observation desert me, like the swallows heading south to warmer climes, leaving the chill behind.

Brian Bousfield lived near a village about twelve miles east of Lincoln, in what I would call a mobile home and an estate agent would refer to as a park home. They are like wooden chalets as seen in the Alps, and their only mobility is when they are initially installed. After that the pair of dinky-sized wheels are redundant, so I reluctantly agreed that park home was a better description. Bousfield's only form was for drunk and disorderly and handling stolen goods, namely half a ton of roofing lead intended for the village church after ten years of fundraising by the dwindling congregation. That's virtually a clean sheet in my book. He wasn't in the phone book, so we were cold-calling.

'Like 'em?' Dave asked as we turned off the lane and passed through a gate into what an ornate sign told us was Wolds View Park. I'd torn myself away from my brick-and-mortar home ridiculously early and diced with the businessmen and reps in the fast lane of the M1 so I could snatch a quick coffee and toast with Dave before the day's work started.

We were in an estate of the wooden houses, linked by narrow Tarmac paths just wide enough for one vehicle. Almost every house had a car parked alongside it but there was no sign that any children lived here. No bikes left out overnight, no football lying in the grass, no basketball net. Little borders had been cultivated around most of the homes, and were alive with coloured flowers that I didn't know the names of, and roses growing up trellising, which I did. You can learn a lot about people by studying the cars they drive. We saw elderly Volvos and newer Daewoos and Skodas, all clean and shiny. These people were careful with their money and had bypassed the daily rat race that most of us compete in, whether we believe it or not. The sun was shining, it was eight-thirty in the morning and there was a dreamy feel to the place.

'It's a different world,' I said. 'An alternative society. Where do they keep all their old lawnmowers and stepladders and stuff?'

'Go left,' Dave told me. 'They don't. You have to be ruthless, living in one of these. That's it, number eight.'

There was no strip of cultivation round this one, but it was tidy. No doubt there were rules about keeping the grass short and not allowing rubbish to gather. The curtains were closed and a ten-year-old BMW, sans tax disc, stood in the shadow of the chalet, three house bricks supporting the front nearside brake disc. A slightly newer Rover 75 was at the sunny side.

'It looks as if our man isn't an early riser,' Dave said as I parked nose-to-nose with the Bee Emm.

There were two steps up to his door. I reached forward without mounting them and tapped quietly, not wanting to wake the rest of the community. The third time I tapped much harder and we heard stirrings from inside.

The curtain behind the window in the door was snatched to one side and we had our first view of Mr Bousfield. I was grateful he hadn't made a death threat against me.

'Handsome chap,' Dave mumbled out of the side of his mouth.

'What do you want?' Bousfield demanded.

I held my warrant card against the glass without saying anything. He knew the score and opened the door.

'What's it about?' he asked.

'A word,' I told him. 'Either in the comfort of your home or at Lincoln nick.'

He was wearing a singlet that showed off his biceps and tattoos, and Adidas shell suit bottoms. Probably the clothes he'd slept in. At any given point in time more men are wearing Adidas bottoms than any other garment available. Adidas bottoms are the chicken tikka masala of *haute couture*. 'You'd better come in then,' he said.

That's when I learned what the tenants, or this tenant, did with their surplus belongings:

they let them pile up. We were admitted into a corridor bounded by mountains of cardboard boxes, bulging bin liners and assorted items whose shapes didn't lend them to being contained. I had a vague impression of an exercise machine and a motorcycle frame as we edged our way through the kitchen area into the living space. A sleeping bag, flung open like a peeled banana, told us that this doubled as his bedroom. A television bracketed on the wall was showing a cartoon. Bousfield picked up the remote and killed the picture. He bundled the sleeping bag and told us to take a seat.

'Is it about the car?' he asked.

I was trying to identify the smells, to separate the cocktail into recognisable components. Body odour was the main carrier, with a hint of pot, a good slug of tobacco smoke and something else that burnt the back of my nose. It reminded me of the paint shop at the local garage where I once had a Jaguar resprayed. God, that was a long time ago. Cellulose thinners, something like that.

'No, it's not about the car,' Dave told him. 'We were wondering where you were on the night of Sunday, ninth of May. That's three Sundays ago.'

He didn't have to think about it for long, as he was a man of habits and his habits were modest. They exclusively involved consuming lager in the company of a few like-minded friends. When it came to supplying addresses for them he had difficulties, because most of them were involved with fairgrounds and moved around, but he readily suggested that the pub landlord would confirm his alibi. Sunday night was Country and Western night, and he never missed it.

'So what's it all about?' he asked, not unreasonably.

'There was a murder in Heckley that night,' Dave told him. 'A man called Alfred Armitage. Your name came up.'

'My name? Why should my name come up?'

'It just did. Does Alfred Armitage mean anything to you?'

'No. Never heard of him.'

But he bit his lip as he made the denial, and started to scratch at a pretend Celtic design on his bicep.

I said, 'We know about your sister Julie, Mr Bousfield. It was a long time ago.'

He turned his gaze to me. His face was tanned through working outdoors and his eyes were surprisingly pale blue. 'Julie?' he repeated. 'What's she got to do with it?'

'It never really leaves you, does it, something like that?' I said. 'Do you still think about her?'

'Yeah,' he replied. 'Every day.'

'I've seen the photographs,' I told him. 'She was an attractive girl. It must have wrecked your family.'

Something through the window appeared to catch his eye, but he was just remembering her, gathering his thoughts. A big patch of sunlight fell on his lap and bulging stomach, illuminating the tattoos on his forearms and sending flashes of light glancing off the half-pound of wrought gold around his wrist. He came back, saying, 'Julie was special. She could have made something with her life. Not like me. Not like dad. Dad was an arsehole, but he loved Julie. She was the apple of his eye. It killed him, too, when she was murdered. He didn't live to see the trial.'

'Do you have a job?' I asked. I wasn't interested, but I needed him talking.

'Not really,' he confessed. 'A bit of this and that. Casual work on the farms, fruit picking, mushrooms, anything. I sometimes go down to Skeggy to work the fairground. Stuff like that. Nothing regular. I do paint jobs for the Angels, now and again.'

'Hell's Angels?' I asked.

'Yeah. I do airbrush designs on their bikes when I can get it. They pay well.'

That's what the smell was. Our man was an artist. I'd seen the sort of thing he did and it amazed me. Dave shuffled in his seat and crossed his legs. He was thinking the same as me.

I said, 'Do you have anything on the go at

the moment?' and he told me that he had. I asked to see it and he left us for a few seconds to retrieve his latest work from the teetering heaps of boxes in the other room. He came back carrying a long, torpedo-shaped petrol tank.

I took it from him two-handed and admired his handiwork. I like to think that using an airbrush is easy and gimmicky, like painting on velvet, but the proportions were perfect, the colours well-toned and the detail immaculate. I couldn't do it, and I went to art college.

'Bat out of Hell,' I said, recognising the album cover.

'Yeah, it's a favourite of theirs,' he replied.

'And mine.' I studied the workmanship for a minute and carefully handed the tank back to him. 'Do you have a bike, Mr Bousfield?' I asked.

'No. Not interested.'

'But you have friends who have?'

'They go in the pub, that's all. Most of them are just posers. They have jobs. Nobody could afford a Harley without one.'

'You were telling me about Julie.'

He started at the mention of her name and gently placed the petrol tank on the cushioned seat where he'd slept. 'Julie? What about her?'

'The trial must have been a traumatic time for you. I believe you made some threats at

144

the end of it.'

'Yeah, well. I was upset, wasn't I?'

'He was called Terence Paul Hutchinson, and you threatened to kill him. Would you still like to kill him, Mr Bousfield?'

'It was just talk.'

'But would you still like to kill him?'

'Yeah, I suppose I would. Scum like him deserves to die.'

'But you weren't in Heckley on the ninth of May?'

'No, I've never been to flamin' Heckley. I don't even know where it is.'

'It's in Yorkshire,' I told him. 'What about your Angel friends? Were any of them in town that night?'

'How would I know? So who was this Alfred Whatsisname?'

Dave showed him the picture but the only reaction it provoked was a shrug of the shoulders. Bousfield said it meant nothing to him.

'Apparently Alfred Armitage bore a strong resemblance to Hutchinson, the Midnight Strangler,' I said. 'What do you think?'

'I don't know. He might do.'

I looked at my watch and went on, 'But it's not the same person. The real Terence Paul Hutchinson is safely locked up in Bentley prison. He'll have had a warder gently shake his shoulder about half an hour ago and should be tucking into a full English about now.'

Bousfield's neck muscles tightened like tree roots at the thought of his sister's murderer lording it in a category C prison. He clenched and unclenched his fists and breathed hard through his nose. Was it because he thought the man was dead? Huge veins ran down the inside of his arms, like strip maps of the River Nile, spreading into deltas at his wrists. In reality, Hutchinson would have been blasted out of his pit by a bell at six-thirty, and breakfasted on mechanically reclaimed pork sausage and lumpy porridge, eaten off a tin plate.

He remembered some more names for his alibi and gave us a couple of addresses, but we knew it would check out. I took Dave back to the services where he'd left his car, and we drove home to Heckley. We weren't fazed by Bousfield's cast-iron alibi. He hadn't done the deed himself, but that didn't mean he wasn't involved. Paint jobs like the one he'd shown us don't come cheap, as our man had admitted, but cash is not the only currency, and Hell's Angels are not affiliated to the Women's Institute. The line of enquiry was still alive.

My phone rang on the way home and I pulled into a lay-by to answer it. The ACC had decided that an appeal on *Calendar* and *Look North* was overdue, and I was nominated to do it. I grumbled but was overruled.

They needed me at HQ by three o'clock. I stopped at Sainsbury's to buy a *Gazette* and a sandwich, and parked near the cash machines while I dashed in.

A black youth and a white girl were before me at the basket-only checkout. I followed them out and they climbed into a Jaguar XK8 convertible parked in a *Disabled* slot, with the hood down. 'They didn't get that on Motobility allowance,' I mumbled to myself. Almost without thinking about it I flipped my notebook open and wrote the number down. It's all about stereotypes. It shouldn't be, but it is, and experience often proves us right. As they drove off another convertible, this time a Mercedes SLK 320, nipped into the space they'd left. It was driven by a tall woman in heavily embroidered flared trousers cut low enough to be barely decent, a skimpy top and the obligatory shades. She had Mercedes written all over her, but the youth and girl were strictly Skoda Octavia. I watched her sashay away on four-inch heels and wrote her number under the other one, simply because I had a pen in my hand and it's what we do.

The newspaper had a half-page photo-collage of the race, with Sonia in two of the pictures. *Return of the Gazelle*, it said. In one photograph she was battling with Eunice Mboto, the girl who came second, and in the other she was with me, surrounded by admirers. Hers, that is, not mine. The caption named me, describing me as her coach. I'd have words with our press officer about that, but it was better than calling me her live-in lover. I carefully folded the paper and drove to the office, where I cleaned my teeth and brushed my hair, ready for the telecast.

They'd prepared a statement for me, saying that Alfred was murdered and we wanted anyone who had seen a white van in the vicinity to come forward. It had been a sadistic crime for no apparent motive and we desperately needed to apprehend the killer. I asked for any unusual motorcycle to be added to the list of suspicious vehicles, and it was. Alfred was well known locally, I had to tell the world, and anyone who had seen him with strangers was asked to contact the police.

I memorised most of it, declined having my face powdered, and we were away. Someone with a slightly familiar face introduced me as Acting Detective Chief Inspector Priest and I made the statement with barely a glance at the notes. Everybody said 'Well done' and I drove back to Heckley.

Eddie Carmichael was in the office when I arrived back, his head in a newspaper. He looked up, saying, 'Hi guv. How did it go?'

'Fine,' I replied. 'No problem.'

He held the paper for me to see, open at the sports page. 'They'll be having you on *Celebrity Squares* next.'

'No chance. Do you want to volunteer as the acceptable face of the force? Your old pal Superintendent Stanwick is looking for someone.'

'Nah, not me, guv. Everybody to his own, I say.'

I said, 'Don't say you weren't asked. You could be the next Michael Parkinson. What have you found?'

'Nothing. Blank faces all round. Maybe the broadcast will jog a few memories.'

'Let's hope so. What do you know about Hell's Angels?'

He looked puzzled. 'Same as anybody, I suppose. They're a bunch of scruffy bikers scrounging off the state. In America they go round killing people, into drugs and what not. Over here they're just a bunch of tosspots. What's brought this up?'

I told him about our interview with Bousfield. 'Have a look into them, please, Eddie,' I told him. 'Have a word with the Serious Organised Crime Agency. They have experts on gangs. See if the Angels are active down in Lincolnshire, or into bumping people off. Anything at all. Bousfield is in the frame, good and large.'

'Great,' he said, glad to have something fresh to work at. 'I'll get on with it.'

Half an hour later, just as I was finishing filling in the log book, Dave came in with a coffee for me. 'How did the TV go?' he asked.

'No problem,' I replied. 'They said they might ask me to do the weather forecast if they're ever short.'

'Only the weather forecast? I'd have thought it would be *Panorama* at least. Have you seen the paper?'

'About the race? Good, innit?'

'*Coach!*' he exclaimed. 'I've heard it called some things...'

I said, 'Now now, Dave. Let's not get personal.'

'Yeah, sorry about that. Do you want me to start looking into the Hell's Angels?'

'Ah!' I said. 'No. I've asked Eddie to get on with it.'

'Oh, right,' he replied, and turned to go. I opened my mouth to call him back, then closed it again without saying anything. He's a big boy.

Half an hour later he brought me another coffee, but apart from me thanking him we didn't speak. Another half-hour later he brought me another coffee, then it was time to go home.

Sonia and I did our laps of the park, showered at home and dined on casseroled pork cutlets. At nine o'clock I took her to the station and introduced her to the staff in the incident room. We had four telephonists manning the phones to gather the responses to the broadcast, which had gone out at 6.25 on the BBC and 6.45 on ITV. They were not being overwhelmed. One was taking a call and the other three were chatting, their chairs turned at angles to their desks. A newspaper was folded with the crossword showing, almost completed, but I resisted the temptation to pick it up and have a go. I studied the reports we had and saw that some might be worth following up but that nothing stood out like a Rastafarian at a Ku Klux Klan tea party. There were the obvious crank calls, and the well-meaning ones that had nothing to say, but in the next few days every one would be chased. We went home and watched *The Shawshank Redemption* on video. OK, so I hadn't caught a murderer, but it had been a near perfect day.

Dave brought me a coffee next morning before I finished the tea I'd made for myself. I asked Jeff Caton to join me in the office and told him about the odd couple I'd seen in the posh Jaguar, taking up a *Disabled* space.

'I don't think it's a crime, yet, Chas,' he said.

'You know what I mean,' I told him. 'It might be worth looking into. They were only in their early twenties. What does a car like

151

that cost?'

'About fifty-five grand.'

'There you go, then. That's the number.' I pushed my notebook towards him and he copied it.

'What's this other one?' he asked.

'Ah!' I started. 'That one doesn't matter. She was rather elegant, that's all. In a nice car, too. A Merc. Very swish. Now she did look the part.'

'You're incorrigible, Charlie. I'll look into it. By the way, you looked great on the telly.'

'Thank you.'

'And in the *Gazette*.'

'I thought so, too, but it's nice of you to say so.'

'Is it true they've asked you to be the new face of *Laboratoire Garnier?*'

'Get stuffed.'

In the incident room I told the team about our trip to Lincolnshire and about the responses to the appeal. We had some leg work to do, but it didn't look promising. Our best bet was still with the Hell's Angels.

'Eddie,' I said, looking at him. 'Have you found anything out about them?'

'A bit, guv, but not much.'

'Well come up here and tell us all about it.'

'I had a word with the Serious Organised Crime Agency,' he told us after he'd come to the front, with all the aplomb of someone who conferred with them every day. 'They have an expert on biker gangs. Hell's Angels is a pretty loose term in this country, unlike America. Over there, they were formed by ex-Second World War bomber crews, disillusioned when they returned home. Call yourself an Angel over there and you could get killed. Over here it's much less organised, but there are three main groups: one is based on the south coast, around Brighton; one up in the North East; and one in the east of England, where our suspect lives. Unfortunately for them the British climate is not conducive to riding around for hours with your arms and legs spread like a jump suit on a washing line. They usually ride old British bikes, mainly Triumphs, on which they lavish great attention. The members themselves are often ageing remnants of the rocker scene, hippies and greasers. There's no doubt that they peddle drugs, but what part of society doesn't? They are not to be confused with the Harley Davidson Owners Group, who like to refer to themselves as Hogs. Harleys start at about ten grand, so these are usually well off, born-again bikers living in a fantasy world. They call themselves *bad asses* and go to Rotary every Wednesday evening.'

'So how would you summarise?' I said.

'In short, guv, the Angels are a bunch of scumbags who'd rob their grandma of their granddad's ashes if they thought they could get a bob or two for them.'

Someone said, 'The weather's warming up, so they're probably coming out of hibernation.'

'Yeah,' Eddie agreed. 'They're all coming out from under their stones.'

'OK,' I said. 'There's a strong possibility that Bousfield recruited one of his Angel friends to nobble Alfred. Unfortunately, Lincoln is a long way away, so we can't dash down there at the drop of a nun's wimple, and while we might have enough to bring him up here for a long and meaningful talk, if he stays shtoom we have no chance of charging him. We'll have to ask Lincoln to do some legwork for us, and maybe spend a day or two down there when we have some names. Anybody fancy a break amongst the sprout fields of Lincolnshire?'

I'd hardly warmed the chair in my office, upstairs, when Dave brought me another coffee. 'What's all this about?' I asked. 'I've only been here an hour and I'm onto my third drink.'

'Oh,' he said. 'I thought you'd be grateful. Would you rather I didn't bother?'

'I am grateful, but you're killing me with kindness. I'm spending more time going for a pee than I am working.'

'Sorry, Chas. I'm only trying to oil the wheels.'

'You're certainly succeeding in that. Could I have the next one at about ten, please, if we're still here?'

He went out and I started looking at the reports from the appeal. One or two demanded immediate attention, so I deployed the troops to look into them. Maggie came in and I told her to sit down.

When I'd finished making a note I said, 'What's going off with Dave, Maggie? He's behaving strangely.'

'Strangely,' she repeated. 'In what way?'

'He brings me a cup of coffee about every ten minutes. I could float a battleship on all the coffee I've drunk since yesterday afternoon.'

'It started yesterday afternoon?'

'That's when I noticed it.'

'Right, well that explains a lot.'

'It doesn't to me.'

Maggie looked at me, tight-lipped, for several seconds, then said, 'When Dave came back in yesterday afternoon, someone had done a drawing on his blotter.'

'A drawing? What of?'

'A poodle.'

'I see. The inference being that he's my poodle.'

'It looked that way.'

'He's been called that before.'

'I know, but this time it rankles.'

'Eddie?' I asked. Maggie shrugged her

shoulders. Crooks are not the only ones who don't grass. It was my problem. I said, 'So Dave's way of dealing with it is to go over the top. Good for him. It's better than pushing him down the stairs.'

'What will you do?'

'Is Eddie upsetting any other members of the team?' I asked.

'You know Eddie, Chas.'

'I'll take that as a yes. I don't know what I'll do, Maggie. Have a word with him, I suppose. Again.'

The phone rang. 'Are you in Chas?' I was asked. 'It's your bank manager.'

I didn't know I had a bank manager. Well, I suppose I had one, someone must manage the place where I use the cash machine, but we weren't on telephone-calling terms.

'It's my bank manager,' I whispered to Maggie, pulling a face.

She stood up. 'Shall I leave you to it...?'

I shook my head 'no' and she sat down again. 'Put him through, please.'

'DI Priest,' I said, after the click. 'How can I help you?'

'Is that Inspector Priest in charge of the murder enquiry?' a fairly refined voice asked.

'That's right. How can I help?'

'My name is Jarvis, Inspector, and I'm manager of the Heckley branch of the York and Durham.'

He paused for effect. I bank with Barclays.

'I'm listening, Mr Jarvis,' I said.

'I heard your appeal, last night,' he continued. 'Well, saw it, actually. I've been on holiday for three weeks, out of the country. Hiking in the Dolomites.'

'That sounds fun.'

'It was. Nothing too strenuous, you understand, but quite energetic enough for someone with my heart condition. I never usually watch television. Not these days. All these reality shows and makeovers. A load of moronic nonsense, if you ask me.' I hadn't asked, but I agreed with him. 'Just put it on to catch up with the headlines,' he went on. 'And that's when I saw you.'

It's amazing how many people never watch television but just happen to see everything that's on it. 'So what can you tell me,' I urged. *Cutting to the chase,* as we say in Heckley.

'The dead chap, Alfred Armitage. I thought the name rang a bell, so I went in this morning although I wasn't scheduled to return until tomorrow.'

'That's conscientious of you,' I admitted, rolling my eyes at Maggie. 'And what did you find?'

'Just as I thought. He was a client of ours.'

'Good. Good. Was he a regular client?' It was another piece of information in the riddle that was the world of Alfred Armitage. We now knew where he banked. Big deal.

'At one time he was. And we are the executors of his will.'

I sat up. 'He left a will?'

'That's right.'

'Can you tell me who he left his estate to?'

'No problem. He left it all to the Church of the Nazarene. Apparently his wife worshipped there.'

'Blimey!' I exclaimed. 'And did he have much to leave?'

'It depends on if you call £342,000 much,' he replied.

'Jeeesus! I think I'd better come round to see you, Mr Jarvis. Will about ten minutes be OK?'

'Yes, that will be fine, Inspector. Officially, I'm not here, so we shouldn't be disturbed.'

I turned to Maggie. 'Get your coat, Maggie,' I told her. 'You've pulled.'

Chapter Six

We walked, so were a few minutes late, but I saved 35p on parking. Mr Jarvis's office was sparse and utilitarian. A plain desk with computer terminal, typist's chair and abstract prints on the wall knocked up by the decorator with a roller and some leftover emulsion. I'd expected a book-lined office in mahogany and leather, with a signed photo of Mrs Thatcher prominently displayed, but I'm behind the times with these things. The bank had recently announced record profits after sacking half its employees in this country and opening a call centre in Ulan Bator. Jarvis's position in the company was probably more precarious than that of the polite young receptionist who led us to his office.

We declined coffee and asked him what he could tell us about the financial affairs of Alfred Armitage. He could have refused, or at least put up a few obstructions until we hit him with a warrant, but he was sensible and cooperative, and the subject of the enquiry wasn't going to complain.

'Mr Armitage opened a savings account with us in 1962,' he told us. 'Nothing special, bread and butter stuff. Saving to get married, I suppose. We helped him with various loans over the years and he made regular payments, never defaulted. He didn't have a mortgage with us. It was all steady business until 1986, when he started making deposits over and above his regular salary. In 1997 he took advantage of our will-making service and appointed us as his executors.'

'His wife died in 1997,' Maggie explained.

'Tell us about the deposits, please,' I urged, anxious to get to the meaty part. Jarvis pondered for a second, then dived into one of the drawers that supported his

159

desk. 'If you won't have a coffee, can I tempt you with one of these?' he said, thrusting a box of Thorntons Continental towards us. Maggie chose a walnut whip and I went for the caramel truffle because the Turkish delight was missing.

'One of your weaknesses, Mr Jarvis?' Maggie asked.

'Actually, no,' he replied. 'Before I went on holiday I bought them for a girl who was leaving. Unfortunately she finished two days early and left me a note calling me a fucking wanker, so I kept them. I'll give the rest to the staff. Sorry about the French, miss.'

'I've heard worse.'

'The deposits,' I reminded him.

'Ah yes. Unfortunately I haven't had chance to investigate our paper records in the ledgers because we don't keep them here, but we started our computerisation programme in 1974 and I've made a few notes. It would appear that Mr Armitage has been making ir-regular but frequent deposits for a long time.'

'How large and how frequent?' I asked.

'Between five hundred and a thousand pounds every week or two. They started tapering off about 1998 and had dried up by 2000.'

'Cheques or cash?' Maggie asked.

'Cheques.'

'So you can tell us who was paying him,' I said.

Jarvis looked uncomfortable. 'Sorry, but no,' he replied. 'As you know, when a deposit is made a deposit slip is completed, but this does not record who the drawer was, unless the customer actually wrote it on the back.'

Actually, I didn't know. My salary goes in, my bills are paid and I draw money from a cash machine. Occasionally someone gives me a cheque for a painting, which I hand over to the disinterested girl behind the glass, she gives me something to sign and that's it. Presumably it appears on my account, but I rarely look.

'I don't suppose Mr Armitage wrote anything on the back,' I said, hoping to be proved wrong.

'I'll have to check, but I doubt it. We keep the deposit slips, of course, stored at our central collecting point for ten years or so. After that they're destroyed to make room. The cheques themselves are sent back to the drawer's bank. The sort code identifies which branch.'

'Would all Alfred's deposit slips be stored together?' I asked.

'Sorry, Inspector. They are bundled by the day. We'd need a date to make it easier. Have you found any of his accounts?'

I shook my head. 'No. Weren't your suspicions ever aroused about the account?' I asked.

'No, Inspector. Why should they be? For a start, the payments were established long before all the fuss about suspicious cash transactions by drug dealers was made, and these weren't cash transactions. As far as my staff were concerned he was just another businessman doing quite nicely.'

'Depositing a thousand pounds a week with no outgoings?' I said.

'It was his profit. He was netting thirty or forty thousand pounds per annum. As far as we were concerned he could have been a salesman or anything. It's not our job to pry into these things. We will no doubt have sent him our small businesses pack, and invited him in for a chat, but as far as I know he never took advantage of our services. As for suspicious cash transactions, I'd say our record at reporting them is as good as anybody's.'

'No doubt you're right, Mr Jarvis,' I admitted. 'But I have to ask.'

The running was becoming serious. Sonia decided she needed more professional coaching than I could provide and had started going to a track session at Huddersfield. It was serious stuff, against the clock. I'd forgotten that Thursday was one of the nights, so was disappointed when she wasn't at my house when I arrived home. I watched TV until seven, to give the takeaway's wok time to warm up, then fetched one of their specials.

She rang me just as I finished it, to say that she ought to go to her own house tonight, so she'd see me after work tomorrow. I asked her how the training went.

'Fine,' she replied. 'Ten intervals, only two seconds outside what I used to do them at. We're getting there. It's not as enjoyable as running round the golf course with you, but it's good to measure yourself against the others. I'd better stay at home tonight, if you don't mind. I have the mail to pick up and the rubbish to put out. They collect it Fridays. I'd better turn the thermostat down, too, now that the warmer weather has arrived, or it'll be like an oven in there. It's a good job I only have cactus plants. I suppose I'd better water them while I'm there. What about you, Charlie? What sort of a day have you had?'

'Oh, so-so.'

'Have you caught the murderer yet?'

'Not yet.'

'Do you have any ideas who it is?'

'He's short and fat and wears spectacles. We've arrested Elton John.'

'Really!'

'I'm pulling your leg, Sonia.'

'Oh, sorry.'

'That's all right.'

'Chas...' she began. She usually reserves

163

Chas for more intimate moments.

'Yes, Sonia.'

'Have you any holidays to come?'

'Months.'

'How do you fancy a fortnight in South Africa?'

'I'd love it, but not in the middle of a murder enquiry. What brought this on?'

'Nothing. Well, not much. I have contacts at the University of Cape Town. They hold training camps, and I've been invited. You could come, too.'

'Sorry, Sonia. No can do. Not at the moment. You go, though, if that's what you want.'

'I'll see.'

'Don't be late home tomorrow.'

'I might be. I still need a dress for Saturday.'

'Just go in a shell suit, like me.'

'Uh! You'd better not!' she exclaimed.

'Goodnight, love.'

'Goodnight, Charlie.'

I put the phone down. We'd been thrown together by tragedy, and that's not a good basis for a relationship. For a while we'd spent seven nights a week in each other's company, and I'd enjoyed every second of them. But now she was going to the track twice a week, mixing with other athletes. He'd be there: the guy who came third in the 10K and invited her over to train with them. 'You need more speed work,' he'd told her, and, 'Perhaps we'll see you at the track?' And now he was seeing her there.

I took a photo of Alfred Armitage's face, taken postmortem, out of my briefcase, found a pad of cartridge paper and sharpened several 2B pencils. I taped a sheet of paper to my drawing board, propped the photo against a jar of coffee on the kitchen table and started the drawing I should have done a fortnight ago.

For eighteen days we'd only seen Alfred with his eyes closed. I opened them on the drawing and tried to put the spark of life in them. For the first time I saw the human being that had been Alfred Armitage: the man who'd been a loving husband and gone to pieces when his wife died; the man who'd worked for forty-five years with the same company until temptation became too much for him. The man who was hurt when someone called him an insulting name, and who died for no other reason than he resembled someone else.

But I put something else there, too. Something that wasn't in the photograph. I drew a sadness in his eyes, in the curve of his mouth, in the hang of his jowls. A sadness that transcended the ridicule he'd endured all his life. Where it came from, I dreaded to think.

It was a good drawing. One of the best I'd

ever done, but it wasn't for public consumption. There was too much of Alfred in it, and too much of me, too. I carefully tore it into quarters and dropped them in the swing bin. The digital clock on the oven was showing midnight and my eyes were burning.

Drifting in a canoe on a lake in Canada, the water's surface mirroring the big sky and the only disturbance the occasional salmon taking a fly. Walking on the moors with the sun setting behind and the lights of a Dales pub beckoning. Lying on a beach. Sitting in a conservatory drinking tea and listening to Dylan, with the rain dancing on the glass roof. I don't sleep well, so I have my favourite places to go when I lie awake, waiting for the dawn to come skulking over the hill. Some of them I keep to myself.

Tonight it was the Olympic Games 1,500 metres final. Starting the final lap I was lying last, but I accelerated as the bell rang and took the lead with 300 metres to go. I held them off down the back straight, let them gain on me round the bend, but I'd programmed myself for one last kick at the hundred-metre mark and won by three metres. I jogged to the girl with the flowers and gave her a kiss on the cheek as she handed me my bouquet. Behind me, the rest of the field was spread-eagled on the track, exhausted. It was a new world record. Two, if you included the fact that I was the oldest winner ever.

Nine o'clock Friday morning I rang Smart Solutions. Bernie Smart was an old super-intendent of mine who left under a cloud after a bribery scam involving one of his sergeants. Bernie's as straight as Watling Street, but mud sticks and he left. He formed a security company called Hawkeye Security, but soon learned that a more low-key profile was required for the work that was coming his way, and Smart Solutions was born. I rang him because I needed information about industrial espionage. It was something we rarely became involved with. I'd always imagined it was high-tech stuff, involving computer files, micro-photography and sleepers planted in companies for years, but now I was having second thoughts. I remem-bered reading about Russia's Tupolev 144, which was their answer to Concorde. It looked just like the Concorde, which wasn't surprising as, if the stories are true, a French spy had furnished them with the blueprints. The Tupolev flew a couple of months before the Concorde, but it ended in tears at the Paris air show in 1973 when it crashed, killing the crew and several people on the ground. Know-alls and conspiracy theorists claim that faults had been deliberately built into the stolen blueprints, and the Russians had copied the plans, faults and all, with fatal results. It's probably all bunkum, but that's the sort of world I imagined industrial spies to move in. I was wrong.

'There was this company in Slough that made babies' dummies,' Bernie told me after we'd exchanged insults, had the obligatory five minutes of reminiscing and I'd explained my problem.

'Dummies?' I echoed.

'That's right. What the Americans call comforters. They made them by the million and sold them all over the country. Every chemist's shop in the land had one of their display cards with the dummies on it. But all of a sudden their sales went into sharp decline. People were having just as many babies but the orders weren't coming in. So the MD went on the road to see what the problem was. It was a small family business and he was a hands-on type of guy. Well, he couldn't see where things were going wrong. Everywhere he went he saw their dummies prominently displayed and the shopkeepers assured him that they were turning them over, as before. Until one day he noticed a card filled with blue dummies. The thing was, they'd never made any blue dummies. Turned out they were being copied somewhere in the Far East, right down to the last detail of the packaging, and the market had been flooded with them, undercutting the originals.'

I said, 'Strewth! You can't get more low-tech than a baby's dummy.'

'That's right, Charlie, but copying the product is the easy bit. You just buy one and give it to your engineers. It's the sales and distribution where the inside information is essential. Ask any businessman. Who is the market? What do they pay? What quantities are we talking about? When you know those things you have a flying start. And it's much easier to pay a bent employee a few thousand pounds for the information than to spend millions on research and development and building up a customer base.'

'So our man didn't just give them the product, he was passing on details about customers?'

'You've got it, but guess what.'

'What?'

'It's not illegal. He wasn't breaking the law.'

Three weeks into a murder enquiry questions are asked. The ACC (Crime) was going on holiday to his villa in the Algarve the following week, so he called the meeting a couple of days early. He was anxious that the division be seen as pioneers with the HMET initiative, and wanted to put us all up on our toes. As always, it was more out of self-promotion and preservation than any desire to see justice done. He came to see us, which is a change, at short notice, which isn't. I heard about the meeting ten minutes early, and barely had chance to change into a sober tie for the occasion. The one with tiny Homer Simpsons on it that Dave's daughter bought me last Christmas.

At ten seconds to ten I paused outside Gilbert's office, knuckle poised, until I heard the first chime of St. Saviour's church clock, over the road. I knocked briskly and swung the door open.

The ACC and Mr Wood were enjoying a laugh with someone that I didn't recognise at first. They coughed and spluttered but didn't offer to share the joke. 'Have you met Superintendent Stanwick, Charlie?' the ACC asked.

'We've talked on the phone,' I said, shaking the proffered hand. He tried to crush my fingers to show what a straightforward type of fellow he was, but I forgot to do the Masons bit.

'I offered Charlie a job,' Stanwick said, 'but he wouldn't bite. Don't know why. That was a first class presentation you did on Wednesday, Charlie. First class.'

'Sorry, Mr Stanwick,' I said, 'but it's not for me.'

'Mark, please,' he protested. 'And we have met before.'

'Have we?'

'Long time ago. When we were both on the

up. The strange case of Old Mother Twanky.'
He turned to the ACC and Gilbert to explain. 'Old Mother Twanky spontaneously combusted. All that was left of her was a pile of ashes, one hand and a foot. Strangest thing you ever saw. I was duty sergeant and arrived a few seconds before Charlie came and took over. He was a rooky inspector, if my memory serves me well. No doubt Charlie has forgotten all about it, but I haven't.'

I hadn't forgotten all about it. I remember the name of every victim I was ever involved with. Edith Tweddle wasn't murdered, but I still remembered her. It was the names of ambitious cops on the up that I forgot.

'It was a long time ago,' I said.

'Can we talk about the case, please,' Gilbert protested. 'I have other places to go.'

'Mind if I sit in?' Stanwick asked. 'See what's happening at the sharp end, eh?'

We didn't mind, and I spent the next half-hour explaining the avenues of investigation that we were following. I told them all about the bad blood that existed between Smallwood and Alfred, and then about Alfred's secret income and the possibility that he was involved in some sort of low level industrial espionage.

'And you reckon that's not illegal?' Gilbert asked.

I shrugged my shoulders. 'I'm informed that it needn't be. If Alfred was photocopying documents it could be construed as stealing, or if he was copying computer files he might be breaching the data protection act, but if he was simply making notes and passing the information on, then there's nothing we can do. It's a grey area and is usually sorted out in the civil court.'

The ACC put his hands over his ears, saying, 'Don't talk to me about the data protection act.'

After that I told them about Alfred's uncanny resemblance to the Midnight Strangler, about Brian Bousfield's outburst in court and his association with the local chapter of the Hell's Angels. They asked questions, I tried to answer them. We kicked things around, didn't come up with any conclusions. But that wasn't the purpose of the exercise. The ACC wanted to go on holiday with a clear conscience and I wanted him off my back. In those respects, it was a successful meeting.

'So what's happening with the Hell's Angels?' the ACC asked.

'I've handed them over to Lincoln,' I said. 'They're looking at individuals named by Bousfield as his alibi. And we've had a word with SOCA's biker gang expert. It's a bit far to keep dashing down there, but we'll have to spend some time with them when we have some more information.'

'I'm glad you're keeping an eye on the

expenses, Charlie,' the ACC said.

'Do you think Smallwood could have done it?' Gilbert asked.

I sat silent for a few seconds, then said, 'I don't know, boss. He's weird, that's for sure. He fits the template, but whether he'd have the balls to do a murder is another thing.'

'What's your gut feeling, Charlie?' Stanwick asked.

I shook my head. 'I don't have gut feelings. I go where the evidence points.'

'Spoken like a professional,' he said.

'Have you asked the economic crime unit to look into the dealings at Ellis and Newbolds?' the ACC asked.

'I've asked, but they were reluctant as there's no complainant.'

'Were they? Well ask again on Monday and I think you'll find them more eager to help.'

'Right. Thanks.'

He stood up to leave and we all did the same. 'Before you go,' Gilbert said, diving into his desk drawer and producing a bunch of tickets, 'who'd like a ticket for the Rotary spring ball, tomorrow night?' He turned to Stanwick, saying, 'Two for you, Mark? It's all in a good cause.'

Stanwick grinned sheepishly and went for his wallet. 'Oh, if it's for a good cause. How much?'

'Only forty pounds the pair.' He turned to the ACC. 'And can I interest you, boss?'

'Not for me, Gilbert,' he said. 'We'll be busy packing.'

Stanwick handed Gilbert two twenties with all the grace of a juvenile orang-utan surrendering its last banana to the alpha male. I said my goodbyes and went downstairs.

Jeff and Maggie were in the big office. 'Any great breakthroughs, boss?' Maggie asked.

'What do you think? At least we're still on the case, and the ACC goes on holiday for two weeks on Sunday.' I told them about Gilbert slow-timing forty quid out of Stanwick, which raised smiles all round. 'What about you, Jeff? Anything I need to know about?'

'Nah. You can sleep easy. I've got Terry Hyson downstairs. I'm letting him stew for a while.'

'Hyson? Hyson?' I said. 'Remind me.'

'Angie's ex-boyfriend, of Angie's Sex Shop fame.'

'Ah, that Terry Hyson. What does he have to say for himself?'

'He says he didn't do it. Denies everything. I've threatened him with an ASBO and the sex offenders' register, but he won't accept a caution. Says it wasn't him, so why should he?'

An adult caution, or reprimand, is an admission of guilt. It is not regarded as having a criminal record, but we keep it on file for at least five years, and the recipient has to declare it to a prospective employer, if asked. An ASBO is an anti-social behaviour order and requires a lower standard of proof than a criminal conviction.

'Has he any other form?'

'Causing an affray, that's all. He was in a punch-up outside the Lamb and Flag, back in 2002.'

'So what are you going to do?'

'Like I said, I'm letting him stew. If he's still adamant I'll let him go. He reckons she's had several boyfriends since him, and it's one of them. He did it the first time; they're just copying him. I'd better get down there.'

'Want me to have a word?'

'Yep. That's fine by me. Then kick him out, please.'

I went downstairs. At the front desk I said, 'Got any fags, Arthur?'

'Not sure,' he replied, pulling a drawer open. The nick is a non-smoking area for the staff, which is OK because just about all of us are non-smokers, but visitors and detainees are allowed to smoke. The right to give cancer to yourself and anybody near you is a civil liberty, and we're big on civil liberties. Sometimes there's a packet of cigs at the front desk, used to pacify distraught victims or prisoners who are gnawing their knuckle joints in despair.

'Here we are, Chas,' I was told as a

crumpled Benson and Hedges packet was produced. 'Just a couple left.' I took them from him, with a plastic lighter, and went to the interview room where Terry Hyson was patiently waiting.

He didn't know it, but I had a certain admiration for him. Modifying the sign over Angie's shop as an act of revenge was something I could imagine myself doing. There was a certain wit to it. He was slumped in the plastic chair, head in his hands, and hadn't put any weight on since our last meeting.

'Hello Terry, remember me?' I asked, taking a seat opposite him and sliding the fags across the table.

He looked up, red marks on his face where his fingers had been pressed. 'Yeah,' he replied, 'it's Mr Priest, innit?'

'That's right. It was me who cautioned you, over a year ago. I hoped we wouldn't see you again. You've let me down, Terry. When I caution someone they're supposed to stay cautioned. Otherwise it looks bad on my record. Have a fag.'

'I'm sorry, Mr Priest,' he said, 'but I haven't let you down.' He took one of the flattened cigarettes from the packet and put it in his mouth. The lighter fired second flick. 'It wasn't me did it this time. They were just copying me. She's a slag, and I'm better off without 'er. I see that now.' He tipped his head back and sent a long plume of smoke up towards the ceiling.

'I believe DS Caton told you that you could expect an ASBO if it went to the magistrates? Do you know what that would mean?'

'Yeah. I'd be banned from going down Main Street or anywhere near Angie. Something like that, but I'm not admitting something I didn't do.'

We talked for ten minutes. He stubbed the cigarette in the tin-lid ashtray and asked if he could have the last one. I asked him if he was working and he said he was waiting to go on a bricklaying course when the new term started. He didn't know anything about who was selling drugs or about any of the day-to-day petty crime that besets any modern market town. I told him to let me know if he heard anything.

'Off you go, then, Terry,' I said, standing up. 'I'll believe you, thousands wouldn't, but you owe me.'

We walked along the corridor to the foyer. Eddie Carmichael and Superintendent Stanwick were standing just inside the door, talking like bosom buddies. I saw Terry off the premises, flapped a hand at the two of them and ran upstairs, three at a time. Since I started serious training it hardly makes me puff.

'I've kicked him out,' I told Jeff, after I'd made myself a tea. 'He may have been telling the truth.'

'Or maybe he's lying like a toad to hide a broken heart,' Maggie suggested.

'Ah,' I said, after taking a tentative sip of near-boiling tea, 'you know what they say about broken hearts, Margaret.'

'No, Charles,' she replied. 'What do they say about broken hearts?'

I'd backed myself into a corner so I came out with it. 'They say that if there's one thing worse than having a broken heart, it's never having had a broken heart.'

There was a silence as it sank in, until Maggie asked, 'So who said that?'

'I did.'

'And did it help?'

'No, not a lot.'

The door burst open and Eddie Carmichael bustled in, carrying an orange and black plastic bag. When he'd made himself a coffee and joined us I said, 'Swapping stories with your old army buddy, were you, Eddie?'

'Army buddy?' he replied. 'Me and Stanwick? Who told you we were army buddies?'

'As a matter of fact, he did.'

'No. We met in the Met.' He paused for a second, then repeated it. 'Met in the Met. That's nearly funny.'

'Nearly,' Jeff agreed, before I could.

'I was in the REME for three years,' Eddie explained. 'Stanwick was in the officer cadet corps at some toffee-nosed school in North

178

Yorkshire. Appletreewick, or somewhere.'

'Ampleforth?' I suggested.

'Yeah, that's probably it, guv. He wasn't in the army proper. We compared notes once or twice, that's all.'

'Right. So what's in the bag?'

He held it aloft. It was a Harley Davidson carrier. 'I've been shopping,' he declared. 'There's a Harley shop in Brighouse so I thought I'd go along to see if I could learn anything. No joy, I'm afraid. The proprietor agrees that they're mainly a bunch of middle class posers. He looked the part, though. Big bushy beard and long hair, but he has letters after his name. He's a bachelor of science from Birmingham. It wasn't a wasted journey entirely, though. I bought this.'

He shook the carrier upside down until a black T-shirt fell from it. He spread it out so we could see the big bald eagle logo on the front, then turned it over. Emblazoned in white letters across the back was the legend:

IF YOU CAN READ THIS
THE BITCH FELL OFF

'Good, innit?' he proclaimed. 'The wife'll go spare when she sees this.'

'Hmm. Not a single spelling mistake,' Jeff agreed.

Maggie stood up and walked away. As she passed me she hissed, 'Tosspot,' but I don't think she meant me.

John Rose's report from the Bramshill boffins was waiting on my desk, but I made a couple of phone calls before I picked it up. My expectations were low, and I wasn't disappointed. There'd been a remarkably similar murder in Belgium, back in 1998, but the killer had died in custody. Dropping an electric fire into the bath was a popular MO, and very fashionable in Switzerland, for some strange reason, but it was usually a partner-on-partner crime. Suicide by self-electrocution had a steady but depressing following, usually after other methods had failed. John had added a note saying that he'd asked them to go back ten years, did I want to extend the period? The contact officer reminded us that we were required to keep him informed of any developments.

I made a note in the log and marked the report for filing. It had to be done, but we were on our own with this one.

Sonia and I went for a run in the park, followed by grilled salmon, new potatoes and garden peas, with apple pie and custard for pudding. It's my favourite meal. We shared a bottle of Barramundi and sat talking, a Philip Glass playing softly in the background. Some say it's wallpaper music, but wallpaper has its place in our lives and it's great for covering cracks. I told her about the meeting and we had a laugh about Terry Hyson. It's a deliberate ploy by me, to keep her interested in my work and hope that she understands what it means to me. In return, I give all the support I can to her running career.

'Tell me about South Africa,' I said.

She placed her wine glass on the low table. 'There's nothing to tell,' she said. 'It was just a thought. I had a month in Arizona, back in '95, and it was terrific. I knocked twenty seconds off my best 5,000 metres time. The facilities were good, but the main thing was the weather. It was perfect. I got a super tan. South Africa is an alternative and it costs less. Arizona was subsidised, but I wouldn't get a grant now. I'm not regarded as a prospect; I'd have to pay my way.'

'You could still go,' I said. 'I'd help you with the money if that's the problem.'

'That's kind of you, Chas, but no. I thought it might be fun if we both went.'

'I'd like that. Perhaps when this enquiry's over,' I said.

'Hmm. Perhaps then.'

Except, I thought, there'd be another enquiry after this one. 'Did you buy a dress?' I asked.

She smiled at me. 'Yes. Cost me a fortune. You can pay for that, if you want.'

'I'd love to. Are you going to show me it?'

'No, you'll have to wait until tomorrow.'
She was silent for a few seconds, then
began, 'I just wish...'

'Wish what?'

'Oh, that I could wear glamorous dresses.'

'What's stopping you?' I asked.

'I'm just too ... you know.' She glanced
down at her chest. 'I can't wear them.'

'Of course you can,' I assured her. 'You've
a figure most women would kill for.'

'No I haven't. I wish I had, you know...' –
she pinched her T-shirt between fingers and
thumbs in the appropriate places and
tugged it outwards – 'a bit more up here.'

I laughed out loud. 'Are you serious?'

'Yes. Don't laugh at me. I think I'll have a
boob job when I finish running. Would you
pay for one of those for me, please?'

'No way,' I told her. 'And you'd need two,
wouldn't you?'

'Yes, I suppose so.'

'Well don't you dare. You're perfect just as
you are.'

'Do you mean that, Charlie?'

I looked at her, held her gaze for a long
time. 'Every word of it,' I said.

The man with shiny shoes was displeased
but not downhearted. Discovering that his
last chosen victim was a black man was a
blow, but it opened up another avenue of
possibilities. He went upstairs to consult his

files, this time for 2004. It was time to come up to date.

He found what he wanted in minutes. Jermaine Lapetite was a twenty-five-year-old Jamaican with the sexual appetite of a horde of Mongols. At thirteen he was accused of raping a girl and stealing her bicycle. He pleaded guilty to the bike, not guilty to the rape, and was acquitted because she was too traumatised to give evidence. At fourteen he sexually assaulted his careers advice teacher and was put in a young offenders' institute. He came out at twenty and since then had fathered six children to four different women. At his most recent court appearance he was accused of dealing in crack cocaine. His defence was that he needed the money to meet his financial responsibilities, although he had never paid a penny towards the upkeep of any of his offspring. He was given bail and the newspapers showed him outside court, wearing more gold than a maharaja's elephant, waving to his friends.

'Fucking parasite,' the man with shiny shoes hissed, and few would disagree with him. He jotted a few notes and turned his computer on. Seconds later he was trawling through the electoral roll for Heckley.

Lapetite lived on the edge of town, where the council houses were being demolished as part of Heckley's Plan for the Future 2000. As blocks were cleared of tenants the buildings were bulldozed because, they said, rebuilding was cheaper than refurbishment, although the rebuilding hadn't started yet. A few hardy old-timers clung to the last remnants of what had once been a community, and a few others lived there more reluctantly because the council had deposited them there. This was a sink estate in its death throes. Two of Lapetite's mistresses lived in adjacent streets with their multi-hued children.

The man with shiny shoes was in his car, not the white van, so he had to be careful. The van, which he kept in a lock-up garage a mile from his home, couldn't be traced to him, but the car could. After an exploratory drive round he parked outside a pub off the estate and walked the half-mile back to Lapetite's house. It was early enough not to arouse suspicion, but dusk was falling.

It couldn't have been better. The estate was quiet, deserted, and had the air of a western town when the baddies are due to ride in. The houses were in blocks of three, with great gaps between them. In a couple of places heaps of bricks indicated the bulldozers' last victims. When the site was totally clear the haggling would start, he thought. Deals would be struck, palms would be oiled, hospitality would flow like communion wine at a God-fest. In a year or two the bijou residences would start to pop up and perhaps a few councillors would relocate into not-so-bijou residences on the outskirts of town. A sudden breeze sent a plume of dust spiralling from a heap of rubble, and the man with shiny shoes felt for the handle of the cosh in his jacket pocket.

This was it, number 133, right at the end of a long street that dissected the estate. There was no gate or hedge, because the owner had a car parked in the front garden. A Subaru Impreza, six years old, with an exhaust pipe big enough to accommodate a family of rabbits. An upstairs window was boarded up and the downstairs ones looked incapable of transmitting light. Washing windows wasn't on Jermaine Lapetite's agenda, along with gardening, painting or opening curtains. The place looked deserted, and the man with shiny shoes felt a pang of disappointment, but he'd try, all the same. This had just started out as a reconnoitre, but if things were favourable, he'd do the deed. There was no time like the present, and the quicker the country was rid of scum like Lapetite, the better.

He knocked briskly on the door and waited, looking round for signs of life. There were none, but he knew that someone would be watching from behind a curtain. It didn't matter. The police had no interest in the estate and the few residents remaining had no trust in the police. If some Rasta drug dealer just happened to be killed their sympathies would be with the killer.

He knocked again, louder, and thought he heard a noise from within. Next time he hammered on the glass and shouted through the letterbox.

'Wha' d'you want?' someone called from within.

'Police,' he called back.

'Whassit about, man?'

'I want a word.'

'You got warrant?'

'No. I just want a chat. It won't take long.'

The door opened on a chain and Jermaine Lapetite peered out. The man with shiny shoes was relieved to see he was quite short, not like the black giant he'd encountered four nights earlier.

'You no got warrant?' Lapetite insisted.

'No, I just want a chat, either here or at the nick. It's up to you.'

Lapetite unhooked the chain, pulled the door open and turned to go into the depths of the house. The man with shiny shoes pushed the door closed and followed, two strides behind. As Lapetite paused to open an internal door the man with shiny shoes brought the cosh down on his head. Lapetite crumpled to the floor without a sound. It was a temptation to hit him again and again, but the man with shiny shoes resisted. If he did, blood would be sprayed about, and blood could tell stories. He checked for a pulse, all the time listening for movements in case anyone else was in the house. When he was satisfied that his victim was dead he locked the door and went exploring.

It was dark when he'd finished, and he was soaked in sweat from his exertions. He left the door unlocked and walked briskly back to where he'd parked the car. A pint would have been welcome, but he resisted that, too. He'd have a celebratory drink when he was safely home. It was a pity about the microwave, though. He'd seen it too late, but perhaps next time... The engine fired first spin and he pulled out into the road. It had all gone to plan, better than to plan, and that was satisfactory in itself. But the real satisfaction was in knowing that Lapetite was dead. He'd rape and peddle drugs no more, and when they heard about it from the papers and television – and they certainly would – all his victims would feel a pang of satisfaction that justice had been done at last. That was the real reward.

There's a word men use to describe certain beautiful women at the height of their attraction that goes right back to the days of the caveman. It's not wasted on the normal, standard bimbo with her oversized boobs and smooth outline. It's reserved for women who have often excelled at sport and have muscles that ripple under the skin and a shape defined by effort rather than years of dieting. Muscles that are understated but useful, not sculpted in the gym by hours of pointless exercise until they look grotesque. Women that hold themselves erect and walk purposefully, oozing self-confidence and sex appeal. The word men use is *fit*.

The dress Sonia had bought was in clingy silk, the colour you glimpse as a kingfisher flashes across a sunlit river. It was high at the front and cut low, really low, at the back, with a diagonal hemline that showed her legs. Sonia's assets were on show and she had enough to fund a medium-sized far eastern bank. Sonia looked *fit*. I took one glance and decided I didn't want to share her with anyone.

'I've changed my mind,' I declared, hardly able to breathe. 'Let's stay in.'

'Will I do?' she asked, giving a twirl.

'No,' I told her.

'No?' she echoed, crestfallen.

'No. You can't go looking like that. I won't be able to fight off all the other poor blokes there, with their worthy wives and their varicose veins and bunions. They'll gang up and murder me.'

'So I'll do?'

'Oh yes,' I said. 'Believe me, you'll do.'

The Rotary club spring ball is an annual

affair, as are the summer ball, the autumn ball and the Christmas ball. *Ball* is putting it rather grandly, disco music being predominant, with an old-fashioned dance band filling in between the DJ's sessions. While he does his stuff with hits from the Seventies they toddle off to the bar and reminisce about the good old days when they played with Joe Loss and Ted Heath.

It was a warm evening, so Sonia's panic about not having a coat for the dash from the car park was unnecessary. She draped a fake pashmina across her shoulders and the problem was solved. We grabbed a couple of drinks and I did my best not to mingle. I'm not very good at mingling. We danced to a couple of Abba records and as soon as the buffet was announced open I steered Sonia towards it.

There were some of those little biscuits with Camembert cheese on them. It smells like an onion seller's socks and has the consistency of coagulated snail slime, but I find it irresistible. I put a respectable quantity on my plate, with some dolls-house sausage rolls, pineapple-and-cheese-on-a-stick, midget pork pies and samosas. I saw the samosas a bit late, and grabbed the last few. I found myself reaching for the garlic bread, but thought better of it. Maybe not tonight.

Sonia filled her plate with salad, rice and various coleslaws. We found a corner near the big fireplace and stood there eating, our drinks on the mantelpiece, until Mark Stanwick found us.

'Charlie!' he said. 'I didn't realise you were coming. This must be...'

'Sonia Thornton,' I told him, and to her, 'Mark Stanwick.' If he thought I was going to introduce him as superintendent he was mistaken.

A woman I took to be his wife was a couple of steps behind him. 'Lovely to meet you,' he said. 'Can I introduce you to my wife, Dorothea.'

We shook hands. 'Hello Dorothea,' I said. 'It's nice to meet you.' I meant it. She had the face of someone who does kind acts and a smile that reached her eyes.

They apologised for interrupting us while we ate and went off to grab some food for themselves. Later, after more Abba and a tribute to Nat King Cole by the band, they rejoined us. A photographer from the *Heckley Gazette* was circulating and he took a photograph of the four of us. The band was playing 'Unchained Melody'.

Stanwick coughed and said, 'This is a favourite of mine. Unfortunately Dorothea is nursing a sprained ankle. Would you mind if I asked Sonia for a dance, Charlie?'

I gave an approving face-pull and looked at her. Sonia smiled and turned towards the dance floor, Stanwick following like an eager pup.

'How did you sprain your ankle, Dorothea?' I asked.

'Oh, I fell down the steps at Heckley General. I do voluntary work there.'

'That's as good a place as any to sprain an ankle. Did they fast-track you through A and E?'

She laughed. 'Yes, I'm ashamed to admit that I did receive preferential treatment. We bypassed A and E.'

'And why not? Does your work there take up much time?'

'You know how it is, Charlie. I'm supposed to do two mornings and two evenings, but it works out at nearly a full-time job. I don't mind, I love it, but we're lucky that Mark can keep reasonable hours, otherwise we'd never see each other. He brings lots of work home with him, but he's fortunate in having men like you to take the pressure off him. He really appreciates you.'

'Right,' I said. He was in charge of career development and I specialised in feeling collars. I wasn't aware of having ever taken any pressure off him. I wondered what line he'd spun the gullible Dorothea about his role in Her Majesty's Police Force, but acknowledged that he wasn't the first to glamorise his role, and he wouldn't be the last. While we were talking I noticed John Williamson, aka Dr Bones, with his wife, looking for somewhere to sit and eat. She didn't know me but I caught her attention and introduced myself and Dorothea. The doc shook my hand and slapped my shoulder. I told him that Sonia was dancing.

'I hope she saves enough energy for one with me,' he said. 'Dancing is the only athletic pursuit I can fully compete in. Wait until you see my tango.'

They came back from the dance floor and it was handshakes all round again. Sonia told Stanwick that the doc was a magician and had saved her career, and Stanwick said that it must have given him a great deal of satisfaction. A couple sitting at a table noticed that the doc was blind and gave up their chairs, and we left them tucking into the buffet. Sonia put her arm around me, just to confirm whom she was with. I liked the feel of it and placed my hand in the small of her back, stroking it lightly with my fingertips.

At functions like this the 'Last Waltz' can never come soon enough for me. We did one circuit of the floor and I steered Sonia towards the cloakrooms. As we walked across the lawn towards the car park the wavering chords of the 'National Anthem' came drifting through the open windows. They like to do things properly at the Rotary Club. No doubt Stanwick would be standing to attention, fist pressed to his heart. Twenty minutes later Sonia and I were in my kitchen, holding each other. I was leaning back against the work surface, with my jacket still on, waiting for the kettle to boil; Sonia was pressed against me, her arms under my jacket, head on my shoulder. We decided not to bother with a bedtime drink, so I turned off the kettle and led the way upstairs.

I was cleaning my teeth when the phone rang. I screamed, 'Don't answer it!' through a mouthful of Colgate foam, but my shout was muffled and I nearly choked. By the time I'd rinsed it away and stopped spluttering Sonia was telling someone that she'd get me for him. It was one-thirty. At one-thirty it wasn't a social call or someone selling timeshare. I went into the bedroom and she handed me the phone.

'Priest,' I said into it.

'Sorry, boss,' someone said. 'I'm not disturbing you, am I?'

'Get on with it,' I growled as I struggled to pull my shirt back on.

Chapter Seven

They'd told me that it was number 133, but the parked police car gave it away. Three-quarters of the houses had been demolished, the survivors standing like mesas in a western desert. The moon had risen and a few spots of rain dashed against the windscreen. A dog loomed into the headlights, standing its ground stoically as I swerved around it to park behind the panda.

'What have we got?' I asked the sergeant who climbed out to meet me.

'Hello, Charlie,' he said. 'Black guy. Murder, if you ask me, but I think you'd better look for yourself.'

'How did it come in?'

'Anonymous tip-off, three nines.'

'That's a big help. Right, point me towards him.'

The door was unlocked. 'Was it unlocked when you came?' I asked, and the sergeant told me it was. 'OK. Wait there and I'll find my own way.' I found a light switch with my torch beam and switched it on. The wallpaper was straight out of somebody's impression of a migraine attack.

'Upstairs, did you say?' I shouted back.

'Yes, boss.'

'Which side did you walk on?'

'Hard over to the left.'

'Cheers.' I have them all trained to be forensically aware. These days, we can identify a footprint on a carpet or a flake of dandruff from a slaphead. It's just a matter of time and money. I found another light switch and turned it on. When I made my report I'd say that the lights were off. It usually doesn't

194

matter, but sometime it might. It's all about attention to detail.

He was in the bathroom, hanging upside down from a ceiling joist with his head in the toilet. A few drips of blood from a wound to his head had made pink clouds in the water in the bowl.

Yep, I thought, that's murder, and made my way back downstairs.

I handed the whole thing over to the geeks. They turned their ESLA equipment loose on the stair carpet to establish who'd been up and down them; sprayed luminol all over the place looking for blood; dusted everywhere for fingerprints and dabbed Sellotape on all the surfaces to collect fibres. The pathologist arrived at seven and spent twenty minutes with the body before we cut it down.

'Are you doing these yourself, Charlie,' he asked me as we sat in his car sharing his flask of coffee, 'to brighten up an otherwise dull life?'

'It looks a bit like that,' I admitted. 'We've certainly upped the weirdness quotient with these last two.'

'Do you think they're linked?'

'I don't know, yet.'

'Or is this one black on black?'

Black on black killings are almost always associated with drug dealing. We're accused of not paying them much attention, and there may be some truth in that, but we have our reasons. The Yardies have some misplaced creed about only living until they are thirty. Anything beyond that is a bonus. And they don't cooperate with the police. This is not to be confused with grassing. They'll grass on their mothers to save their own skins, but anything else is just not done. A wall of silence descends that we can't penetrate.

So we leave them to it, with perhaps just a little interference. Drugs multiply several-fold in price at every stage of the dealing. When a newspaper report says that a million pounds worth of marijuana has been seized, someone somewhere has had to pay for it. Say a hundred thousand pounds. That would be a thousand per cent markup; not bad, except the Mr Big can't sell it in one deal for a million. He divides it into smaller lots, dilutes it with milk powder or Polyfilla if it's heroin, and sells it to his own network of smaller dealers. They take the drugs on a *high now, pay later* basis.

That's where we come in. Every time we seize a consignment someone is in deep shit, and the higher up the line we can intervene, the deeper the shit. Mr Big wants his money. He's delivered the goods and now it's payback time. If little Winston or Kevin on the street corner loses his stash before he can sell it on, and therefore can't pay for it, he has the life expectancy of a kamikaze pilot. We find him with a bullet in his neck and shake our heads sadly for the press whilst rubbing our hands behind our backs.

'So was this a black on black?'

'No, I don't think so, prof,' I replied. 'They don't mess about.' I made a gun with my forefinger and thumb. 'Bang, you're dead. That's good enough for them.'

'Sounds as if this is one for Dr Foulkes.'

'I know. I'll ring him as soon as the streets are aired.' Adrian Foulkes is head of clinical psychiatry at Heckley General, and a so-called expert on psychological profiling. He's as mad as a hatter, and I'm not a great believer in what is a rather inexact science, but it's always good to have a second opinion.

'Well,' the professor went on, 'for what it's worth the blow to the head was probably the cause of death and ToD was sometime Friday evening. PM Monday morning, if you can wait until then?'

'Yeah, that's fine,' I said. 'Thanks for the coffee.'

It was nearly ten when I arrived home, and Sonia wasn't there. I found her note saying that she'd gone for a run pinned to the fridge door. 'Back about ten-thirty,' it said.

I was whacked. All that dancing was too much for me. I had a shower, towelled myself nearly dry and crawled into bed. I was running over things in my mind when the door banged. I imagined Sonia pouring herself an orange juice and gulping it down, before sitting on the stool in the kitchen and removing her trainers. She came to the bottom of the stairs and shouted, 'Are you back?'

As my car was on the drive it was a reasonable deduction. I'll make a detective of you yet, I thought, and shouted, 'In bed,' down at her.

She came in, looking pink and sweaty, her hair sticking to her head and dark stains of perspiration soaking through her vest.

'Good run?' I asked as she sat on the edge of the bed.

'Mmm. And you? Have you been in long?'

'No, not long.'

'Was it a murder?'

'Yes.'

She put her fingers on my forehead and rubbed it. 'Poor thing,' she said. 'You must be worn out.'

'I am.'

'Do you want something to eat?'

'No.'

'Shall I leave you alone?'

'No.'

'What do you want?'

'I want you to come to bed.'

'Do you?'

'Yes. Desperately.'

She looked at me for a long while, then her eyes crinkled into a little smile and she said, 'OK.'

Brendan and Maggie went to the post-mortem examination while I had a word with the coroner. Sunday afternoon and Monday we had the foot soldiers out learning what they could about the deceased, and it was a sorry tale. He was called Jermaine Lapetite and had a record that wouldn't have fit on an old floppy disk. He needed a whole 700Mb CD to himself. We found the mothers of two of his children living nearby, and they described him using words straight off their kids' birth certificates. He kept a small amount of crack cocaine under his mattress, a few ounces of pot behind a drawer in the kitchen and twelve hundred pounds cash under a loose floorboard.

Les Isles, the chief superintendent standing in for the ACC(Crime), rang and asked if I needed any help. I explained that we hadn't decided if this was a new enquiry or part of the ongoing one and asked him to hang fire until the reports were in. Before I went along the road linking the two murders I wanted to clear something up about Alfred Armitage. His old sparring partner Eric Smallwood was still in the frame, but I was having my doubts. I needed to see him.

I'd rung him, so he was waiting for me, still jacketed and helmeted as if about to go wobbling off to the library on a bicycle with a basket on the front. He'd have looked more at home in Cambridge, riding down the Backs. He invited me in and gestured for me to sit on a leather armchair while he took the matching chesterfield.

'What's it about, Inspector?' he asked. 'I thought I answered all your questions the last time we met.'

'Since then I've been to see Mrs Newbold,' I told him, 'and now I have a few more.'

'Josephine? You've been to see Josephine?' He sat up, interested, his guard lowered. 'How is she?'

'She's fine. Asked how you were,' I lied.

'And what did you tell her?'

'I said you were fine, too. That's all.' It looked as if Mr Weirdo had a crush on the boss's wife. And why not? 'A few things came to light in our discussions about the company,' I told him. 'It appears that in the last few years Ellis and Newbold were being robbed blind. I want to know what part you and Alfred Armitage had in that.'

Now he looked flustered. 'I – I don't know what you mean.'

'I mean: which of you had his hands in the till?'

'It wasn't me. I never had anything from the company that I wasn't legally entitled to.'

'That sounds a rather loaded statement, Mr Smallwood,' I said. 'I could ask our economic crime unit to come and have a word

200

with you – they know much more about these things than me – but I won't. It would be a waste of resources. Mrs Newbold wants to wash her hands of the whole thing, not prefer any charges, which lets you nicely off the hook. But there is still the little matter of Alfred's death. That won't go away so easily. If you weren't robbing the company, it must have been him.'

He shuffled in his seat and his little pink tongue licked his top lip. He was realising that he was in the clear. 'I, er, had my suspicions,' he said.

'Go on.'

'Well, one day, back in about '93, I caught Alfred doing some photocopying. Order lists, sales projections, that sort of thing. I couldn't imagine what he wanted them for at first, then I realised: he was passing information about our customers over to our rivals.'

'So you reported him to the boss.'

'Um, no.'

'Why not?'

'I was going to, but he threatened me.'

'What with?'

He ignored the question, found something outside to attract his attention and looked towards the window.

'Violence?' I suggested, but he still didn't answer. 'Or did he threaten to expose your own little scam, Mr Smallwood, whatever it was?'

Smallwood stood up and straightened the Shepherd print hanging above the fireplace. 'I didn't do anything. I told you that.'

'I know, but I don't believe you. What were your feelings about Alfred?' I asked.

He turned to face me. 'My feelings?'

'Mmm. Did you like him, hate him, think he was alright, or what?'

'None of those. He did his job and I did mine. We didn't socialise, if that's what you mean.'

'You were indifferent towards him?'

'Yes. Indifferent.'

'So you didn't compare notes. You just both kept robbing the company in your separate ways.'

'No. I never took anything. It was only Alfred.'

'And you didn't kill him?'

Panic flared in his face. 'No. No. Of course not. Is that what you think?'

'It's a possibility,' I said, pushing myself up from the chair. 'Don't leave the country, will you?'

But it wasn't a possibility. It takes certain qualities to get somebody drunk, wire him to the mains and put the power on. I don't know what the qualities are, but I was convinced that Smallwood didn't possess them.

Back at the station there were more loose ends to clear up. Lincoln had been talking to the Hell's Angels and Bousfield's alibi was as tight as a 747's wheelnuts, with just enough slack in there to make it believable.

The economic crime unit were more cooperative after a word from the boss, and had discovered that after leaving Ellis and Newbolds Alfred had gone to work for their rivals, AJK. They, in turn, had sacked him during a period of belt-tightening after that company started going down the tube. As Alfred had probably been selling their secrets, there was a certain irony there. He'd left with a stainless reputation after less than a year in office, and his bank deposits had quickly dried up after that. There was nothing to suggest that his paymasters put any pressure on him: he hadn't paid any money back, changed accounts or moved house.

I was cutting corners, painting with a broad brush, but decisions had to be made. If Alfred wasn't killed because of his industrial espionage links, and if the Angels and Bousfield were in the clear, we were swimming in treacle.

But was Alfred the intended victim or was he killed because of his unfortunate similarity to Terence Paul Hutchinson, the Midnight Strangler? Hutchinson and Jermaine Lapetite both came from the shallow end of the gene pool, so were they both murdered because someone was doing unofficial pool maintenance? It was a strong possibility.

I went down to the incident room and did a big chart on the whiteboard, linking all the scenarios. After a few seconds admiring it I reached out and erased Smallwood's name. I was about to do the same with Bousfield but hesitated. Instead I left it there but drew a line through it, so it wasn't gone completely.

Sonia had developed a routine with the training. Mondays and Wednesdays, if I was home in time, we'd drive to the golf club and do our laps; Tuesdays and perhaps Thursday she'd go to the track for some serious stuff against the clock; Saturday and Sunday mornings we'd go for a jog from home. My presence was optional, but I was there when I could manage it. Her next race was another 10K, in Durham at the weekend.

On this Monday I couldn't face it. I arrived home just as Sonia was about to leave, so I drove her to the golf club and sent her off on her own. The lady with the dog returned from her walk shortly after Sonia started her second lap and mouthed *hello* to me as I sat in the car, making notes, with Vaughan Williams on the CD player. I smiled and waved back. She walked to her car, opened the back door so the little dog could leap inside, and came back to me. I wound the window down and rolled the volume right off.

'Has Miss Thornton gone off running

without you?' she asked.

'Yes,' I replied. 'She's too fast for me so I decided to have a rest.'

'She's a wonderful athlete,' she told me, as if I didn't know. 'I told you I saw her win a race at Roundhay Park, in Leeds. I used to run there myself, many years ago, on Children's Day. Just the hundred yards sprint. I never won, but I've loved athletics ever since. I was so disappointed when Sonia didn't go to Atlanta.'

'A lot of people were.'

'Is she fit again, now?'

'She's getting there.'

'I have my camera in the car,' she said. 'Do you think she'd let me take her photograph?'

'Oh, I don't think she'd mind. She's quite shy, but I suppose she'd be flattered.'

'Oh, good. Shall I wait for her to get back, or would she prefer it some other evening. She might be upset to have it dropped on her, so to speak.'

'Might as well wait,' I replied, 'if you have the time.'

She went to sit in her car and wait, and ten minutes later Sonia came steaming up the hill for the second time. I jumped out with a towel and a drink and told her, nodding in the appropriate direction, about the lady with the Scottie. As predicted, she turned a pale beetroot colour.

'Me?' she said.

'Yes.'

'A photograph?'

'Yes. She's a fan.' I waved to the woman and she came across to us.

'Do you mind?' she asked.

Sonia laughed, still blushing. 'No, of course not.'

The woman produced a small digital camera and spent several seconds making adjustments until things were to her liking. Finally she gave the 'smile' command and pressed the button.

'Let me take one of the two of you,' I said, and reached for the camera. Sonia posed next to the woman, although *posed* is hardly the word. She stood like a prize fighter, feet slightly apart, whereas a model would have placed one ankle neatly behind the other to produce a tapering effect. The sun was low, casting the yellow light that photographers love. I repositioned myself so it was illuminating their faces and squat down, one knee on the ground. By now their smiles had slipped and the two of them looked as if they were up for execution.

'For God's sake SMILE!' I shouted, they laughed and I pressed the button.

The woman took her camera back with profuse thank you's, and I drove Sonia home. 'There,' I said as I buckled my seatbelt, 'that's two people you've made happy today.'

Tuesday morning we had a big meeting in the Portakabin we were using as an improvised incident room. Professor Foulkes was one of the first to arrive and we asked each other about our love lives. His was going through an extended rocky patch; I reported that mine was doing quite nicely, thank you.

'And what does it feel like to be a celebrity?' he asked. 'You know that it's a drug, don't you? The more publicity you attract, the more you want.'

'Don't you start, Adrian,' I said. 'It's all uninvited, I assure you.'

'Ah, you say that,' he went on, 'but would the delightful – and she is truly delightful – Miss Thornton, aka *La Gazelle*, still find you attractive if you were a nonentity?'

'That's the least of my worries.'

'Is it? So what is the most of your worries?'

I laughed out loud. 'Good try, prof, but mind your own business. I'm not on your couch.' It was the twenty-year age gap, and no amount of psycho-babble could alter that.

'Just warming up my finely tuned analytical muscles, Charlie. But if you ever do happen to fall out with her, remember an old friend, won't you? What time does this meeting start?'

It started then. While we talked the team, plus extras, had drifted in, armed with notebooks and beakers of coffee from the machine. I'd brought us two from the office,

207

made with real Nescafe. Chairs scraped as they were manoeuvred into position and everyone made themselves comfortable. Dave came in and headed for me, a folded newspaper in his hand.

'Have you seen this, Charlie?' he asked.

'No. What is it?'

'*UK News*. You'd better read it.'

I took the tabloid from him. It was supposedly a report about the finding of Jermaine Lapetite's body, but the headline read: *Dead druggy's penis amputated.*

I turned the page towards Adrian so he could read it.

'Amputated,' he said. 'That's a big word for the *UK News*. Is it true?'

'Not that I know,' I told him. 'I never looked. It's not the sort of thing I do.'

'Does it say it was stuffed in his mouth?'

'Yeah,' Dave replied. 'Lower down.'

'Even you would have noticed that, Charlie,' Adrian said.

'I'd have thought so,' I agreed.

'Maybe old sawbones will know if it was chopped off,' he suggested.

'The pathologist? He's not coming but I have his report here. He doesn't mention it.'

'Hmm. I imagine it's the sort of thing he would mention. Sounds like poetic licence to me. Or wishful thinking. It's the sort of rough justice that would appeal to a *UK News* reader.'

'Let's hope you're right.' I turned to Dave. 'Ring the paper, Dave,' I said. 'See where they got it from.'

'Can I tell them it's not true?'

'No problem. Let's get on with it.'

I jumped up onto the little stage and everybody stopped talking. 'Good morning,' I said. 'This won't take long. First of all can I introduce Professor Adrian Foulkes, from the psychology department at Heckley General. He's here for background knowledge and then he will hopefully look into the parts we mortals can't reach. If you're very good he'll make his bow tie rotate.' Adrian gave a languid wave of acknowledgement. 'The pathologist can't be with us, unfortunately,' I continued, 'but I have his report here.' I gazed down at the front row and picked on Brendan. 'Here you are, Brendan,' I said, handing him the folder, 'this morning you can be the patho. Read that and be ready to answer questions.

'We're here to discuss the death of Jermaine Lapetite,' I told them. 'As you know, he was found suspended upside down from a roof joist. Two holes had been knocked through the plasterboard ceiling to access the joist. We haven't found the tool that did it and one would expect the perpetrator to be covered in plaster. The victim was hanging by an old clothes line, knotted around his feet with the other end around the toilet overflow pipe.'

'Have you seen this morning's *UK News*, boss?' somebody asked.

'I have. Dave brought it in.'

'Is it true?'

'No, apart from the bang to his head there was no sign of mutilation. Maybe this is a good time to hear what the PM disclosed. Brendan, it's your stage.' He stood up and half-turned towards his audience. 'Just the relevant stuff,' I said.

'Right,' he began, rearranging the pages of the report. 'Time of death was approximately thirty hours before the body was found, say sometime Friday evening. Cause of death was a single blow to the head, probably struck from behind by a right-handed person. There are marks on the victim's neck as if manual strangulation was applied, again from behind, until the killer was certain the victim was dead. The murder weapon was a heavy, blunt instrument about four centimetres wide, with a rounded end.'

'Sounds like a cosh,' we were told.

'It does, doesn't it. Anything else relevant, Brendan?'

'No, boss, that's about it. He had score marks on his arms and various other scars. That's all.'

'What did he weigh?'

'Hang on, it's here somewhere. Um, 67 kilograms.'

'What's that in old money?' I asked.

There was a rustling of papers until someone shouted, 'Ten stone four, boss.'

'Thanks. He wasn't what you'd call strapping, was he? Would it be possible for one man to lift a body of that weight on that clothes line?'

There was a silence while they thought about it. After a while they agreed that it was possible but difficult. 'Do we have anyone who weighs just over ten stones?' I asked, and one of the SOCOs raised a nervous hand. I beamed down at him. 'How do you feel like being hung up by your feet over a toilet?' I asked, and he agreed to be the guinea pig.

'Just be grateful he didn't have his willy chopped off,' one of his colleagues told him.

After that we had the technical teams give us their findings. Bloodstains showed that the killer blow was struck downstairs, in the hallway. There was very little blood but a trail had been found leading up the stairs to the bathroom. According to the ESLA expert only one person had dragged the body up the stairs, no mean feat in itself. Unfortunately he'd worn shoes with smooth soles, not trainers. That was nearly a first, but not much help. 'We've taken the stair carpet away to look for trace evidence,' he reported.

Hundreds of fingerprints were found, but there was no concentration on the stairs or in the bathroom that might have come from the killer. Just the opposite. It would be expected that he'd steady himself against the wall as he dragged the body, but only smudges were found. The bad news was that it looked as if he'd worn cotton gloves.

The clothes line was ancient and the knots in it were amateurish. Just a double granny at his feet, and looping over and over several times around the pipe. We weren't looking for a sailor or a boy scout.

'Any questions?' I asked, and pointed at the first raised hand.

'Do we think this killing is linked to the Alfred Armitage one, boss?'

'We don't know, but that's why Adrian is here. Now that he's filled in with the details I'm hoping he'll tell us all sorts of things, but we'll have to give him time.'

I pointed again. 'Yes George.'

'Have you dismissed that it might be a gangland execution, boss?'

'No, we haven't dismissed anything. It could be, but it's not the normal gangland MO.'

'It could be a first.'

'It could indeed.'

Eddie Carmichael was sitting at the end of the front row. 'You anything to ask, Eddie?' I said.

'Um, no guv. I was just wondering about the gangland thing, but you've covered it.'

'That's it, then,' I said. 'See your sergeant or me if you're not sure what you're doing. First thing is to continue looking into the background of the deceased. He apparently let his assailant into the house, so he probably knew him. The MO is unique, so we have no usual suspects from that angle, but there's no doubt he had some shady friends. Get it all down in your reports and be careful: we're dealing with dangerous people. I'll be upstairs for the rest of the morning, if anybody wants to see me.'

I took Adrian up to my office. One or two photos of the murder scene were pinned on the incident room wall, but they're the expurgated ones. I took a folder of the full set out of a drawer and passed it to him. I also had a set taken of Alfred Armitage, but I didn't show him them just yet.

After he'd perused the photos for a while I said, 'Speak to me, Adrian.'

He shoved them back towards me. 'I've nothing to say, Chas. Taken in isolation, this is simply someone who fell foul of someone else and got himself murdered. It might be over drugs – that must be the favourite – or a girl, or money. Anything.'

'It won't have been over a girl,' I said. 'Their creed is to impregnate as many as possible, that's all.'

'A noble aspiration. And are we so different, Charlie?'

'Speak for yourself. So what's all this hanging him over the toilet about, then?'

'Ah,' he began, leaning forward on his hard chair. 'Now this is interesting. I've never seen it before but there is a certain symbolism. The murderer went to great pains to create this little diorama, lugging the body upstairs, knocking the holes in the ceiling, threading the rope over the joist and hoisting the body aloft. It obviously meant a lot to him. He could have hung him anywhere downstairs, or not hung him at all, but he chose to do it over the toilet. He invested a great deal of effort in it. Now what does that say to you, Charlie?'

'That he thought Lapetite was a piece of shit?' I suggested.

'Exactly. And I'd say we were looking for a white man, wouldn't you?'

'Well that narrows it down,' I said.

A shadow fell over my desk and I looked round to see Dave's considerable shape looming at the other side of the glass door. 'Come in,' I yelled before he could knock.

'Hi prof,' he said. 'Have you sorted it for us, yet?'

'Nearly, David,' Adrian replied. 'Just a few minor details to fill in.'

'What have you got?' I asked.

'I've had words with the deputy editor at *UK News*,' he told us. 'The information came in by telephone from someone claiming to be an officer on the case. They have a recording of the conversation and I've asked Tower Hamlets to collect it. They've also said they'll try to trace if the call was billed to anyone. It was probably made on a mobile, but it's worth a try.'

'Good stuff,' I said. 'Have a seat while Adrian fills in those minor details he mentioned.' I turned to him. 'Earlier, Adrian, you said "Taken in isolation". What did you mean?'

'Well, we were looking at one murder. When we consider the earlier death, and consider the strong possibility of it being mistaken identity, a different picture emerges, which, of course, is why you asked me to be here. Can I see the other photographs, please?'

I passed the folder to him and he took out the wad of ten-by-eight colour prints that showed poor Alfred frozen in his death throes.

'Are these taken on a digital?' he asked, and I told him they were.

'Good, aren't they?'

'Mmm.'

'I've just bought one. Haven't used it yet.'

'Are they linked?' I asked, before he started quoting pixels and megabytes.

'Do you really need me to tell you, Charlie?'

'You're saying they are?'

'Look at them. Two murders in what, three weeks? And less than three miles apart. Then there's the methodology. OK, so they're different, very different, but the mind behind them is the same. It's someone who likes ritual.'

'You mean, like a defrocked vicar?' I suggested.

'That's the obvious choice,' he said, 'but I doubt it.'

'Oh. Sorry to be obvious. What else is there?'

'I'd say he's married,' Adrian said. 'Happily married, although some people would say that's an oxymoron. Not me, of course, but often, in so-called happy marriages, one partner is completely subjugated by the other one. This will be one of those, but outside the marriage he's a bit of a loner. He's never fitted in with the society around him. He lives locally. He's middle class, moderately successful and has had a decent education.'

'University?' I asked.

'Um, not sure. Probably not. Serial killers are often in their thirties, but this one could be older. He's on a mission. He's seen the way the country is perceived as going, thanks to scaremongering by the media, and has decided to do something about it.'

'Voices in the head?' I wondered.

'Possibly.'

'Why isn't he content with just killing them?' Dave asked.

'Because he wants the publicity,' Adrian replied. 'I was telling Charlie about it earlier. It's like a drug to him. He does what he does for maximum impact.'

'So I can safely tell the chief that we have only one murderer loose in the town?' I said.

'Almost without doubt.'

'Thanks for that, Adrian. It simplifies things. Of all the other stuff you've told us, the bit that appeals to me most is this ritual thing.'

Dave said, 'The phone caller claimed he was a police officer. Do you think he could be?'

'Good question. He's forensically aware, as you have no doubt realised. And he has a certain competence. He can do things. He could be a police officer. That might explain how he gained admittance. How keen are you on rituals? Are they instilled deep into every fibre of your psyche?'

'Not in Heckley,' Dave replied with a grin.

It was a relief. We'd been barking up the wrong rabbit holes with Alfred, but now I felt we were on the right scent. As Dave put it in his usual succinct way, we had an executionist loose in the town. I had a long talk with Mr Wood and Les Isles, the acting ACC, and they agreed that the investigations be combined, so I went down into the incident room and spent an hour redecorating the walls and arranging for a HOLMES terminal to be installed. All the stuff about Hell's Angels and industrial espionage was moved to an end wall and was replaced by the photos of Jermaine Lapetite from the Portakabin. I marked the location of his house on the map and sat staring at it for several minutes, wondering where and when I'd be sticking the next coloured pin.

Criminals have a choice of where they commit their crimes, and that choice tells us something about them. Sometimes it's all we have to go on. Murderers rarely travel far, unless they are lorry drivers or such like. Most murders are committed less than a mile from the killer's base, which is usually, but not always, his home. The scale of the big map was six inches to the mile. Freehand, I drew half-mile circles round the two murder scenes and joined them up in a big oval. There was a better-than-average chance that the Executioner lived inside it, and the next person to come through the door would get the job of listing everybody in there. I studied the street names, noted the positions of churches, schools and telephone boxes. There was a pub, a library and a fire station, too, which didn't help a great deal.

We made a few arrests for carrying drugs

and weapons, discovered more details about Lapetite's sordid past, upset certain quarters of our community. More of the troops carried guns when they went to conduct interviews.

I hadn't carried a gun for nearly eight years. His name was Willy O'Hagan, the man I killed. He'd have been thirty-four, now. I wouldn't want any of the team going through what I went through. It was too big a price to pay. But they were carrying the guns, not me. It wasn't right. I was the boss, so the responsibility was mine. I reached for the internal directory and looked for a number.

'Firearms,' I was briskly told, after I'd dialled.

'Is that the handsome, young PC Damian Lord?' I asked.

'Speaking.'

'Hello, Damian. It's DI Priest at Heckley. Charlie Priest. My firearms certificate expired years ago and I'd like to renew it. What do I need to do?'

'You'll have to come on a course and requalify.'

'I realise that. How long will it take?'

'For just an authorised shot? Two two-day courses, if you're not specialising.'

'I can't afford the time. Can we condense it?'

'You could just come for one day of each, I suppose, but you'd still have to achieve the pass mark.'

'Which is what?'

'Fifty rounds, eighty per cent.'

'Strewth. I thought it was only seventy per cent.'

'It was, but we tightened it. Presumably you're only interested in the Glock 17.'

'I imagine so. Thanks a lot, Damian. Any chance of my coming down one afternoon for a spot of practice before then? I've never fired a Glock. Not this week, though. We've a murder enquiry on.'

'I've heard about it. You can come down anytime, Mr Priest.'

'Cheers. I'll give you a ring.'

I obviously couldn't go down anytime. He had courses to supervise, tests to conduct, but he'd fit me in. The range is in the grounds of a swank hotel near Huddersfield. It had once been a minor stately home with extensive grounds, but impoverished descendants bequeathed it to the local council and it fell into disrepair. The authorities – whoever they are – appropriated it for anti-terrorist training in the wake of the Iranian embassy siege and for a while the grounds echoed to the sound of running boots, thunderflashes and barked commands, late into the night. We used it, as did the army. I believe joint exercises were held with the SAS, but it was all hush-hush and I was never involved. I don't look good with my face blacked. A fifty-metre indoor shooting range was built in the grounds, and then the hotel chain bought the whole estate, except for the firing range. The golfers at the thirteenth hole look at the building, see the police vehicles parked outside, and wonder briefly what it's all about. Then they drive off and forget it exists. Inside, hot lead is flying through the smoky air and streams of spent cartridge cases are clattering on the concrete floor. As well as instructing, tests are conducted on things like shotgun spread and bullet penetration. Damian has found himself a fun job, most of the time, but he's also an expert with a sniper rifle.

I'd wondered what it would feel like to hold a gun again, but two weeks ago I'd picked up the Glock 17 issued to Eddie Carmichael and wasn't struck by lightning. I didn't start shaking like an agoraphobic bungee jumper or find it impossible to lift the gun off the counter. It was no big deal.

Wednesday morning my picture was in the *Gazette* again. This time it was the photo taken at the ball, with Sonia and the Stanwicks. There was half a page of them, covering just about everybody present, and ours looked good – I was smiling – but the caption wasn't designed to please Stanwick. It said: 'Sonia Thornton and Charlie Priest, with two of the other guests.' Ah well, I thought, some have greatness thrust upon them.

Jeff Caton came into my office holding a rolled-up magazine. 'Have you seen this, Charlie?' he said, placing it on my desk under my nose and smoothing it out. It was *Hello!* magazine, and some wag had cut me out and pasted me on the front, neatly nestling in a lissom soap star's decolletage. I shook my head and dropped it in the bin, but after he'd gone I retrieved it to show Sonia.

Bits of information were dribbling in from all corners of the enquiry. The scientific branch testing the stair carpet found traces of shoe polish on it, coinciding with the footprints detected by the ESLA tests. The pattern of these indicated that they were left by whoever dragged the body upstairs and that he was acting alone.

Best of all, voice print analysis indicated that the person who rang 999 to tell us about the body was the same one who rang the *UK News* with the false gory details. That call was made at 23:32 Saturday night, from a pay phone in Heckley bus station. Unfortunately the cash box had been emptied, so we couldn't check the coins for fingerprints, but they still had their CCTV tapes. I rang Adrian Foulkes and left a message.

He caught me at home, just as I was testing the chicken.

'Sorry to disturb you at home, Charlie,' he said, 'but I've had a busy day.'

'As long as that's the real reason,' I told

him, 'and you weren't hoping that Sonia would answer the phone.'

'Ah, you caught me out again, Charlie. Is she there? Can I have a word?'

'Sorry, Adrian, but she's not home yet.' It was a lie: she was upstairs having a shower, but if I'd told him that he'd have had a cardiac arrest. 'Can we talk about work?' I said.

'Fire away.'

I told him about the phone calls and he was silent for nearly a minute. I could hear piano music in the background. Something slow and classy. A Chopin nocturne at a guess, but I'm not an expert. Eventually he said, 'The clothes line, Charlie. Did the killer take it with him or find it at the house?'

'It belonged at the house. He cut it down from outside. And we've found a hammer that he used to knock the holes in the ceiling. He probably found that there, too.'

'So he was extemporising, making it up as he went along.'

'It looks that way.'

'He did the deed, and then he looked for materials to perform his ritual. Shall I tell you something, Chas?'

'Go on.'

'No matter how many statements you issue to the contrary, the entire population of this country will believe that young Mr Lapetite was found with his severed knob in his mouth.'

'I'm sure you're right, Adrian, so where does that leave us?'

'It leaves us like this: the killer didn't sever the penis, but afterwards, he wished he had. It came to him, as an afterthought. Hey! *La Petite!* – the little one. Was it, do you know?'

'It depends what you call little.'

'Ooh! That hurt! So, Charlie, the killer didn't mutilate his victim in a frenzied attack. He was cool and calm, and afterwards he thought to himself: *I could have cut his willy off. And stuffed it in his mouth. That would have been a nice touch.*'

'But why, Adrian? What's motivating him?'

'I told you yesterday: he's on a mission. And he enjoys the publicity. That aspect is probably taking over. He'll start enjoying the killing, if he isn't already, and that side of it, and the notoriety, will become overwhelming until he's caught. His next victim might not be another villain, but simply an easy target. What was the interval between the murders?'

'Nineteen days.'

'He won't wait that long, this time.'

'So there'll be a next time.'

'Bet your life on it. And guess what?'

'What?'

'Next time he'll be prepared. He won't be extemporising his ritual – he'll have it all worked out in advance.'

'Thanks a bunch.'

'It's a pleasure. Anything else I can help you with?'

'Mmm. How do you tell if a chicken's cooked?'

'How do you tell if a chicken's cooked?' he echoed. 'They come cooked, don't they? What other sort is there?'

The man with shiny shoes gave them a final buff with a yellow duster and placed them on the rack inside the porch. He pulled his leather slippers on and went upstairs to the tiny spare bedroom that had been furnished as his office. He switched on the light and the small fan heater and pulled his typist's chair close up to the desk, pushing the computer's keyboard out of the way. A pile of newspapers was in a wire tray at the right-hand side of his desk. He retrieved them, one at a time, and leafed through each until he found the report on the Lapetite killing. He snipped the articles out and placed them in the matching tray at the left-hand side of his desk. The remains of the papers were dropped in a neat pile on the floor.

He stood up to reach for his current scrapbook on a shelf and sat down again. The book was nearly full, but there was still room for this week's harvest of cuttings. He took a tube of PrittStick and a roll of Scotch magic tape from a drawer and started positioning the cuttings on the page, moving them around until they fit neatly, with no empty spaces. The photos taken at the Heckley Rotary Club ball posed a minor problem. Should he stick the whole half-page in his book or just the relevant ones? He cut around the photo of Charlie Priest and his woman and placed it in the top right corner of a new page, then he cut one other picture out and placed it alongside. That would do.

Priest was smiling, he noticed. A smug, self-satisfied smile. He was in his element, in the middle of a high profile murder case with all the kudos that that brought, plus having a beautiful girl on his arm. Well, he wouldn't be smiling for much longer, that was for sure.

Chapter Eight

Sometimes we get it wrong and sometimes we get it right but for all the wrong reasons. Jeff came into my office and sat down with a weariness that looked as if he were laden down with the cares of the world. He placed his chin on his fist and stared at me until I finished my phone call.

'Yes, Mr Caton,' I said, briskly. 'What can

I do for you?'

'Um, well, stop collecting car numbers, for a start.'

'Explain, please.'

'The odd couple in the fancy Jaguar. Ebony and ivory. They just happen to be the adopted children of the owner of the City Lights shopping centre outside Oldfield. The car is registered to their mother. Their own vehicles are more modest hot hatches, so they came out in mummy's convertible because the weather was warm.'

'Oops!' I said. 'Sorry about that. Have we upset them?' Something like this could have repercussions: accusations of racism and a chop suey of other implications. Careers were destroyed by less. We're often accused of picking on stereotypes and figures are thrown about to back this up, but nobody ever quotes the percentage of times we get it right.

'Nah, don't worry about it. When we saw who it was I asked the local collator. They're well known and respected locally. We kept it in-house.'

'Thank goodness for that, Jeff. And thanks for looking into it.'

'Do you want to know about the other one?'

'What other one?'

'The elegant piece in the Mercedes.'

'Um, no, Jeff. I think we'd better draw a

discreet veil over that one.'

'Fair enough. It's just that a silver SLK 320 with that number is registered to a book-maker down in Eastbourne, who swears he's never been anywhere near Heckley and the car has never been further than Brighton.'

This was more like it. 'You mean, it's a ringer?'

'No doubt about it, unless you were in a state of high agitation and copied the number down wrongly.'

'A strong possibility. Have you found it, yet?'

'No, but we're looking.'

'Let me know when you do.'

The killer's shoes were size nine and he used black Cherry Blossom polish. The Path-finder electrostatic lifting apparatus – ESLA – picks up dust from the carpet using electrostatic attraction. In other words, a voltage is applied to a sheet of special lifting film and any loose dust is attracted to it. Ionising filters work on the same principle, I believe. Dust particles that have been compressed down into the ground or the carpet by a shoe are not lifted, so a negative of the shoe sole pattern is made. Except in this case there was no pattern. The curve of the front of the heel was detected but anything else was outside the capabilities of the apparatus. It would have been useful to say that he was lame in his left leg, weighed seventeen stones and carried too much loose change in his trouser pockets, but we couldn't.

I rang Sonia at the sports centre where she works and told her not to wait for me – I had work to do. She wasn't going to the track so she said she'd drive to the golf course and do two laps there on her own. Later, we'd have a takeaway.

After everybody had left I spent an hour looking through reports. The report reader prepares a summary for me but I like to have a closer look at what the troops are uncovering. Rarely anything leaps up and slaps me in the face, but I feel as if I'm doing what they pay me for. They report the facts, but I like to look for the story behind them. Feelings, opinions, judgements all have a part to play, especially when you're floundering. At half-past six I washed my coffee mug and closed the shop for the day.

I drove to the bottom end of the Sylvan Fields estate, where Jermaine Lapetite lived. The Sylvan Fields were built in the Thirties, when Britain was supposed to be a land fit for heroes. It was a happy place for many years, giving young couples the home that they'd dreamed about. Big Dave was a product of the Fields, as were several others at the nick. The decline was slow to begin with – nobody could put an exact date on the start of it – but once it was underway it was unstoppable. What was once a community became a sink estate, where the council dumped undesirable families, single parents, the dispossessed and the deranged. It's a common story, enacted around every city in the country, and nobody knows the solution. The bottom end, as we called it, was the leper colony. You don't go there unless you have to.

But it was changing, I discovered, as I drove slowly down the Avenue towards where Lapetite had lived, past the Windermeres, the Wordsworths and the Shelleys, where only the dogs outnumbered the satellite dishes.

It was changing because the bulldozers had moved in. The empty, vandalised tenements were being demolished, leaving only the occupied ones standing. It was a drastic but effective solution, and meant that there were big gaps between the house numbers. Saturday night I'd found the house I wanted because a police car was standing outside it. When the killer came, Friday, he wouldn't have had that luxury. He'd have to use his eyes, read off the numbers, make deductions to allow for the gaps. The number 133 was displayed at the side of Lapetite's front door, in small painted figures, not easy to see. The killer could have been an acquaintance who had been before, but I didn't think he was. Let's assume he was a stranger, I thought, who came looking.

Did he come by car or by other means? The pins in the map often give this away – did he kill near bus stops and railway stations, or were the killings in remote places miles apart? – but we had only two pins. He could have walked between victims. I'd go for the most likely, that he came by car. And a white van had been seen near Alfred's place. Maybe he came by white van. A purple Porsche would have been more useful to me, but white van it was.

Would he park outside, once he'd identified the house? No. The vehicle would be seen. A strange car would stand out like a wooden leg on a parrot. He parked nearby, where suspicions wouldn't be raised, and walked the last bit.

Number 133 was still cordoned off with scene of crime tape and a panda stood outside. We were giving it twenty-four-hour protection until we were certain we couldn't glean another speck of information from the place. Then, as soon as we withdrew, the vultures would descend and tear it apart. I nodded to the driver of the panda and made a U-turn, trying to decide where I'd leave my car if I were on a similar errand to the killer.

Right on the edge of the estate is the Mitre hotel. It's a big, run-down, pre-war pub but is surviving because of its position. It has a good regular clientele from the estate and also attracts passing lunchtime trade. Heavy metal and Country and Western nights help boost the profits, and the landlord probably takes a cut from the teenage prostitutes and dealers who use the premises. It's called diversification, and is to be applauded. The car park is not too big, but the road outside is wide and free from yellow lines. That's where I would park, I decided, were I on a murder mission. I pulled the handbrake on and killed the engine.

I crossed the road and stopped to gather my bearings. I was probably about half a mile from the house, and could go there a number of ways. The estate was laid out in a grid pattern, so I could either walk in a series of left and rights, or do one long leg in one direction, turn left and do another long leg down the Avenue, the way I'd driven. I opted for the series of left and rights, on the grounds that the scenery would be more varied.

The houses looked good at this end. They had clean windows, tidy gardens, and efforts at individuality were apparent. Some looked a bit naff, like the ornamental lych gate, but people were trying, and deserved to be congratulated for that. An old man with a walking stick, making slow progress in the opposite direction, probably going for his nightly brown ale, said ''Ow do,' to me.

232

It soon changed. Big gaps appeared where the houses had been cleared. Some school kids, five of them, aged about twelve, were kicking a ball about on a triangular patch of grass, two sticks marking a goal. One of them took a shot, the goalie missed it and the ball came bouncing across the street to me. I flicked it up and booted it back. He missed that one, too.

'Thanks, mister,' one of them shouted, followed by, 'Want a game?'

I waved a hand and pressed on.

A youth came by in a Ford Fiesta with a door that didn't match and a faulty exhaust. He slowed down to look at me, but when I stared back, clocking him, he tore off with more noise than speed. He was wearing a Burberry baseball cap. If ever a company sold its soul for a *mess of potage,* it was Burberry.

Most estates like this are littered with house bricks lying in the road, abandoned shopping trolleys and cars on blocks. A big Vauxhall stood on the verge with its bonnet raised, a gaping cavern where the engine should have been. The owner came out of his garden carrying a spare part and a socket wrench, the front of his overalls the colour of burnt crème caramel.

'Sorted it?' I asked as I strode by and he rolled his eyes and grinned in reply.

I passed through that zone until I was at the bottom end, where Lapetite had lived.

Here, anything metal has been sold to the scrappies and the dogs are too wary to come sniffing. A burnt-out shell of a house looked as if it belonged in a Middle East newsreel. The PC in the panda saw me coming and reached across to open the passenger's door. I slid in alongside him.

'Any problems?' I asked.

He had none. A few sightseers came, now and again, then left. Some spoke to him hoping for a titbit of information that would give them status in the eyes of their friends, and a few took photographs. *Good riddance* was the general attitude, but none wanted to enlarge on that. The press had long gone, concerned more with the England captain's possible affairs than with the actual death of a drug dealer. Reality TV sells more papers than reality. I told him to stay loose and walked up the garden path towards the house. The key fit and I was inside.

The wallpaper was still a shock. It gave *fallen off the back of a lorry* a bad name. The next blow was the smell, but I couldn't do much about that. I set my breathing control to *shallow* and wandered round downstairs, room to room, opening cupboards and drawers, not expecting to find anything. He had a settee that probably harboured more wildlife than the rain forest, a couple of non-matching hard chairs and a rickety table. The floor was partly covered with worn lino, but the troops had lifted it and not bothered returning it to its previous pristine state, which didn't help. He still had floorboards, though. At the bottom end, floorboards are a luxury. They'd be the first things to go, after any remaining copper piping.

In the kitchen a stub of a lead pipe coming out of the floor marked where the gas stove had once stood. It had been flattened to seal it, but they needn't have bothered: the meter was missing and all the pipes ripped out. The gas had been turned off months ago. I wondered if the water supply to all the houses was through lead pipes. It probably was, which could explain a lot. There was a grease-covered microwave on the work surface, in case he ever invited any of his girlfriends around for a bite, and a few items of cutlery in a drawer. The soft bloom of the aluminium powder used by the fingerprint boys covered everything and added to the squalor.

It was the same depressing scene upstairs. He slept on a mattress on the floor, in a sleeping bag. It had been thrown to one side when the room was searched and lay there in a huddled heap. There had been clothes in a closet but these had been taken away. I found a few CDs but resisted the temptation to borrow them. I didn't think Benzino, Chilli Dog and C-Bo would be to my taste.

Downstairs, I sat on one of the hard chairs

and reminded myself why I was there. This was a murder scene. The boys had done the usual good job, so I knew there was nothing left for me to uncover, but a house has an ambience. There's something there intangible, something that you can't measure or put a name to. Well, there usually is. I tried to visualise how anybody could live in a place like this, but failed completely. It wasn't fit for a pig. This was a squat, a last resort, a desperate refuge. Lapetite didn't live here, nobody did. He lived on the streets, on his wits, slipping from friend to friend, woman to woman, like a virus flits between victims or a feral cat between dustbins. He was the registered owner, placed there by a council obliged to give him a dwelling, but it was never his home. It was his mail box, that's all.

We'd do a reconstruction. Friday evening we'd place a white van up near the Mitre and see if it jogged anybody's memory. We'd invade the pub, take the name of everybody present and interview them individually the following week. 'Did you see this van?' 'Did you see any strangers that night or any other time?' 'Did you know Jermaine Lapetite?' Criminals hang around near their crime scenes before doing the deed. They look out for things, check the possibilities, pluck up courage, and someone always sees them. We'd talk to everybody on the estate, concentrating on the route I'd taken, and collate their answers. But I wasn't optimistic. 'No', 'no' and 'never heard of him' could be pre-printed on the forms to speed things up.

It was dark when I went outside, so the kids wouldn't still be playing football. I wouldn't have minded a kickabout with them. I said goodnight to the PC, declined a lift back to my car and went the other way, up the Avenue and turned right at the end. The Mitre car park was almost empty and mine was the only vehicle in the road. Tonight evidently wasn't music night. I drove home slowly, enveloped in an emotional cocoon that I didn't understand at first. I was strangely on edge, but content at the same time. Then I realised what it was: gratitude. Plain and simple, straightforward gratitude. Whether to my parents, or some god, or my friends, I didn't know. But it was gratitude for the life I led. That's all.

Sonia didn't train Friday or Saturday, resting before Sunday's race, but I was working so couldn't spend much time with her. The reconstruction went off reasonably OK but the usual wall of silence descended when we asked the drinkers in the pub about Lapetite's acquaintances. He was Mr Invisible. Nobody knew anything about him and nobody mourned his demise. We took names and addresses and asked if they'd been in the Mitre the previous Friday. If they hadn't, we wanted to know where they had been. A few punters finished their drinks and tried to fade away when we announced our presence, nine o'clock sharp, but we had the place surrounded and they didn't get far. The sniffer dog gave a positive response to two of them and they were handcuffed and put in the van. I stood on the stage where a Kenny Rogers tribute act was about to do his stuff and explained to the audience that we were investigating the unfortunate killing of Jermaine Lapetite and wouldn't keep them a moment longer than was necessary. I thanked them in advance for their cooperation and hoped we hadn't spoiled their evening. It's a balancing act, and I'm the chief juggler.

We took 139 names and addresses, including the ersatz Kenny Rogers, whose Barnsley accent didn't go with the stetson, and on Saturday morning started visiting them for a more substantive interview. I stayed in the office, dishing out the work, waiting for the phone call from one of the troops saying that he was onto something, but it never came. At three o'clock I rang Sonia to say I was tearing myself away.

The race was another 10K, this time in County Durham. Sonia had booked a room for herself at a Travelodge and I went with her. We had a pasta meal before we left and took sandwiches and breakfast cereals and bananas with us. Energy food. There was a video in the room and Sonia had brought *Finding Nemo*. We watched it sitting up in bed, sipping cocoa and eating bananas, listening to the rain.

Sunday morning Sonia woke up complaining that she had a headache and a cold, possibly caused by the air conditioning being set too warm. I gave her some aspirin and opened the window. 'That's the trouble with thoroughbreds,' I told her, 'you're too prone to infection, not to mention the temperament.'

The rain had stopped. I suggested that she withdraw if she wasn't feeling good, but she said she was better. She dressed carefully in her neatly pressed kit, her number sewn on the front of her vest. It was a double-figure number, showing her to be among the elite. Two tracksuits, towel around her neck, water bottle, comfy trainers on her feet, the lightweight ones for the race in a bag that I carried. We parked the car where we could and made our way to the start.

Sonia finished tenth, bless her. From the start she didn't latch on to the leading group and allowed a gap to open. At the halfway mark she broke away from the main pack but couldn't make any headway on the leaders, so she had to run the final 5K on her lonesome ownsome. Her finishing time was half a minute slower than at Oldfield.

I gave her a peck on the cheek and draped the towel across her shoulders. She wasn't disappointed. It was a classier field and a tough course, and she'd done her best. We skipped the presentation and went looking for a motorway services that had shower facilities for lady lorry drivers.

All the names from the Mitre were put through the PNC to check on backgrounds, and we scored hits with twenty-nine of them. Offences were evenly spread between drunk and disorderly, drink driving, receiving, theft and possession of class C drugs. We had odd hits for more serious drugs offences, burglary and GBH. Three girls were under age, one being only fifteen, and they were dressed like whores from the cheap end of Marseilles docks. The DC who spoke to them thought they were on the game. I detailed Maggie to have a word with whatever parents they had.

I had egg and chips in the café over the road and went to see the GBH offender. He lived in the twilight zone, where I'd seen the kids playing football, with a woman who wasn't his wife and her two sons. He'd beaten up a previous girlfriend, a long time ago, and put the man she'd been having an affair with in intensive care, for which he'd received four years.

He sat me down and his lady friend made herself scarce.

'How's things, Malc?' I said.

'Not bad, Mr Priest,' he replied. 'I'm settled, these days. Not much money, what with t'kids, but we get by.' I knew he was on sickness benefits because of epilepsy and asthma, and was on constant medication.

'You've put weight on,' I told him.

He laughed and tugged at the waistband of his trousers. 'I know. Rich living, not 'elped by the steroids. What about you? You look like a whippet. I've seen more meat on a butcher's pencil.'

'Stress, Malc. Pure stress. What can you tell me about Jermaine Lapetite?'

'Stress! You? Pull the other one. He was a nasty piece of work, that's for sure. Not what you'd call real evil, if you know what I mean, but bad.'

I said, 'No, I'm not sure what you mean.'

'Well, you know, he wasn't mixed up with the 'eavy boys, didn't get people whacked, anything like that. He was small-time, but he 'ad about ten kids all over the estate. That can't be right, can it? He poked the women-folk of Heckley as casually as the rest of us poke the fire. It was what proved him a man, he thought. He used to come into t'Mitre dripping in gold, dressed up like Tommy Ward's donkey, and t'young birds were attracted to him like moths to a candle. Mind you, way they dress, these days, they're asking for it. If it's not on offer they shouldn't put it in t'shop window, that's what I say.'

'So he had enemies?'

'I suppose so. How would you feel if your fifteen-year-old pride an' joy, the apple of your eye, suddenly presented you with a little curly headed piccaninny? Some'd call it a killing offence, don't you think? An' that chopping his dick off and sticking it in 'is mouth... It all fits, dunnit?'

'I suppose so,' I agreed, not bothering to put him straight. We chatted for another fifteen minutes but I didn't learn anything. Malc had stepped out of line just once, but big time. He'd done his bird and settled down. Sometimes, now and again, the system works. I thanked him for his help, wished him all the best, and left.

Sonia rang me on my mobile, so I pulled off the road.

'Heckley Help the Aged,' I said.

'Oh, I'm sorry, I must have...'

'It's me, dumbo!'

'Is that you, Charlie?'

'Of course it is.'

'What are you doing in Help the Aged?'

'I'm not in Help the Aged. I'm in my car.'

'Were you having me on?'

'Yes. I'm sorry. I've had a stressful day and had to take it out on somebody.' It wasn't true but I thought it might placate her. Sonia isn't slow, but she is naïve. She believes everything she's told, trusts everyone. It had hurt her in the past and it could hurt her again, but it was one of the qualities that made her so loveable. 'I'm missing you,' I said. 'What time will you be home?'

'I should be early,' she replied. 'Are you coming for a run?'

'I don't think I'll be finished in time. Why don't you give yourself a rest day? You had a hard day yesterday.'

'Discipline, Chas. Start knocking the sessions out and soon you're missing more than you're doing.'

'Nobody would know.'

'I'd know. It's all psychology at the top. You've got to convince yourself that you've done everything possible. Some go out on Christmas day, because one day, when they're battling for a place, if they've missed a session for Christmas they know it and it eats away at their confidence. I'll just do a couple of steady laps at the golf course to keep loose.'

'OK. You've convinced me. I'll be home as soon as I can. What's for tea?'

'Um, I'm not sure. Any chance of you calling in Marks and Sparks for something quick?'

'Can do, but I get to choose.'

'Fair enough.'

I was back at the office, reading somebody's *Daily Express,* when Maggie walked in. I watched her hang her coat on the back of a chair and lift her hair from under the collar of her blouse. As she walked over to the table in the corner where we keep the electric kettle I poked my head out of my office and shouted, 'No sugar in mine, please.' She flapped a hand to say she'd heard me and I pulled a chair across to the end of her desk.

'Any joy?' I asked, when she brought the coffees and sat down.

'I've been to talk to the underage girls. Who said they were on the game?'

'I've forgotten. They certainly looked as if they were on the game.'

'Blame Christina Aguilera and Britney Spears for that. It's what they wear, these days. If you've got it, flaunt it. Subtlety isn't in the vocabulary.'

'You can say that again. I wouldn't let my daughter, if I had one, go out looking like that.'

'But Charlie,' she began, 'you haven't seen their mothers. You can't always go on appearances, you know.'

'Don't remind me,' I told her, remembering the two posh cars. 'Did they have anything to say about Lapetite?'

'One of them thought he was wonderful, the other two said he was a creep. Take your pick. I suspect he was shagging one of them and had turned down or finished with the other two. He was good fun; always had some pot; never tried them with anything harder.' Pink spots appeared on her cheeks as she added, 'Drugs, that is.'

I said, 'Maggie, you blushed.'

'Sorry.'

'I didn't know you had a blush in you.'

'Neither did I. They think Jermaine was killed by a jealous boyfriend.'

The door banged and there was a burst of voices as Eddie, George and Brendan came in. They hung up their coats, complained that the kettle was empty, scraped chairs and said their hellos. When they were settled I asked if they had anything interesting to report, but the question was answered with headshakes. 'You find anything, guv?' Eddie asked.

'No,' I replied. 'General consensus is that young Jermaine was a human sex machine with the morality of a goat, and that's what got him topped. Except, of course, the local populace doesn't know that we are linking his murder with that of Alfred Armitage.'

'You mean, they were both executions,' Eddie said.

'That's right.'

Dave came in, saw us in a cluster, and sat down at his own desk, yards away. George asked Eddie what his wife had thought of the T-shirt from the Harley shop.

Eddie laughed. 'She's threatened to cut it up if I ever wear it.'

George said, 'One day she'll cut you up.'

'Nah,' Eddie assured him. 'She knows which side her bread's buttered on.'

Brendan turned to me, asking, 'Did the psychiatrist have anything to say, boss?'

I nodded. 'Yes, he's convinced both murders were done by the same person, and he said he'll kill again. According to Adrian, the killer – the Executioner – is getting his act in order and next time it will be a bit special.'

'Special? What did he mean by that?'

'I dread to think.'

'We'll catch him then.'

'I wish I had your faith.'

I picked up my mug and walked over to my office. 'A word, Dave,' I said as I passed his desk, and he followed me.

I closed the door.

'Fancy a pint, later?' I asked him.

'Mmm, could do. How did the race go?'

'She finished tenth. Poor thing woke up with a cold, didn't feel too good. She did well. I notice that you studiously didn't join us, just now.'

'Nothing personal, Chas. I prefer not to be in the company of that arrogant sod if I can help it.'

'Any more poodle drawings?'

'Who told you about that?'

'I have my spies. You don't have to work with him, as long as it doesn't interfere with the job, but I know what you mean. I wish he'd stop calling me guv.'

'It's a military thing,' Dave told me.

I said, 'You mean, like, he says it to keep a distance between us?'

'That's right. In the army, on exercises, you might drop most of the bullshit, use first names, that sort of thing. But if you didn't like an officer you'd keep it formal.'

'Well that's reassuring. Thanks for that, Dave.'

'Don't mention it. What time tonight?'

'I'll give you a ring.'

I spent the rest of the afternoon reading reports and processing all the other stuff that piled up on my desk. Jeff came in with a smile on his face and his ears more prominent than usual.

'I've been to see Angie,' he told me.

'Angie of the sex shop fame?'

'That's right.' He stroked each side of his head twice with his fingertips. 'Gave me a trim, on the house. I've told her that we've given young Terry Hyson a good talking to but he denies it was him. She says he's a lying toad. Anyway, she's changing the name of the shop to Kurl up and Dye.'

'In memory of Hyson?'

'Probably. I told her that it isn't very original, so she said we've to think of something better.'

'You mean like Herr Kutz, the Hair Port, and all those?'

'Mmm, but original.'

'Right, if I can't sleep tonight I'll give it some thought. How's everything else?'

'No problems, except we haven't traced that Merc yet.'

'Keep at it.'

I decided on lasagne and bread and butter pudding and sneaked out to buy them before they sold out for the day, but I was too late: they'd had a run on the bread and butter pudding. M & S bread and butter pudding is my favourite, next to homemade apple pie, but they were right out of it. Ah, well, it would just have to be rhubarb crumble. I put the bag in the car boot and went back to the office. I could have finished reasonably early and made it home in time for a run, but I didn't feel like it, and being late in from work was the easiest way of dodging it. I went upstairs and talked with Gilbert, reminded him of the way we were tackling the case. Going over things sometimes helps, but not this time. When the rush hour traffic had subsided I placed everything in neat piles on my desk and drove home.

I decided I'd do the crumble and the lasagne in the oven rather than the microwave. Microwaves are quick but they are savage. Rhubarb crumble requires gentle treatment, and there was plenty of time. Sonia's run would take her about an hour and a half, including driving to and from the golf club.

Men were walking about in their shirt-sleeves and shorts, the women in miniscule tops with thin straps. I wound the car window down and started to sing a happy song, out loud, but not loud enough for anybody else to hear:

'Sometahms Ah feel like a mudderless chile,
Sometahms Ah feel like a mudderless chile...'

That one always cheers me up. A girl in a cotton dress was approaching a zebra crossing in front of me, so I slowed and gestured her across. She gave me a smile and I flashed my lopsided one at her. It would be a good evening for a steady run. I could have done it bare-chested, worked at my tan. I'd need a tan if I went to South Africa with Sonia. I'd prefer to go to Arizona, I thought, but *Sith Ifrica* would do.

Curlew! It just came to me, out of the blue, like being hit by an aeroplane door. *Curlew Hairdressing,* with a curlew logo. I'd tell Jeff in the morning. I'd never seen a Curlew Hairdressing salon anywhere. Why doesn't inspiration like that come to me about important things, though, I wondered?

'Sometahms Ah feel like a mudderless chile...'

I was pulling into my driveway as I reached the end of the stanza...

'A long wa-ay from home.'

Sonia's car wasn't on the drive, but she'd left a note under the kettle, where I couldn't miss it. 'Back about half seven. Have the tea ready,' it said. The clock on the oven was showing 19:09 and the lasagne needed 30 minutes at 190 degrees. The oven would take at least five minutes to reach that temperature, so Sonia would have enough time for a quick shower before we ate. Perfect. I switched the oven on and washed my hands. Our breakfast things were on the draining rack, so I put them away and removed the lasagne and the pudding from their cartons. There was some broccoli in the fridge's salad tray, so I decided we'd have that too. It was hardly five portions, but I sometimes wonder if the people who come up with these recommendations live in the real world.

When the little red light went out I put the lasagne on the top shelf of the oven and set the timer for 14 minutes. The pudding only needed 16 minutes, so it could go in then. When the broccoli came to the boil I turned the heat off and placed the lid on the pan. That would cook itself in thirty minutes. I could have been a chef, if I hadn't made the grade as a cop.

I placed knives, forks and spoons on the table, with an empty glass for each of us. When the pips went I placed the pudding on the middle shelf and reset the timer for another 16 minutes. The clock was showing 19:28, so *La Gazelle* should have finished her run and be setting off home. I had a drink of water from the tap and settled down to snooze in the rocking chair.

The timer announced that the lasagne was cooked at 19:44, but Sonia still hadn't arrived. I went in the front room and flicked round the channels, with the usual disappointing result. Back in the kitchen I put Sonia's Robbie Williams in the player and settled down to wait. He's no Frank Sinatra. After a couple of songs I went outside and sat on the bench with the sun on my face until the character next door started his petrol mower and began to chug up and down his garden. Some people are never content to let nature take care of things. They trim and prune, dead-head and weed, and their gardens don't look any better than mine. Not if you're a bird or a hedgehog. Maybe we'd have to have a blitz on it, next weekend, before the neighbours organised a petition.

Marks and Spencer's lasagne contains beef, egg pasta, tomatoes, milk, water, onions, mushrooms, cream, wheatflour, cheese, butter, olive oil, cornflour, oregano, pepper, bay and nutmeg. All good stuff. A portion of their rhubarb crumble provides fifteen per cent of the daily energy requirement of an average man. I worked it out from the figures on the box. I opened the oven door to stop our dinner drying out and put the kettle on. She must have met someone she knew, and perhaps they'd called for a drink in the clubhouse. When she hadn't arrived home or rung me by 8.30 I began to worry. What if she'd fallen in the woods and sprained an ankle or damaged her knee again? I gave her another ten minutes, then drove to the golf club.

The dog-walkers had long gone and her car was standing all alone where we always park. The doors were locked and the engine cold. I walked round it, as if expecting it to speak to me, but it didn't. All four tyres were inflated. It just stood there, enigmatic, like the Mary Celeste. The steward of the golf club wasn't much help. No, nobody in running kit had been in for a drink that evening. From the clubhouse you can see right round the golf course, and she wasn't there. I decided that she must be in the woods.

It took me nearly 40 minutes to walk our route through the woods, and it was almost dark when I arrived back at the cars, without Sonia. I rang Dave.

'Dave, it's Charlie,' I said. 'I'm worried stiff. Sonia's missing.'

'Missing? What do you mean by missing?'

Poor Dave. He thought I was trying to tell him that Sonia had walked out on me. 'She went out for a run,' I explained, 'and she's lost somewhere. She should have been back two hours ago. I'm at the golf club and I've walked her route, but she's not there.'

'Where are you now?' he asked.

'I'm in the golf club car park, standing next to her car.'

Dave was silent for a few moments, then he said, 'OK, Charlie, how's this sound: her car wouldn't start, or she lost the key, and she's jogged home?'

It sounded so obvious. 'Yeah,' I agreed. 'It's a possibility.'

'Right. So you go home and see if she's there. Ring me on my mobile, either way.'

'I'm on my way,' I told him, convinced he was right. The simple explanation is always the right one.

But she wasn't there. I shouted her name, dashing from room to room, upstairs and down, turning lights on. There was no sign of her, no sound from the bathroom of a running shower, no pile of running kit on the bed, no other note. I re-read the one she'd left, double checked the time, and found myself soaked in a cold sweat.

'She's not here, Dave,' I told him.

'OK. It's all in hand. I've sent for Jeff and alerted uniformed. Task force are standing by so I'll tell them to get here – I'm at the golf course. She's probably fallen and hurt herself, or perhaps her knee has let her down. You stay there and wait in case she comes home.'

'No,' I told him. 'I'm coming back.' Dave's a good pal, wouldn't try to pull the wool over my eyes, but you don't send for the task force for someone who's sprained an ankle. He was daring to think what I was too terrified to consider.

Monday's are our quietest night, so three pandas were there when I arrived back, as were Jeff Caton and several others of the team. Gareth Adey, my uniformed counterpart, arrived, wearing jeans and cowboy shirt, fresh from his line dancing class. Jeff had brought the Ordnance Survey map and I tried to indicate on it the path she would have taken. Heckley Wood isn't Sherwood Forest. It's about one mile by half a mile, but is ancient woodland with lots of fine big trees, mainly oak, birch and ash, that must be centuries old. The ground is pockmarked with craters, the remnants of bell-pits where ancient monks mined for coal. Brambles and bracken choke the spaces between the trees, with a network of paths criss-crossing the area. In spring the wood is ablaze with blue-bells, but tonight they were well past their best.

Under Gareth's direction the uniformed boys armed themselves with torches and set off to follow her route. It was fully dark as the task force van arrived and the searchers straggled back into the car park. There were eight of them in the van, under the supervision of a sergeant. His first suggestion was to send for a dog handler. Why hadn't I thought of that? He was with us in ten minutes, saying he needed something worn by Sonia to give the dog a scent to find. Her tracksuit was inside the car. I unlocked it with the spare key I had brought with me and handed the suit to the dog handler.

'Find him! Find him!' the handler urged, burying the dog's muzzle into the tracksuit top, and the dog started running round in circles, nose to the ground, tail wagging. It zigged and zagged a couple of times before plunging off into the darkness.

'OK,' the task force sergeant said, summoning his troops, after I'd told him Sonia's probable route. 'Let's get on with it. We'll do a systematic search of that half of the wood first. Form your line that side.' He turned to Gareth and asked if he could borrow his men, and Dave and Jeff said they'd join the line, too.

Gareth had sent for reinforcements and the park was surrounded, in case anybody tried to escape from it. It wasn't explained to me, but I knew what everybody was thinking. The searchers spaced themselves at five yard intervals and slowly moved into the wood. Their torches sent beams of light flashing on the tree trunks and illuminating criss-crossing branches that flickered bright for a moment, cutting the blackness into an ever-changing cubist nightmare of shapes. The shadows danced and swayed and closed in again behind the searchers.

'Sonia! It's the police, where are you.' It was Dave, shouting her name. Their torches had vanished apart from the occasional stray beam of light as someone examined the undergrowth. A minute later he called again, fainter. The third time he was barely audible.

'Thanks for coming, Gareth,' I said.

'They'll find her, Charlie.'

'Of course they will.'

I've never believed in all this positive thinking stuff. Not when it's about events you have no control over. It's one thing for someone like Sonia to believe that she can train to make herself the best, but no amount of positive thinking or self-hypnotism or any other mumbo jumbo will help you overcome gravity or change the mind of a madman. There was no moon. We leaned on the bonnet of my car and didn't speak again. Away to the left were the windows of the clubhouse, and beyond the golf course we could see the orange glow of the lights on the bypass. Otherwise, the darkness was near total.

The torches appeared again, a couple of hundred yards away, and we heard the sergeant shouting instructions. Within seconds they had vanished back into the wood. Over at the clubhouse car engines were starting. Headlights swept round, dazzling us briefly before driving away. It was going home time. Call it eleven-thirty. Sonia had been out for over five hours. Half of the clubhouse lights went out, then the other half.

I thought of her, and how I'd felt, two weeks ago as she pranced her way to victory. She was almost apologetic, while I nearly exploded with pride. *La Gazelle* was back! But I was just as happy about how she handled defeat, and as she'd pounded her lonely way on the last half of yesterday's race the crowd recognised they were watching someone special, and gave her the biggest cheer. Was it only yesterday?

High above us the stars were a blazing trail across the sky and I was looking for constellations, wondering how many billions of light years they were away, when the warbling of a phone brought me back from where I was trying to escape to. I turned to Gareth but he already had it to his ear.

'You have?' he said, and, 'Right. Where are you...? Yes, he's with me... A couple of minutes. Right.'

He closed the phone and said, 'They've found something, Charlie. They want you round there.'

Chapter Nine

'What?' I demanded, dreading the answer, not sure if I wanted to know. 'What have they found?'

'A shoe. C'mon, we'll go in my car.'

They were on the road that borders the northern edge of the wood, near the park gates. The searchers were standing around in groups, waiting for my pronouncement. The dog had found the shoe, nowhere near the route she would have normally taken. It was a Reebok Premier, in her size. The lace was still tied and it was cold and wet.

'Yes,' I confirmed. 'It's hers.'

Gareth and I joined the line and the quartering of the wood resumed. We moved off at the sergeant's instructions, picking our way between the trees and around the clumps of brambles, our torches casting giant shadows that reared and swam before us. The going was uneven and full of obstacles. Brambles dragged at my trousers, low branches hit me in the face, bracken spores made me choke. The idea is to move slowly in a straight line, regardless of the terrain, examining the ground to your left and right every stride. A pheasant exploded into flight between the next man and me, sending our pulse rates off the scale, and went clattering off into the unknown. I dropped into a bell-pit, pulling fronds of bracken to one side, and hauled myself out of it again. The pits would be a good place to rest or hide, but this one was empty.

The sergeant was behind us, controlling the line. We were drifting to the right, he told us, and one end was getting ahead. We stopped, measured our spaces and moved off again.

Now there were clouds in the sky, building up to the west. We came out of the wood onto the golf course and the chill smell of rain was in the air. The sergeant strode out sixty yards and formed us up again. When we were ready he gave the order and we moved slowly and purposefully back into the wood. This is what the task force are good at. It's menial work, tedious and uninspiring, but just as important to any investigation as fingerprinting, post-mortems, or any other process we rely on. In daylight they'd be assisted by the mounted police. I said a little prayer that it wouldn't come to that.

The going was smoother for my stretch, this time, and the trees more widely spaced, but the floor of the wood was deep in dog's mercury and a dew was developing, so my feet were soon soaked. Orchids grew here, I remembered. They'd be out about now, if we hadn't trampled them. I took a stride, swung the torch to my left, another stride and swung it to my right all the time willing the beam with all my might not to find anything. It worked, thank God. Maybe there is something in mind over matter, after all.

The moon had risen when we came out of the wood again, onto the road. I was wet up to the knees and I knew Gareth, Jeff and the others would be the same. The task force were wearing boiler suits and Wellington boots. They carried poles for poking about, and six-cell Maglites. The sergeant realised the situation and came up to me.

'I appreciate your feelings, Mr Priest,' he said, 'but my men are more used to this work, and better equipped. Why don't you wait in your car and let your men go home, eh? We'll manage. If she's in here, we'll find her.'

I was about to say that the others could go but I was staying, when someone behind me said, 'What the devil...'

There was something in the way he said it that cut through everything else that was going on. I turned to see where he was looking. Everybody fell silent and did the same, and fifteen torches switched on and sent a concentrated beam of light down the road.

A figure was visible, right at the edge of the pool of light, walking slowly towards us. A tall pale figure that raised an arm to shield its eyes from the glare and staggered, as if slightly inebriated.

I was paralysed. Something stopped me racing forward to embrace her, swing her off her feet and plant a kiss on her mouth. It was relief beyond anything I've ever experienced, mixed with confusion and embarrassment. A million questions flashed through my mind, none of them important. Torches were lowered, some switched off. I stepped forward, then strode to meet her. Sonia was limping, wearing one shoe. Her knees were bleeding, her T-shirt muddy and her face bruised, but she was alive and she was here.

I threw my arms around her and hugged her. She hugged me, great convulsions pumping through her body as she realised the nightmare was over.

'You're safe, now,' I told her as she sobbed onto my shoulder. 'You're safe now.'

I led her to where the others were standing and a car door swung open. I helped her into the traffic car and the driver poured her a cup of something from a flask. Sonia thanked him in a squeaky voice and gulped it down, both hands around the cup. Somebody else handed a blanket to me and I did my best to spread it over her knees.

'What happened, love?' I asked, after I'd slid in beside her. 'Did you fall and hurt yourself?'

Sonia mumbled something I couldn't interpret.

'What was that?'

I still couldn't decipher her sobs, but I thought the word 'attacked' was in there. 'Did you say you were attacked?' I said, and felt her nod against my shoulder.

I held her arms and looked into her face. 'Are you saying you were attacked, Sonia?'

'Yes,' she sniffed. I found a tissue and held it against her nose. She took it from me and had a good blow.

'By a man?'

A nod and a sniff.

'Did you know him?'

'No.'

'Is he still in the wood?'

'No. I don't think so.'

'OK. Let's get you home.' I made a better job with the blanket, wrapping it around her shoulders, and led her back to where the team were waiting, big grins on their faces. It wasn't the result they expected, not what they were used to. The sergeant gave her his sweater to wear as I introduced them, and I handed him the blanket.

'She was attacked,' I told him. 'We may have to do another search of the wood in the daylight.'

'Right,' the sergeant said. 'Meanwhile, are you going to ... you know...'

Sonia was standing next to us, leaning on me, and what he was trying to say was would we be taking her to the rape suite for a full medical, with swabs, antibiotic injections and counselling.

'I don't know,' I said. 'We'll see.'

I told him that I'd either go to the station with her or phone in a report, and thanked everybody for their help. Gareth shook my hand and Jeff squeezed Sonia's arm, told her it was great to see her. The traffic car took us back to the golf club while the others set off to walk there. Sonia had stopped sobbing and shivering and was coping better than I would have thought. When we were in my car I asked her what had happened.

'I think there must have been a trip wire,' she told me, her voice soft and slow. 'I was really flying on that downhill stretch where the fallen tree is. Just past there. Suddenly I hit the ground. Really hard. I think I may have been concussed. Next thing I knew I was sitting up and this man was all over me, pulling my arms behind my back. My hands were hurting like hell.' She showed me her palms, with the skin grazed away. 'And my knees hurt, too. And I must have bumped my face.'

'Your cheek is swollen,' I said. 'Go on. You're doing well.'

'He tied my hands behind me, with one of those plastic things. All the time he was saying, "I won't hurt you, I won't hurt you." I said, "Well you are doing," and he apologised. It was weird.'

'Then what happened?'

'He dragged me to my feet and pushed me into the wood. Off the path. He took me to one of those holes in the ground. He had some stuff there, as if he were camping, or living rough.'

'What sort of stuff?'

'A sleeping bag, and one of those orange bivvy bags, and some food. On the way I managed to pull one of my trainers off, thought I'd leave a trail.'

'We found it. You were thinking well, very brave. Then what?'

'Not much. He said he wanted to talk, that's all. He'd seen me run, remembered me from the Nineties, was my greatest fan. It was pathetic. I said I couldn't talk with my arms tied behind me. At first he refused, but after about an hour I said I had cramp in my arms and was in agony.'

'You talked for an hour?'

'It must have been at least that long. He knew all about me, knew I went out with Tony. Said he didn't deserve me. He said you didn't either. He said he'd written to me, years ago, but I hadn't answered. I did receive a few crank letters. I told him that all my mail was vetted by my manager.'

'Did you have a manager?'

'No. Then I told him that I thought I remembered him from one of the meetings at Gateshead. He was at the presentation and had asked me for my autograph. I said I was sure I recognised him from somewhere.'

'That was a good move,' I agreed. 'Have you been on the training course?'

'No, but when it's real you learn fast. Anyway, I said my arms hurt and started crying. After a while he said he'd tie my arms in front of me if I promised not to try to run away. Would you believe, I had to think about it? But I agreed. He cut the tie and pulled my arms to the front.'

'What did you do?'

'I kicked him in the face with my good shoe and ran for it. I knocked his spectacles off. It was pitch black by then and I couldn't see where I was going, but neither could he. I could hear him shouting my name, pleading for me to come back, promising not to hurt me, but I hid in another one of those holes. After a while he went away. I stayed for ages, then wandered about. I was lost. I came out on the road and saw the lights.'

I leaned across and put my arm around her. I didn't say anything. Couldn't say anything. After a while I asked if she'd be able to describe her attacker.

'He was only little. That's why I wasn't afraid of him. He was little and weedy, with wire-rimmed spectacles.'

I said, 'You're amazing, Sonia. I'm staggered by how you're taking this, but I have to ask a few questions. This is DI Priest asking, not Charlie. Do you understand?'

'Um, I think so.'

'Right. I have to ask this: did he rape you?' She shook her head. 'No.'

'Did he sexually assault you in any way?'

Sonia hesitated. 'I'm not sure. He was a bit free with his hands when he made me stand up. He sort of ... fondled me, but it could have been accidental.'

'It wasn't,' I assured her. 'Did he threaten to rape you, or suggest you have sex with him?'

'No. He said he just wanted to talk. He wanted to be my friend. That's all.'

I heaved a big sigh. Sonia is to naïve what Santa Claus is to generosity. 'No he didn't,' I told her. 'He wanted sex with you. He wanted it more than anything in the world, except that he wanted *you* to want to have it with him. *Expected* you to want it. That was his dream. It's what happens in the world he lives in. You're attracted to someone, and there's a universal rule that says they will automatically reciprocate the attraction. Newton's tenth law, or something. But life's not like that, as we both know. When you didn't play his game, Sonia, he'd have settled for second best. He'd have raped you, believe me.'

She squeezed my hand. 'I've had a lucky escape.'

'Luckier than you'll ever believe.' Because, having raped her, he'd have strangled her to cover his tracks. If there was no need for a medical I could take her straight home. I turned the key and fired the engine. 'We'll collect your car tomorrow,' I said. As we pulled into the drive I said, 'The lasagne will be ruined.'

I made us both a cocoa and asked Sonia to put everything she was wearing in a bin liner. I phoned in a brief report and told them to expect me at lunchtime. It might have been smart to have the car park cordoned off to preserve any tyre marks, but I decided it would be a waste of time, and this wasn't a murder hunt.

'Why do you want all my clothes, Charlie?' Sonia asked.

'To look for any fibres left by the kidnapper.'

'But won't they also find fibres from that blanket and this police sweater?' She was still wearing the one the task force sergeant loaned her.

'Yes,' I replied. 'They'll just think that you're a popular girl, that's all.'

'I see.' She stretched her arms out, demonstrating that the sleeves of the sweater were miles too long. 'Does it suit me?' she asked.

'No.'

'No?'

'No. I don't like you in it.'

'Why?'

'Because I have a rule about my private life and relationships with police women. Take it off, please.'

'Ooh. Right.'

I said, 'Go have a shower, love, and you'll find some aloe vera in the cabinet. Put it on all your grazes. It's good stuff. Put plenty on.'

She moved towards the stairs but I called her back. I put my hands on her shoulders, moved one behind her head and ran the fingers through the short hairs at the nape of her neck. 'Sonia,' I said. 'Are you all right?'

She nodded.

'Positive?'

'Mmm. I'm all right, Charlie, honest I am.'

I wanted to say, 'I thought I'd lost you. I really thought I'd lost you,' but I didn't. Instead I said, 'Do you want me to sleep in the spare bed?'

'No. I want you to sleep with me.'

'Good,' I replied. 'I hoped you'd say that.'

The task force found the plastic bivvy bag and lots of footprints in the hole in the ground where Sonia had been held. The bag might have fingerprints, but it was possible that our man had never been in trouble with the law. The big romance in his life had come to nought, and now he'd sink back into the swamp where he would wallow in obscurity for the rest of his life, surrounded by memorabilia of the woman he loved and lost, dreaming of what might have been.

Oh! It was a feeling I was all too familiar with.

I brought Sonia into the station at lunchtime and she was interviewed and made a statement there. A female inspector from the sex crimes unit at HQ came to give the case an overview, but she had a full workload and was happy to leave it with me. Afterwards I sat down with Sonia and my sketchpad and produced what she said was a reasonable likeness of her attacker. It was just a caricature, but the secret is to keep it simple, don't put in too much detail which may not be accurate. He made Woody Allen look like Clark Gable.

Mr Wood took a fatherly interest in the case, asking Sonia if she'd like a coffee when we went up to see him, pulling a chair over for her, getting the chocolate Hobnobs out.

I winked at her as I dunked mine, saying, 'We're not offered these normally; you'll have to come more often.'

'They're for special visitors only,' Gilbert said. 'Proper sports people, not washed-up ex-footballers who never made the grade in the first place.'

I said, 'Ouch!' and reached for another one.

'So you don't think there's any link with the two other cases, Charlie?' Gilbert was saying.

I shook my head and mumbled a no. When I'd swallowed my biscuit I went on, 'According to Sonia our man is about five-foot six and slightly built. When they tried hoisting a body over the toilet it was possible for one man to do it, but difficult. The murderer is fairly powerful, we think.'

Sonia looked pale. 'Were you thinking I'd been attacked by the murderer of those other two?' she asked.

'No,' I assured her. 'We considered it, but you were attacked by a nutcase who's been stalking you. He's nothing to do with the others.'

'What's this about cars in the car park?' Gilbert asked.

'It's a favourite place for dog-walkers,' I told him. 'They go there every night. We'll see who's there this evening, ask what they saw, the usual stuff. One woman in particular speaks to us. She may have seen something.' I couldn't resist adding, 'You know what women are like,' which earned me a scowl from Sonia.

I took her over the road for a late lunch and then we collected her car. After she'd driven off I had a look for tyre prints but the ground was as hard as bell metal, so I had a wander into the wood. It was a different place. The trees were newly into full leaf and the sun was lancing down through the canopy, like the light through a stained glass window in a cathedral. I thought of the poem from my schooldays, about dappled things, but couldn't remember any of it. I'd have to make a return visit, sometime. Gerard Manley Hopkins, I believe it was.

I found the fallen tree we jumped over, near where Sonia said she'd tripped. Mud from our trainers was dried on top of the trunk. A wood pigeon ceased its monotonous calling as I approached, then rattled away through the branches. I wafted away a bumble-bee that came enquiring. About fifteen yards further on was the place where he'd felled her with a wire across the track. It was downhill, and she'd have been running flat out, galloping recklessly, her long legs raking over the ground as she rejoiced in the sheer joy of it.

Poor kid would have hit the deck like a ton of bricks. I sat on the log and quietly fumed. Someone was going to pay for this.

I didn't find anything. You never do. Task force had been and gone, and if there'd been anything to find, they'd have done it. I walked back to the car and drove to the nick.

Dave and Maggie volunteered to interview the dog-walkers. 'There's three or four of them at that time,' I told them. It was nearly five o'clock, and the office was full. Spirits were high, with everybody sharing the relief I'd felt when I saw Sonia limping out of the darkness. 'The only one I remember,' I continued, 'is a woman in a Citroen Picasso who has one of those Scotties. A white one.'

'Vicious little things,' Eddie said. 'Got bitten by one, long time ago.'

'Little dogs are the worst,' Brendan informed us. 'I was once bitten by a shih-tzu.'

'What's a shih-tzu?' George asked.

'It's a zoo with only a budgie and a white mouse,' Dave informed him.

Dave rang me. I'd grounded Sonia, forbidden her to train for at least three days. Events caught up with her, reaction struck, and she was in bed when I arrived home. I lay alongside her, on top of the duvet, for an hour, holding her close. Like I said, it's all about gratitude. I made us pork fillet, roast potatoes and vegetables, and we'd just finished eating when he called.

'She didn't turn up, Charlie,' he reported.

'Damn!' I said. 'That's a set back. What about the others?'

'One German shepherd, one spaniel and one mongrel. They've all seen the woman in question, but none of them know her. They're all strangers to each other. Some of them come quite a distance to walk the dog there.'

'What about other cars?' I asked.

'A red one, sometimes, two of them reported. Oldish, possibly a Nissan. Didn't see the driver. I've asked them to think about it, let us know. And we'll do a follow-up, of course.'

'Of course,' I said. 'I wonder what happened to the woman with the Scottie.'

'Possibly had a night off. We'll find her tomorrow.'

We couldn't keep it out of the *Gazette*, but were too late to include an appeal for the woman with the dog to come forward, so we asked local radio to do the job. I couldn't imagine her listening to their mixture of football, rap, football, phone-ins and football, but it was the best we could do. And she may have grandkids who listen.

But she wasn't there Wednesday or Thursday evening, and she didn't come forward. It was another juggling act, dividing myself between the two cases. We were doing repeat interviews on the murder case, and still investigating Jermaine Lapetite's contacts, but not making much progress. I put Dave in charge of Sonia's attack, but that was only for official consumption and to keep him away from Eddie. I was keeping a close eye on things myself.

Friday morning I rang the *Gazette* and asked to speak to the chief photographer. We've met a few times, and he's always been helpful.

'Do you use a digital camera?' I asked him, after the usual pleasantries.

'These days, we all use one,' he told me. 'Wouldn't be without it.'

'After the Oldfield 10K race you published some photos of the finish, including one of Sonia Thornton and myself.'

'I remember it,' he said.

'Can you remember if you cropped it?'

'I can't remember, but I can assure you that I almost certainly did. Do you want me to dig it out for you?'

'That was my next question.'

'No problem. Do you have an email address?'

Technology. This was where I came unstuck. 'Um, would it be possible for me to come to the *Gazette?*' I asked. 'Then maybe I can look at anything else you may have.'

'No problem. When are you coming?'

'Ten minutes?'

Ten minutes was OK, so I was soon in his tiny corner, scattered with documents, photos, camera paraphernalia and bags to carry it all in. A flat screen VDU was showing a screensaver of a crashing surf, but in pride of place above his desk was a photo of

Princess Diana, taken when she came to open the new children's wing at Heckley General, back in '93. She looked gorgeous.

He pulled another chair next to his for me and shoved a CD into his computer. After a few clicks thumbnails of all the pictures that he'd taken at the race came into view and he asked me which ones I was interested in.

I scanned the mosaic of tiny images until I found a familiar one. 'There,' I said, pointing.

He clicked on it, the thumbnails vanished and a new, full size picture began to scan down the screen. In seconds I was faced with a photograph of Sonia and myself as I'd seen it in the paper over two weeks ago, but I wasn't looking at us. I was looking at the man standing to the left of Sonia, half-turned to gaze at her, one arm reaching out so he could touch her elbow. His mouth was stretched in a wide, adoring grin, but I couldn't see his eyes because the sun was reflecting off the lenses of his wire-rimmed spectacles. An icy hand gripped my stomach and squeezed, and a muscle in my throat started to twitch.

'Him,' I croaked, and my hand was shaking as I pointed. 'Can you blow him up for me, please?'

He brought the man to the centre of the screen and zoomed in on him. I took a copy of the sketch I'd done from my pocket and held it alongside the VDU.

'How does that look?' I said.

'Pretty good,' he agreed.

'Can I have a print of that, please? And a disc with it on?'

'No problem. Is there a story in it for us?'

'You bet there is.'

Sunday I took a day off and we drove to Kilnsey in the Dales. Kilnsey Crag was a great spot to watch climbers dealing with a huge limestone overhang, back in the days when they carried Rawlbolts with them and could have scaled a cooling tower. Now sanity prevails and the sport had reverted to more natural methods. We crossed the Wharfe and hiked up over Featherbed Moss onto Conistone Moor, through the lines of shake holes and disused mineshafts. The shake holes are depressions in the ground caused by the limestone being dissolved or reacting with elements in the sandstone that underlies it in places. That's the theory. The miners were looking for lead. It started with the Romans and lasted until about 150 years ago. It's impossible to imagine that the moors once rang to the sound of miners' clogs on the rocky tracks, but they must have done. The desperation that made them want to burrow underground, following the vein so they could feed their families, is beyond belief. Now, potholers go down there for amusement. The whole area is like a giant Gruyère cheese, riddled with holes, more porous than a string vest.

'How did they know where the lead was?' Sonia asked, after I'd given her the fifty-cent history lesson.

'I don't know,' I replied. 'They were clever people. Something about the landscape, or the geology, told them that it was probably here.'

The idea was to have a break, a change of scenery, and to leave the traumas of the week behind, but inevitably we talked about things. We were eating our sandwiches, seated on some rocks, when Sonia raised the subject.

'I've been thinking, Charlie,' she said.

'What about?'

'That car. At the golf course. I think I remember it, unless the idea has been planted in my head. But I can see it. A dull red colour, shabby. It was there two or three times when we left. I'm sure of it.'

'I know,' I agreed. 'I can see it too. It was forlorn-looking, as if abandoned. I'm supposed to be the observant one, but I didn't take any notice of it.'

'Do you think you'll catch him?'

'Yeah. We'll get him through the photos.'

'Then what will happen?'

'Uh!' I snorted. 'That's when the problems will start. If he doesn't plead guilty he'll say you led him on. It won't be easy for you.'

'But I've never met him before. Well, I didn't think I had. It's all in his mind.'

'I don't think it will come to that. It won't if I get my hands on him first, that's for sure. Let's change the subject. There's a rather nice tea shop in Burnsall. How's the knee shaping up?'

'No problem,' she said.

'Right, then. It's your turn to carry the rucksack.'

Dave rang just before the gruesome bit at the end of *Seven*. Brad Pitt has his gun on the killer, and you're doing the maths. Two more, you're thinking. Two more, but which two out of the three of them? Then he opens the box...

Except Dave rang.

'Hiya, Shagnasty,' I said. 'Great timing.'

'You weren't ... were you?'

'No, we're watching a video. What can I do you for?'

'I found her, the woman,' he replied.

'The dog-walker?'

'Who else?'

'That's brilliant! When was this?'

'She came this afternoon. She remembers seeing the red car on several occasions, but never saw the driver. And never looked at the number, of course. I said you'd probably want to talk to her tomorrow.'

'That's great, Dave. I hope you haven't

spent all weekend on the golf course.'

'Of course I have. That's what I do best. See you in the morning.'

'See you then.'

I put the phone down and turned to Sonia. 'Dave's found that woman with the Scottie, and she remembers a red car. Doesn't help much, but it's another piece of the jigsaw. If he has no plausible reason to be there it all helps to indicate he was stalking you.'

We started the video again and watched the credits scroll up the screen. When we got to Mr Pitt's secretary I hit the rewind button, switched the telly off and asked Sonia if she'd like a drink of any sort.

She said, 'I wonder if the pictures came out.'

'What pictures?'

'The ones she took in the car park, the other night.'

It was like a big light went on in my brain. You work at a case, get nowhere, then suddenly it all falls into place. Someone in charge decides that you've made the effort and deserve the reward, so he pushes a pile of goodies your way.

'The photos!' I gasped. 'I forgot the photos!' I grabbed the phone and dialled Dave's number.

'It's me,' I began. 'About a fortnight ago the woman with the dog took a photo of Sonia, in the car park. Then I took one of the two of them together, on her camera. The cars were in the background. I'm sure of it. Get round there as early as is decent and get the film or whatever off her. Please.'

'Is that you, Charlie?'

'Did you hear me?'

'It's as good as done.'

'Thanks. I'll remember you in my will.'

The sanctity of marriage is a thing of the past, if the statistics are anything to go by. Every week there are about a dozen wedding photos in the *Gazette*. At least six of them have the couple's children on them, and four of the remaining couples already share the same address. The brief captions don't indicate which are second or third marriages, and there's little to indicate how long each one will last. And for every wedding there are two other people deciding to move in together, to see how things work out. Usually, they don't.

All this is bad news for us. Kids are being brought into the world and raised without a regular man in the house. A succession of uncles is a poor substitute for a dad who's always there to help you build a kite or pull out a loose tooth. Or, more likely these days, to debate the possibilities of intergalactic travel or the rival merits of X-wing fighters and Millennium Falcons. The kids run wild, without fear of authority, and we reluctantly feed them into the legal system that blights them for the rest of their stunted lives.

But it's not all bad news. For every broken marriage or failed relationship there's an aggrieved partner. Usually, but not always, it's a woman left to raise the kids while dad sneaks off somewhere out of reach of the Child Support Agency. She struggles along for a year or two, the resentment gradually building up inside her, until one night, when the kids are playing up and she's too tired to deal with them, she reaches for the phone and dials Crimestoppers. Revenge, plus a small fee, helps ease the burden. More than a few murderers have fallen into our welcoming laps that way, plus a steady succession of burglars and other felons. But mainly it's drug dealers.

We'd just finished the Monday morning briefing when George, one of my DCs, approached me. He'd interviewed Lapetite's ex-girlfriend and mother of one of his children, and she was ready to point the finger at the dealer who supplied him. He hadn't wanted to announce it to the meeting because, he said, walls have ears.

'Do you know something I don't?' I asked.

'No, boss. Just being super-cautious. I don't think he's what you might call a Mr Big, but he could be a Mr Medium.'

'Have you told her about the informer programme?'

'No. She doesn't know much and wants to be out of it all. She'll be content if she gets a couple of hundred from the Crimestoppers. She blames this guy for all Jermaine's problems, thinks they'd have been OK if he'd kept away from him.'

'Silly girl. When will they learn? Are you going to see her today?'

'Later this morning. I was wondering if you'd come along.'

'Can do, but you've been working with Eddie, haven't you?'

He shrugged his shoulders.

'What does that mean?' I demanded.

'Nothing, boss. Eddie's OK, but he's a bit of a one-man band. Likes to do things his way. We went to interview her together, first off, but he came on a bit heavy. Got her back up. When I went to see her on my own she opened up a lot more.'

I could imagine Eddie having an unsympathetic approach towards an unmarried mother. He was much more experienced than George, good at reading character, making snap judgements and taking shortcuts, but sometimes his judgement would be clouded by his prejudices. Cops like him sometimes don't like passing on their expertise. Eddie was old school, George wasn't.

I remembered the sergeant I was under when I first went on the beat. We visited this old lady who'd been burgled, and I removed my hat when she invited us inside. Afterwards he told me off about it. Apparently, if there'd been an altercation, holding the hat would have impeded me. 'Keep it on your head, lad, where it belongs,' he told me. It was the only advice he ever gave me, and totally useless.

'Have a word with Mr Adey about a snatch squad for tomorrow morning,' I told George. 'If we get a name we'll hit him early, catch him in his jim-jams. I'll come with you this morning and if she coughs I'll organise a warrant.'

George went off as happy as a wasp in a bun shop window and I went upstairs. Dave had already returned from the errand I'd given him and I wanted to see what he'd found.

Not much. It was a digital camera, thank goodness, and he'd already mastered how to display the pictures on the little screen at the back of the camera. One of the advantages of having children is that you learn things like that. The woman had spent a few days visiting her daughter in Berkshire, so there were photos of the grandchildren playing with the dog, of the dog begging, scratching its ear and doing all the other things dogs do. Well, not all of them. The photos were taken in a big garden with lots of roses, a pergola and a water feature depicting a watering can apparently supported on nothing more than the column of water pouring out of its spout. Eventually, straight after a fetching shot of the dog rodgering the son-in-law's leg, there was Sonia standing next to the camera's owner.

Two cars were behind them. One was a Ford Mondeo with the number plate clearly visible, but only the offside front wheel arch of the other one could be seen at the edge of the photograph. Dave fiddled with the tiny buttons on the back of the camera, adjusting the position of the cars on the screen, and zoomed in on the Mondeo's number until it was readable.

'That looks familiar,' he said.

'Yes, I know,' I snapped. 'It's mine. What about the other one?'

He zoomed out, brought it across and zoomed in again. All I'd caught was the front headlight and tyre. 'Sorry, Chas,' he said. 'That's the best we can do. It's obviously red, and one of the petrol heads will identify the make and model. It's a start.'

'Bugger!' I snorted.

'Exactly. What are you?'

'A useless prat. Take it to photographic, please, and ask them to run it off. Run a few of the others off for her, too, if they'll do them. And keep tomorrow morning free if you fancy coming on a bust.'

It had been a long shot, and sometimes they come off. We were narrowing the field down, but had a long way to go.

Jessica Ripley had two children: one espresso and one latte. I didn't enquire about their surnames. They were beautiful, with all the advantages that genetic diversity brings, and if the toys scattered around the house were anything to go by they weren't deprived. Except they had no dad and shortage of money was a constant problem for their mother. The DSS pays for the necessities, but where do you turn when the washing machine floods the kitchen?

We sat on hard chairs and Jessica sent the kids to watch a video in the front room. She was blonde, but not natural, and twenty years old, looking fifteen. She offered us coffee but we declined.

'How long had you known Jermaine?' I asked.

'About six years,' she replied.

'So you met him while you were at school?'

'Mmm.'

'Did he hang around the school?'

'Not really. I met him at the youth club. We didn't go – it was crap – but we used to hang about outside, near the pavilion. A gang of us. He was there.'

'Did he offer you drugs?'

'Not me, but he did some of the others, I think. Except pot. He always had some pot. We used that, a bit, now and again. It gave

285

me a headache, so I didn't bother.'

I thought of Richard Burton. He said that if God had given him headaches he wouldn't have become an alcoholic. The burnt-out pavilion stands at the edge of Heckley recreation field, or the rec., as it's known. The walls are covered in graffiti, the surroundings littered with empty cans, broken glass and takeaway rubbish. The council workers refuse to clean up because their union's risk assessment procedure gives it a red flag due to the danger of needle-stick injuries or diseases from condoms. We send regular patrols there, but the denizens simply fade away across the playing field.

'Did you live with him?' George asked.

'For a bit, until I was pregnant with Jasmine. He couldn't deal with it.'

Despair gnawed at my bones like a hungry rat. It always does when I try to talk to someone like Jessica. Where did the 1944 Education Act go wrong? *She* was pregnant; *she* was scared and on her own; *he* couldn't deal with it. So that was OK. Why do they perform contortions to protect wasters of oxygen like Lapetite? He couldn't deal with it because he'd found somewhere else to gratify his appetites. Having a pregnant girlfriend was inconvenient, so he moved on. I wondered if she knew about his several other children but decided not to mention them, just yet.

'When did you last see him, Jessica?'

'Two days before he died. We'd been trying to get back together.'

Or to put it another way, he'd been nipping round for his nooky again. And I thought Sonia was naïve.

'Do you blame his death on his drug dealer friends?' I asked.

'Who else?' she replied. 'Everybody liked him. He was good fun. I think he must have owed them some money. He said he did. Asked me if I had any. Wanted me to get a credit card. I got a form from the bank.' She was quiet for a few moments, then she asked, 'Is it true about ... you know...'

I shook my head. 'No, it's not true. The newspaper made that up.'

'Why would they do that?'

'To sell more papers. Did you loan him any money, Jessica?' There was £1,200 from under his floorboards in the safe at the nick, looking for a good home.

'No,' she said. Naïve again. Why is it that when pensioners are mugged they usually have about £800 in their handbags? Ah well, I thought, it's not my job to tell her to modify her story.

'Do you know the name of the man you think Jermaine owed money to, Jessica?'

She nodded.

'Are you going to tell us his name?'

She nodded again.

Chapter Ten

Lapetite's sponsor in the drugs industry was called Jason Coombs and he lived in a fine Victorian mansion on the main drag from the motorway into town. The houses along that stretch are sturdy examples of the architecture of the time, when ornament-ation was back in style and the wealthy merchants of Heckley were keen to outdo each other. Entrances like proscenium arches, with classical columns, fluting and ornate entablatures were the favoured look, whilst others went for the Egyptian touch, with enigmatic sphinxes, prowling cats, and plain, angular columns. It's an eclectic stew of styles, a crash course in design, and I've heard it said that bus trips come all the way from Florence to admire.

Unfortunately, they planted trees, too. Trees are a good idea at the time, but they have this habit of growing. Now, the absentee landlords won't pay for their removal, and the itinerant tenants don't care at all, so most of the houses are in perpetual shade and invisible from the road.

Coombs' house was one of the few still tenanted by the owner, but he hadn't chopped the trees down. He had, however, installed high metal gates and surrounded the property with spike-topped railings. I parked a few yards away and George went for a casual walk past. It was all a bit grander than I expected.

'He's got security lights and CCTV,' George reported as he climbed back into the car. 'It'll be like getting into Fort Knox. Do we have enough for a search warrant?'

I shook my head. 'Probably not. He wouldn't let us in so we'd have to force our way, and we've only Jessica's word to go on. I was expecting a doss house in the project, not a mansion.' What I was saying was that I could have bullied my way into a project house, but this tenant might have friends in high places, and he'd most certainly have a sharp-suited lawyer on call. There was also the possibility, God help us, that we were in the wrong place completely.

'Plan B,' I said. 'Back to the nick.'

I arranged 24-hour surveillance of the house. It costs money, is not taken on lightly, but this was a murder case. We had two vans parked at either side of Coombs' gateway: a scruffy Transit and a shiny new gas board lookalike, both fitted with CCTV cameras. The operators don't have to peer through the windows any more, or through a peephole cut in the side, trying not to be seen themselves. Now, they sit on easy chairs in the back, drinking coffee and watching the screen. It's a bobby's job.

'Do we have an operation name, boss?' one of them asked when I set it up.

I was standing in the office, looking down on the street with the phone to my ear. A long line of schoolchildren were crossing the road, two by two, on their way to the municipal swimming pool.

'Yes: operation crocodile.' I gave them my mobile number and left them to it.

I took Sonia to the golf club in the evening and she did four laps of the course, missing out the woods. I managed two circuits without being lapped by her. It was her first run since the attack, and it went well. She'd made a good recovery.

The man with shiny shoes parked in the multi-storey and clicked through the car's computer display. He'd done 126.3 miles at an average of 41.9 miles per hour and 37.2 miles per gallon. Not bad, he thought. He parked on the third floor and followed the covered walkway that led into the shopping mall. He was wearing his poplin jacket, with a flat cap and sunglasses, and didn't bother trying to avoid any CCTV cameras that were around. He was on a mission, but wouldn't be coming back for a while and wasn't doing anything illegal. His step was carefree, almost jaunty. He'd done the research, was ready to act, and this time would be special, really special. But he couldn't use the pay phone in the bus station again. Surveillance had been stepped up there, higher definition cameras installed, which was why he was here, now. In five minutes he'd found the shop he was looking for and went inside.

If *inside* was the word. It was open-fronted, a carpet delineating where the mall outside ended and the shop inside began. The walls were hung with every imaginable accessory for the mobile phone user, plus a few hundred others that a normal person would never imagine. Most of the colourful goodies seemed to be false fronts. Why would anyone want a false front on their phone, he wondered? Behind the counter the expensive stuff was on display. Most people regarded a phone as a convenient way of talking to someone miles away, and wouldn't pay £150 for something that would only do the same as a similar item costing £50, but the man with shiny shoes didn't think like that. He enjoyed the technology. To him, the mobile phone was more than a means of conversation. It was a lifestyle indicator. He looked more closely at what was on offer.

There were phones that took pictures, phones with video screens so you could see the person you were addressing (providing they had the suitable equipment, of course), phones that connected to the Internet.

Some had receivers that fitted around your ear, so you could hold a conversation and microwave your brain at the same time. They had flashing lights on them, in case you fell into the river whilst deep in conversation. He smiled with satisfaction. The phone he carried in the pouch on his belt was six months old, but it was still at the cutting edge, where he liked to be.

The young man in a turban behind the counter said, 'Can I help you, sir?'

'Yes,' the man with shiny shoes replied. 'I'd like to buy a phone.'

The phone call I was waiting for came next morning, during my second tea break. It was from the boys in the gas board van.

'Crocodile two here, boss,' they reported. 'They must have had visitors staying over. A blue Merc SLK 320 convertible left three minutes ago with a man and a woman in it. We've run it and it belongs to a chap in Eastbourne. Do you want the details?'

I grabbed my notebook and scrambled through the pages. Sometimes, Lady Luck deals us the aces. 'Eastbourne, did you say?'

'That's right.'

I read a number out to them. 'Is that it?'

'Yep.'

'OK. The car's a ringer. It's Coombs and his wife. It came to our attention about three weeks ago. Here's what you do. Park the Transit across their gateway so they can't get in and all sit in your van. I'll send back-up. I want them both arrested as soon as they get back, but he could be dangerous. Leave it to the back-up. Don't you accost them. Understood?'

'Right, boss.'

'And keep me informed. I'm in the office. Which way did they go?'

'Towards town, so they may have just gone shopping or something.'

It went like a dream. Coombs and his lady friend came back an hour later and stood around, indignant, wondering who had the effrontery to obstruct their driveway. The answer came in the form of the cavalry, charging down the road and blocking it from both directions. They were trapped. Guns were pointed, orders barked, arms raised. I'd instructed that they be immediately separated and she taken to Halifax, he brought to Heckley. Crocodile one gave me a running commentary of the whole thing. Sometimes, now and again, this job is a load of fun.

The arresting officers had the authority to enter and search Coombs' house, but I told them just to make sure the place was safe and nobody was inside destroying evidence. When they returned to the station that authority passed to me, but first I wanted to interview him.

The clock was running so we gave him twenty minutes with his solicitor while we looked into his background and set up a formal interview. It was a waste of time. He just sat there, throughout, with a silly grin on his face. Nowadays, silence is not acceptable, but we still have to have a case. The caution makes it clear that if he refuses to answer our questions he can't come up with the answers at a later date to defend himself, but the burden of proof is still with us.

With one big exception.

'OK,' I said to him. 'Play it your way, but you're not helping yourself and I'm not convinced you are receiving the best advice.' It's just a little quirk I employ: make them wonder if their brief is any good. 'We now intend to search your house from top to bottom. Is there anything there that you wish to tell us about?'

He spoke for the first time: 'I want to see your search warrant.'

'I don't need one. The process will be videoed but your legal representative is entitled to be there and I'm happy for you to come along, too, in handcuffs. I'm asking you, once again, is there anything at the house that you wish to tell me about?'

'Yes. There's some valuable stuff there, and you'll pay for any damage you do.'

We collected the keys from the custody

sergeant and we all decamped to chez Coombs, accompanied by the ARV and a couple of pandas containing our house search experts. I unlocked the gates and the front door and they went to work.

Coombs and I sat in a neat sitting room, with a big comfortable settee and easy chairs covered in a bold floral print, while his brief went off with the search team. The furniture looked antique. It had bowed legs and marquetry, if that means anything. A modest chandelier hung in the middle of the ceiling and a TV peeked out of a reproduction sideboard. A painting of what might have been Coombs himself, standing alongside a Tiger Moth aeroplane, hung over the fireplace and another portrait, not as expertly done, hung on the end wall, this time of his lady friend or wife. It was the room of a man who liked good things, and knew how to get them.

'If there's anything here you want us to know about you ought to declare it now,' I advised him for the third time, but he didn't reply. He just gave me the superior grin. It said he knew something I didn't and we'd be off his premises just as soon as he decided. He was in control.

'Keeping silent isn't helping your case,' I said.

'Uh!' he snorted. 'What case?' Keeping silent isn't easy. It takes practice, like those

Yes/No games they used to play on radio. Now that he'd spoken it would be easier.

'The murder of Jermaine Lapetite,' I said. 'We explained at the station.'

'Never heard of him.'

'Perhaps he had a street name.'

'What if he did?'

'I'm told he owed you money. Did he?'

'How do I know if I don't know who he is?'

'So some people do owe you money?'

'It's what I do. I run a credit agency. It's a legitimate business.'

'What rate of interest do you charge?'

'That's a commercial secret.'

'I bet it is. How much did Lapetite owe you?'

'How much did you find?'

'What do you mean how much did we find?'

'You heard.' He switched the grin on again.

'Where were you on the night of Friday, 28th May?'

'Wincanton, for the races. We stayed the weekend. Now will you take these off please, and leave me alone.'

'Why didn't you tell us that at the station?'

'Why should I? I haven't done anything wrong. The onus of proof is on you. Will you unlock these and go, now?'

'No. There's still the little matter of the Mercedes.'

'I bought it in good faith. I was done. Why aren't you looking for them?'

'How much did you pay for it?'

'I don't remember.'

'Or is that another commercial secret? About ten per cent of its market value is the usual rate, I'm told.'

'Listen,' he said, leaning forward conspiratorially. 'What did you say your name was?'

'Priest.'

'OK, Mr Priest. You think that I killed this Lapetite character because he owed me money, right?'

'Or had him killed.'

'Or had him killed. Fair enough. Would you be kind enough to have a look in the second drawer of the sideboard over there.' He pointed across the room.

I stood up and walked over to the piece of furniture he indicated. 'This one?'

'That's right. At the back.'

I pulled the drawer all the way open and saw a bundle of twenty-pound notes at the back. 'There's some money,' I said.

'Could you bring it here, please?'

'No. You fetch it.'

He struggled to his feet and took the bundle from the back of the drawer. They were twenties, about four or five hundred pounds' worth. This was getting awkward.

'Worried about prints, hey?' he said. 'Well

let me demonstrate something. This is how I count money.' He removed the rubber band from the bundle and pressed them out flat. The pile was about a centimetre thick. He licked his thumb and peeled the top note off, flicking it with his fingers like a card sharp, to make sure there was only one. 'Twenty,' he counted, 'forty, sixty, eighty, a hundred, one twenty, one forty...'

I wasn't sure if I was expected to say 'when' at an appropriate amount, so I said, 'If you think I'm going to salivate at the sight of a couple of hundred pounds you're sadly mistaken.'

'And you underestimate me, Mr Priest. What I'm demonstrating is that my prints will be on any money I loaned your Mr Lapetite. On every single note. Did you find any money?'

'A small amount.'

'If we're talking about the same person, I loaned him £1,500 a few days before he was murdered. Have you checked his bundle for prints?'

'We will have done.'

'There you go, then. Why would I have someone murdered who still had the money I'd loaned him in his pocket? What's my motive, eh?'

Coombs was the type of person I joined the police to put behind bars. His credit agency was a front for drug dealing, no doubt about it. But he covered his tracks well. He had no contact with the drugs. He just put up the money. They did the dirty work and he charged ten per cent per week interest, at the minimum. Sometimes, when a big deal was going down, he'd make that overnight.

And I was going to have to let him go. It hurt, oh, how it hurt.

One of the searchers poked his head around the door, saying, 'Come and have a look at this, Mr Priest.'

I asked a uniformed PC to babysit Coombs and followed our man through into a kitchen. The doors of the units were wide open and crockery was piled up on the work surface. The brief was there, and he looked a worried man.

'Down here, boss,' the searcher told me and I knelt next to him on the pale wood-laminate floor.

'See this front row of crockery?' He picked up a cup and saucer, white with a blue pattern, like Wedgwood, and lifted them out.

'Yes.'

'Well, could you pass me a cup from the next row. Please.'

I tried, but couldn't lift one. 'It's stuck down,' I said.

'That's right. It would be such a drag lifting them out every time, so they're glued down. Now watch this.'

He gripped the woodwork base of the unit

and pulled. It came right out, cups and saucers and all, revealing a big hole underneath the units. 'How's that for a cubby hole?' he declared, his face pink with triumph and exertion.

'And is that what I think it is?' I asked, looking into the void.

'If you're thinking suitcase, yes it is.'

'Get Coombs in here.'

We lifted the shelf of crockery out of the way and manhandled the suitcase from the hole. It was one of those plastic Samsonite-style ones, in a sickly lime-green colour, and weighed a ton. Coombs arrived, the PC holding his arm, as we heaved the case out onto the kitchen floor.

'Key?' I said, but didn't get an answer.

'Somebody pick it,' I said, and in less than a minute the lid was thrown back to reveal the biggest sum of cash any of us had ever seen in one place. 'OK, seal it again, and put it in an evidence bag. Let's do this properly.' I turned to Coombs' brief. 'I'd like you to attend the station when this is counted, sir. In the meantime, perhaps you ought to tell your client all about the Proceeds of Crime Act, 2002. I'm told that a Samsonite suitcase like this can hold about half a million pounds. That should be enough to qualify.'

The Proceeds of Crime Act is the one that puts the onus of proof on the villain. If he has in excess of £5,000 and can't say where it legitimately came from, the balance of probability says it came from crime or was intended for a crime. It's a civil law so we just sit back and let it take its course.

I reminded Coombs that he was still under caution, to keep his brief happy, and noticed that the grin had vanished. 'Nice colour,' I said, patting the lurid suitcase. 'Matches your complexion.'

Back at the nick I telephoned our Regional Asset Recovery Team to let them know we were doing their job. There's always a chance that you've blundered into a larger enquiry and scuppered the whole thing, but we hadn't. Coombs was known to them but they had nothing on him. It was a result. A good result. Under normal circumstances we'd be cracking open the brown ale and celebrating, but we were on a murder enquiry, and Coombs wasn't the Executioner, of that I was certain. I looked at my watch and saw that if I hurried I could go for a run with Sonia and take her out for a meal afterwards, but then I remembered it was Tuesday, and her night for the track. I'd picked up the phone, so I put it down again.

Athletics is big up in the north east, building on the popularity of local heroes like Brendan Foster and Steve Cram, who won countless middle distance titles back in the

Seventies and Eighties. The Great North Run is the largest sporting event in the world, with over 40,000 entries, and the Gateshead International Stadium hosts regular topflight meetings, attracting the world's best to the city. The spectators there are probably the most knowledgeable in the country.

But occasionally there is one who doesn't understand where adulation ends and obsession begins. Letitia Pringle was the third-fastest female hundred-metre runner the world had ever seen, and she had all the looks and style of a supermodel. Lycra was made for Letitia Pringle, and she used it in ways nobody else imagined. Except, possibly, Norman Easterby.

1999 wasn't Olympic year, so the athletic community were free to wander the globe, competing wherever fancy and appearance money took them. Letitia came to Gateshead and hit the headlines as soon as she peeled off her tracksuit. Her right leg was clad in red and white stripes, her left arm in blue with white stars, and there was very little else joining the two. The photographers abandoned the pole vault and jogged across centre field, dodging the javelins to get to her.

She won by a distance, not hampered by her lopsided costume, and the crowd went wild. She accepted the winner's bouquet, waved to the spectators and turned to shake hands with her fellow competitors. That's when Norman Easterby could contain himself no longer. He leapt over the barriers, ran forward and threw his arms around the bewildered girl. Afterwards, he said he embraced her; she said he groped her. It was a disappointing end to the day's festivities.

Five years later the PC – now sergeant – who arrested him saw a familiar face peering up from the papers on the front desk. 'What's our Norman been up to now?' he asked out aloud, as he reached for the photograph taken by the *Heckley Gazette* photographer. He read the accompanying report and request for information, wondered what some men saw in skinny birds, and reached for the telephone.

999 calls come through to the switchboard at HQ where they are prioritised. The crank calls are filtered off and the rest designated according to resources. Blues and twos are dispatched where necessary the rest have to wait. Ten o'clock Wednesday morning is not peak time for triple nines. Drunken slappers have usually made it home by then, so they don't ring to enquire about late buses; teenage burglars are still curled up in their pits; and suicidal loners are fuelling their depressions with daytime TV. So when the call came through with a message for me, the telephonist passed it on personally.

'Read it again,' I said.

'He said, "Tell DI Priest to get himself to 14, Canalside Gardens, Heckley, as soon as he likes." I asked his name but he was gone.'

'And you said the voice was muffled.'

'That's right, sir, with a radio playing in the background.'

'But it's been recorded.'

'All calls are recorded.'

'Of course. Will you bring this to the attention of your supervisor, please, and have the tape taken out of the system and saved. It could be important. Thanks for letting me know, and I'll get back to you.'

We have an out-of-date electoral roll hanging by a piece of string under the notice board in the main office, and a more up-to-date one available on the computer. The office was deserted, desks strewn with papers, outdoor coats hanging behind the door because the sun was shining, coffee mugs left where they'd finished with them. Screensavers revolved and swam and swooped silently, lights blinked on telephones, the morning's tabloids poked out of waste paper bins. I unhooked the electoral roll and sat down at the nearest desk.

The tenants of 14, Canalside Gardens were John Wesley Williamson and Miriam Williamson. Doc Bones. Somebody was telling me to get down to where Doc Bones lived. And his wife. The bundle of sheets fell out of my fingers to the floor. The screen-saver where I was sitting showed snowflakes hurtling towards me, as if I were driving into a blizzard, and I felt dizzy.

Back in my office I found his home number and dialled it. There was no answer. I wrote *Ring me* in big letters on a sheet of A4 and left it propped against Dave's VDU, but as I burst out into the sunshine he was walking away from his car towards the front door.

'With me,' I shouted to him, and he changed course.

'Where are we going?' he asked, fastening his seat belt as I bullied my way out into the traffic. I told him about the call and we drove the rest of the way in silence.

Canalside Gardens is a small development of detached houses near enough to the canal to claim an interest, far enough away to avoid the flies and the smell. You could probably see it from the upstairs windows, but I wasn't there to admire the location. Number fourteen was one of two across the end of the cul-de-sac, with a pair of pergolas dominating the front garden.

'She must be the gardener,' I said.

'Not necessarily,' Dave argued, adding, 'they probably grow smelly flowers so he can appreciate them.'

We'd tried ringing again, sitting outside his house, and also dialled his clinic, but a recorded message told us that the clinic was closed on Wednesdays. The paintwork was bright and the garden immaculate, straight from an estate agent's brochure, but the windows were dark against the bright sun, and implacable to our enquiring eyes. I didn't know if Miriam worked. I unfastened my seatbelt and we walked up his short drive. I peeked through the garage window but there was no car inside. Dave raised his hand and looked at me. I nodded and he hammered on the door. Four hammers later he tried the handle with a fingertip and it swung open.

You're never quite ready for the smell, but this one was more of a surprise than usual. The door led straight into the kitchen, and somebody had been cooking. It reminded me of when my mother cooked Sunday roasts. Dad was a roast beef man, and I follow his example.

'Mmm, that smells good,' Dave said, doing his Bisto kids impression.

We stepped inside and I shouted Doc Bones' name. 'John,' I called. 'It's Charlie Priest. Are you in?' but there was no reply We looked at each other and shrugged our shoulders. 'You look down here,' I said. 'I'll have a look upstairs.'

There were gaudy prints of Caribbean beach scenes on the walls of the staircase. I felt for each step with a foot, looking upwards, calling; 'John, are you there?' in a wavering voice. There was something about the silence that unnerved me. At the top, on the landing wall, was a big glossy photograph of the doc in his prime, three feet off the ground as he dropped the ball into the basket. Slam dunk.

'Are you there?' I called, more quietly. A bedroom door was open and I was drawn towards it as if by magnetism. 'John? Are you there?'

His bare feet were towards me, white underneath, and he was sprawled across the bed. 'Doc? Can you hear me?' I touched the sole of his left foot, but it was cold and there was no reaction. It looked as if he were asleep, with his head dangling over the far side of the bed. I moved round the bed, so I could check for vital signs, then realised that there was nowhere I could check, and it would be a waste of effort. My guts convulsed and bile rushed upwards to fill my mouth, as bitter as henbane. The doc's head was missing.

I made it downstairs without falling, trailing my hand down the banister, stumbling on each step, mindless of it being a crime scene. As I reached the bottom I heard Dave retching. He was leaning over the sink, doing his best to deposit his stomach lining in it.

'Don't look,' he pleaded, as I entered the

room, his hand held out towards me. 'Don't look, Charlie. For God's sake, don't look.'

But I had to look, hadn't I. I turned to where he was unconsciously indicating, towards the microwave oven. The door was ajar but not closed. I placed a fingertip on the corner and eased it open, and saw what was left of the good doctor, his big teeth grinning at me.

I grabbed Dave by the arm. 'Oh my God, Oh my God,' I could hear myself crying. 'Let's get out of here. Let's get out of here.'

We sat in my car for ten minutes without saying anything, staring blankly through the windscreen, trying to comprehend the horror behind the front door with its climbing clematis and pretend stained glass. Eventually I broke the silence. 'Miriam. His wife. We don't know where she is or what time she'll be back. See if a neighbour knows if she works, Dave, and I'll make the call.'

I rang Les Isles, acting ACC, told him it was a murder enquiry linked to the other two, and that I was too close to the action to make rational decisions. He said he'd get straight over and take command.

Sonia was scraping new potatoes when I arrived home. 'Hi Chas,' she called as I closed the front door behind me. 'I'm in here.' I walked through into the kitchen and gave her a peck on the cheek from behind.

'Don't do any for me,' I said.

'Oh, have you eaten?'

'Erm, yeah. I'm not hungry.'

'What sort of a day have you had?'

'So-so. And you?'

'Not bad. I managed half an hour on the ice wall this morning, and the run went well tonight. I went from work, halfway round the bypass and back again, on the cycle path. One of the girls – Amy – chased me on her mountain bike. I think I'll train there more often, until ... you know. I reckon it's about five miles. Will you measure it for me, please, on your big map at work? I can always go further round, if necessary. It's not as much fun as the golf course and the woods, but there's always plenty of traffic passing by. I like running through the woods, and the golfers usually give me a wave, but it can be a bit spooky. I'm not keen on running in the woods on my own again. Not for a while.'

'Sonia.'

'Sorry. Was I gabbling again?'

'No love, you weren't gabbling. Come and sit down, please.'

I led her by the hand through into the front room and told her that Doc Bones was dead. That he'd been murdered, and his death was linked to those of Alfred Armi-

tage and Jermaine Lapetite. I didn't tell her
that his head had been sawn off and cooked
in the microwave oven. Sonia shed a few
tears, said that he was a lovely man and that
she owed him a lot.

'And you, Charlie,' she added. 'Between
you, you got me running again.'

I made a little 'Huh' noise, and said, 'I'm
off the case because I know the victim. So
that's my news. That's what sort of a day
I've had. Now finish telling me all about
yours?'

'My day? It doesn't feel important, now.'

'What doesn't?'

'Oh, nothing.'

'Tell me. Tell me, please. Tell me about
what you had for lunch or what the other
staff have been gossiping about. Tell me how
the traffic was on the way home, or about the
weather. Anything at all, please, just anything. Bring some normality into my life.'

'I...'

'You what?'

'I received a letter this morning.'

'Tell me about it.'

'It's from South Africa. My friend who
coaches at the University of Cape Town.
She's pregnant and there's a temporary post
available while she has maternity leave. She
says it's mine if I want it.'

I didn't sit in on the big meeting, Thursday

morning, but I heard all about it. I may have been off the case, but the rest of the team weren't. The doc had died some time earlier that morning from a single blow to the head, same as Lapetite. His head had been cut off with a pruning saw that was found in the bedroom.

'He was a big man,' I said. 'It would have taken a bigger man to have carried him up the stairs.'

'He was killed upstairs,' Dave told me. 'In the bedroom, near the bed.'

'So it was someone he knew?'

'Or someone who talked him into going upstairs. Those phone calls to the *UK News* claimed to be from a police officer. Maybe he pulled the same stunt, then asked to use the toilet; something like that.'

'Mmm, I suppose so.'

'I haven't told you the best bit.'

'Go on.'

'A cigarette end was found at the far end of the landing, beyond the bedroom door. It looked as if it had been flicked there. It's gone to the lab. If he's left DNA on it we could have him. The doc didn't smoke, did he?'

'I doubt it.'

Les Isles appeared at my door, so Dave stood up and left. Les sat in the chair Dave had vacated. 'Did Sparky tell you about the cigarette butt?' Les asked.

'Mmm.'

'Let's hope the boffins can work their magic on it; then we'll have him.'

'Let's hope so,' I agreed. 'Do you want my log book?'

'Please.' I pulled it out of the drawer and handed it to him.

'Charlie...' he began. 'I don't know how to put this...'

'Do I think the doc was killed because he knew me? How does that sound?'

'Yes, I suppose that's what I wanted to ask.'

'I don't know, Les. I really don't know. I'm desperately trying to convince myself that he wasn't, but it isn't working. And I want some sort of low-key protection for my girlfriend.'

'Is there anywhere she can go for a week or two?'

'I don't know, and it might cause her unnecessary alarm.'

'It's tricky,' he said, 'but we'll organise something.'

Les sat there, leaning forward, his hands clasped. He's not a murder man, was out of his depth. I asked him if he wanted a coffee and he shook his head. After another minute or so he said, 'The pathologist reckons it would have taken about fifteen minutes to saw his head off. He said it was done inexpertly. What's going through the mind of someone who could do that?'

I said, 'Jesus Christ. Do we have experts in that sort of thing?'

'His wife's under sedation. She'll never get over it.'

'No.'

He stood up and opened the door. 'I've told them to give the cigarette end everything they've got; spare no expense. They've taken it down to Leicester University. It's our best chance.'

'That's where the experts are. Thanks for telling me, Les.'

He went away and I found the list of other crimes that had troubled the good citizens of Heckley in the last week. I read through them mechanically, and when I reached the end couldn't have described any one of them. Sonia holds a level-four coaching certificate, and Cape Town University had offered her a one-year contract coaching their ladies' athletics team. I told her to snap it up.

If Leicester found any DNA on the cigarette we'd have him, that was certain. First of all we'd check the database, which had three million entries at the last count, and was growing daily. If that failed – if he wasn't in there because he'd never been arrested for burglary, or wagged his willy on the bus, or asked a policeman for the time – we'd start a programme of testing the local population. Eventually, we'd find a match. It might be in ten or twenty years, but we'd have him. And the chances of us being wrong were one in ten trillion.

Except for one thing. It was all too easy. I didn't believe for a second that the murderer had a fag dangling from his mouth when he killed poor Doc Bones.

'He's called Norman Easterby and he's done something similar before. Well, he groped an American sprinter, back in '99. Letitia Pringle; you might remember her.'

'I remember,' I said. I was talking to a DI at HQ, who'd rung me to say that a sergeant up in Gateshead had recognised the figure in the wire spectacles. 'Where is he now?'

'We're having him brought down, then hopefully we can organise an ID parade. Do you think Sonia will be up to it? He should be with us sometime after lunch.'

'No problem. She's taken it well.'

Sonia may have taken it well, but I hadn't. I'd have to find an excuse to be at HQ when the inadequate Mr Easterby arrived. I was pondering on what I'd do to him when Sparky's phone started ringing in the outer office. I dialled the intercept number and took the call. It was the editor of the *UK News,* asking for DC Sparkington.

'I'm Acting DCI Priest,' I explained, 'Dave Sparkington's senior officer. How can I help you?'

'Oh, hello, Mr Priest. Mr Sparkington said to speak to you if he wasn't available. We have some information which may be of assistance.'

I grabbed a pen, checked that my recorder was working and turned to a clean page on my telephone pad. 'Fire away,' I said.

'We've had another phone call, about fifteen minutes ago. Same as before. Obviously muffled, with traffic noise in the background. He claimed that he was an officer working on the recent murder case in East Pennine division, and that it was the work of the man you are calling the Executioner. He says that the victim's head was severed and cooked in the microwave oven. Can you vouch for the veracity of that statement, Mr Priest?'

'No,' I stated, 'I can't. And I'll take all the necessary steps to prevent you from printing the information. Presumably you have taped the message?'

'I understand your concern, Mr Priest, and assure you we have no intention of printing it. Yes, we've taped the message. The last one went to Tower Hamlets, I believe?'

'That's right. I'll arrange for them to collect the tape.'

'That's OK; we'll send it by courier. All I ask is that you keep us informed of any developments.'

'I'll ask DC Sparkington to contact you,

and thanks for your cooperation.' I clicked the cradle and immediately rang Dave's mobile. 'Get your backside back here,' I told him. 'We need your expertise.' Sometimes, I have to remind him who's the boss.

Chapter Eleven

Lord St Bertrand, owner of Sandal Priory, a stately pile outside Wakefield, thought a rock festival over the spring bank holiday weekend was a great idea, and so did hordes of fans. Thousands of them turned up, driving converted buses, VW campers and every imaginable vehicle that could convey a small family and their menagerie. A town of tents sprang up overnight, like toadstools in October, and the air was pungent with exotic fragrances that enhanced the potency of the music. For three nights the sky above the priory vibrated to the beat, and the fabric of the building groaned and creaked under the assault. On the fourth day Lord St Bertrand did his sums, decided the venture had been worthwhile, and looked out of his window to wave goodbye to the parting fans.

Nobody moved. The fans decided they liked it there, and stayed put. Two weeks later they were still there. Complaints were made, strings pulled, and the police called in. Arrests were made for possession, social services notified of possible cases of child neglect, vehicles confiscated for being unroadworthy. They got the message, and at noon on the seventeenth day a convoy of assorted vehicles moved off the once-manicured lawns of the stately home and the good lord heaved a sigh of relief and poured himself a stiff one.

The travellers had heard of Heptonstall thanks to Ted Hughes, Sylvia Plath and PJ Proby, and decided that the place held some sort of spiritual significance. Maybe it did, but their creaking vehicles could not cope with the one-in-three gradient, narrow cobbled streets and lack of parking places. They immediately de-camped and relocated to a less spiritual but more practical playing field outside Halifax.

Halifax immediately fought back. There was an altercation, involving police in riot gear, and many arrests made. Twenty-two recalcitrant New World travellers were being processed at HQ by a small team of over-stressed custody officers ('Yes, sir, I have noted that you are a vegan') when the un-marked car containing Norman Easterby arrived. They immediately diverted him towards the nearest vacant cell, which was at Heckley.

I was arranging my magic marker pens according to their colours when the phone rang. Dave had returned and was at his desk in the big office, head down, on his phone. 'DI Priest,' I said.

'Oh, I was hoping to speak to acting DCI Priest. Do you know if he's available?'

It was my opposite number at HQ. 'Hiya, pissquick,' I said. 'It's an honorary title, strictly for the press. What can I do for you?'

'Nothing. I just thought you'd like to know that Norman the groper is on his way to Heckley. Our cells are full of hippies, junkies and assorted peace warriors. Come over if you fancy a party.'

'He's on his way to Heckley?' I repeated.

'Be with you in about fifteen minutes,' he confirmed.

'Right. Thanks for telling me.'

I took several deep breaths, then moved the yellow to the left of the pale green. My mind went back ten days to the worst night of my life, and I had a pain, right in the middle of my forehead. I moved the yellow back to where it had been and looked in my drawer to see if I had any aspirins. Negative. Who uses yellow highlighter anyway?

Something was troubling me. Unpleasant thoughts were making me uneasy. I looked at my watch and went into the big office. Dave was talking to the boffins at the Met about the telephone call, so I stood by his desk and waited. When he'd finished he looked up at me, saying, 'They've had a listen and are convinced it's the same person, but they haven't done the tests yet so it's not confirmed. And they're onto the phone companies.'

'Good. Keep on it,' I said. 'Here's another little job for you. Can you get me a transcript of the television appeals I've done, please, plus the radio and the press, and also transcripts of the telephone calls from the Executioner? Anytime.'

'No problem. We have them, somewhere.'

'Cheers. I've just heard that they're bringing Norman Easterby here. All the cells are full at Halifax.'

'Blimey. When's he coming?'

'Anytime.'

I stood at the window in my office, looking down into the street. The weather was changing, alternating between sunshine and showers, and a sprinkling of rain was blowing in the breeze. Umbrellas were out as shoppers darted between the mall and the market, threading between the stationary cars. The lights changed and the traffic came to a standstill on the High Street and moved off on Station Road, as if choreographed by some great Eric Smallwood, up in the sky. I sat down at my desk and sharpened two pencils, then stood up again and resumed my vigil at the window.

They brought him down in an unmarked car, handcuffed to an officer in the back seat. As the car pulled into the car park I turned and strode towards the door of the big office. I heard the scrape of Dave's chair behind me.

I yanked the door open and headed for the stairs, my feet noisy on the tiled floor. I could hear footsteps following me. I took the stairs two at a time, the footsteps behind growing closer. I hit the door into the foyer and it banged back into the wall. I was through it before the rebound but heard it hit the wall again behind me.

In my hurry I'd timed it badly. He wasn't here. I stood inside the door waiting. A few seconds later he was there, flanked by two officers who dwarfed him. I didn't care. Size had nothing to do with it. The hurt you cause isn't related to your size. I took a step forward as a big hand clamped itself around my arm and Dave was pulling me away, placing himself between Easterby and me. The two big Geordie officers ushered their charge towards the custody suite and I shrugged off Dave's hand.

'Don't think you've done me a favour,' I said as they vanished through the doorway.

'Maybe not,' he replied.

I went over the road for a sandwich and a mug of tea while Dave went upstairs to finish what he was doing. I'd have got away with it. They'd have said I was stressed, the red mist came down, I was at the end of my tether. Easterby, once his broken jaw had mended, would have gone along with it, to save himself from further charges. I'd have been sacked, of course, but it would have been done quite decorously. One day I'd have been there, the next I wouldn't. The gap I left would heal over in a week while I'd be enjoying the benefits of a full pension. There'd be nothing to stop me going to South Africa with Sonia.

The transcripts I'd asked Dave to find were on my desk when I returned. I read through them and they weren't the damning evidence I was hoping for. Never mind, I thought. They'd do. I walked over to Dave's desk with them in my hand. 'Thanks for these,' I said. 'Are you in a hurry to be off at five o'clock?'

He shook his head. 'No.'

'In that case,' I told him, 'be in Mr Wood's office at that time, and bring Maggie with you. Don't mention it to anyone else, though. OK?'

He raised his eyebrows and nodded. 'OK.'

I was supposed to be off the case, so I had more time on my hands. I rang Sonia to organise our meal but she reminded me that it was her track night and she'd be late home. We chatted for a while and she said she'd have a pub meal with some of the others. I said I'd probably do the same.

Next I rang Damian at the shooting range. As I listened to the ringing tone the door behind me opened. I was about to turn to see who it was when he answered.

I said, 'Hello Damian, It's DI Priest. Things are a bit slacker, so can you put me down for the next suitable course, please, if you have any coming up.'

'Hello, Mr Priest. We can fit you in next Wednesday and Thursday. How does that sound?'

'So soon? OK, put me down, please. What about some extra practice?'

'Monday teatime? Five o'clock?'

'That's fine, Damian. Five o'clock Monday. It's in my diary and I'll let you know if I can't make it.'

I swung my chair round and saw it was Superintendent Stanwick standing there. 'Hello, Mr Stanwick,' I said. 'This is a surprise.'

'Just passing through, Charlie,' he replied. 'Organising some shooting practice, were you?'

'That's right. My authorisation's expired but I don't like leaving it to the men if firearms are involved.'

'No, I can imagine you'd want to lead from the front. I hear that the kidnapper has been caught and you have him in the cells.'

'We have. They recognised him up in Gateshead.'

'A good result, hey? That's what it's all about. No doubt he'll be put away for a few years.'

He'd have been eating hospital food through a straw for a month if Sparky hadn't read my mind. 'I imagine so,' I agreed.

'I could murder a chocolate biscuit,' I said as I sipped my boiling coffee in Gilbert's office, five minutes to five.

He took the depleted packet from his drawer and handed them over. 'So what's it all about?'

I passed the transcripts over to him. 'Have a read through those,' I said, 'while we wait for the others.' Dead on five there was a knock at the door and Dave and Maggie came in.

'This won't take long,' I assured them, when we were all seated around the boss's little conference table. 'It's been plain for a while that information is being leaked to the press. It started with the photograph of Alfred Armitage, and the latest example was today, with the information telephoned to *UK News*.'

Dave said, 'There's a bit of difference, though, Chas. Sending the photo of Alfred was just mischief, done for a bob or two, perhaps. The info about Doc Bones was different. That was from the person who alerted us to his body, in other words, the killer.'

'You're right.' I turned to Maggie and slid my A4 pad across to her. 'Make a list, Maggie, please. OK, what have we got? First leak is to the *Gazette*, with a photo of Alfred.'

Maggie wrote it down. 'Got it,' she said.

'Then I made an appeal on the TV.'

'You want me to put that?'

'Yes please.'

'OK.'

'Then we received a phone call about Jermaine Lapetite. Triple nine, anonymous.'

'Yep.'

Dave said, 'Then the same person, now claiming to be a police officer, rang the *UK News* to say that Jermaine had been Simonised, which wasn't true.'

'No. I then did another TV appeal and one for local radio. Put all that down, Maggie.'

'I have done. What next?'

'The call about the doc,' Dave said, quietly. Like me, he was having trouble with the images that the mere mention of the name brought gurgling up out of the darkness. Up to then it had been a game, an exercise – it was what we did – and it aroused almost as little concern in us as completing the five-minute crossword. Until Doc Bones. We hadn't had a wink of sleep between us since then.

'Triple nine,' I said, 'asking for DI Priest.'

Maggie wrote it down. Gilbert said, 'And earlier today the same person as before rang the *UK News* to describe what had happened to Mr Williamson.'

'That's right.'

'So what do you make of it?'

'I'll tell you one thing,' Dave said. 'My opinion of Professor Foulkes has gone up. He said the Executioner would be planning something special, and he wasn't joking.'

Gilbert looked at Dave, then at me. 'So what will he do next? What's Foulkes had to say about that?'

I said, 'Hang on, let's go back to where we were. We've got a leak. That's the first thing. Then we have the killer ringing us with messages. The first two were from the bus station, the next, about the doc, from a mobile. Chances are that the last one to the *UK News* was from the same mobile.'

'They're checking,' Dave informed us.

'Good,' I went on. 'I think we can forget about the leak of the Alfred photo and concentrate on the phone calls. About a hundred people had access to that picture, including dozens of civilians, and any one of us could have passed it on. It's the phone calls that bother me. He claims to be a cop. What does anybody else think?'

'Everybody's a cop, these days,' Maggie

reminded us. 'It's the new rock 'n' roll. There's more crime scene programmes on TV than you can shake a stick at.'

'That's true,' Gilbert agreed.

'Dave?' I asked.

He was quiet, staring blankly at the polished top of the table. A patch of sunshine glowed like a Titian painting around his clasped hands. 'I think he's a cop,' he pronounced, after a long silence. 'Or maybe he's an ex-cop.'

'Explain,' I said.

'I'm not sure if I can. He's clever; knows enough to keep us guessing. And he's inconsistent, changing for every job. We look for patterns, and he knows it.'

'So what's his motive?' Gilbert asked him.

'Who can tell? He's killed three people that we know about and probably has three different motives. I'm not big on motives for psychopaths. Bank robbers have motives. They want the money. Husband stabbers have motives. They want to be out of a violent relationship. Psychopaths are different. He probably killed Alfred because of mistaken identity and he wanted to avenge that girl's murder. Lapetite was different. The killer convinced himself that he was on a mission, ridding the world of rubbish. There's plenty in this job who think like that.'

'Mr Williamson wasn't a criminal, Dave,' Gilbert reminded us. 'He was a fine citizen, unless you think there's a racial element. Is that it?'

Dave shook his head and picked at a thumbnail, his hands still in the patch of sunlight. He was wearing a short-sleeved shirt, and his arms were covered in blond hairs right down to his wrists. 'No,' he said. 'The doc was different.'

'How different?'

'Personal.'

'Personal? What do you mean?'

Dave turned his head and looked at me. 'I think it was done to hurt Charlie. I think the killer is a cop and he's a lot closer than we realise.'

Gilbert rocked back in his chair; I shuffled my papers; Maggie dropped her pen.

Gilbert's chair clunked back onto four feet and he said: 'Any thoughts about who it is?'

'Thoughts, that's all,' Dave replied.

'What do you make of that revelation, Chas?'

I riffled through the transcripts with a thumbnail. 'I brought these with me because I thought they would tell us something,' I replied. 'They do, but not quite as forcefully as I'd hoped. For more years than I care to remember I've been known in the job as DI Priest. DI Priest is almost part of the furniture. A month ago, when I was given the HMET job, I was lifted to acting detective chief inspector, and that's what I've been introduced as throughout. That's what the public have heard me called on TV and radio and in the press. But the three nines call about the doc asked for the message to be passed on to DI Priest. *"Tell DI Priest to get himself to 14, Canalside Gardens, as soon as he likes."* That's what he said. I agree with Dave. I think our man is a cop, and he's a lot closer then we think.'

Angie thought *Curlew* was a stupid name for a hairdresser, Jeff told me when I saw him Friday morning. She was staying with *Curl Up and Dye*. There's no pleasing some people. Dave and Maggie came back from the morning briefing down in the incident room but they had little to report. Leicester were taking their time with the cigarette butt, and Superintendent Isles was depending on it for a result.

I don't know where I am with DNA. I grew up with it, and saw how DNA fingerprinting changed the face of criminal investigations, but lately it's gone from being a fairly complicated but understandable technique to being little short of magic. The things they can do nowadays are beyond belief, stretching the incredulity of police officers and defence barristers. The DNA molecule is about six feet long but only a millionth of an inch wide. One of them, tightly rolled up and compressed, is found in every cell in the human body. All ten trillion of them. In every cell in every living thing, if we're going to be pedantic.

Except, we were led to believe, there was no DNA in red blood corpuscles, or in the shaft of hair, or in fingernail clippings, or in the semen and saliva of people who weren't secretors. But now anything appears to be possible. DNA is obtained routinely from flakes of dandruff, droplets of sweat and fallen strands of hair. If you've got split ends or dry skin, don't commit a crime. Murderers and rapists who did the deed twenty years ago are living in fear of a knock at the door. Some of them have led productive, blameless lives ever since, but the law's egg-timer never runs out. If they dragged nervously on a cigarette and flicked the stub into the undergrowth, or peed on their victim, or spit, we'll have their genetic fingerprint on file.

I'm not much wiser when it comes to mobile phones. We're moving onto something called Airwave Tetra, which is a bells and whistle communications system that combines a police officer's radio with a mobile phone and a terminal that gives him access to various databases like the PNC. It's a national system and outside parties like villains cannot, we are promised, eavesdrop on our conversations. Each unit will also contain a location chip so any officer's position can be monitored at all times, and a destruct device that can be triggered from base, should one fall into the wrong hands.

It sounds good, but the phones available to business and the public are probably ahead of the game. Taxi and lorry firms use similar techniques, and companies employing salesmen now know exactly where, when and how long their man spent over lunch. The chance that the Executioner used one of these phones was slim, but psychos often have a blind spot as big as a mountain. Their minds are on other things. It's what catches them, in the end. I rang Sonia and suggested we go for a curry after her training spin.

Next morning I brought her to the nick for an ID parade, except it wasn't a parade. They showed her video shots of twenty men, all selected to fit a rough description of her attacker: small build, dark hair, thin features. The wire spectacles would have been too defining, so Norman the groper was allowed to remove them. The faces were shown to her randomly in full frontal, in profile and three-quarter view. Sonia said, 'That's him, that's him, that's him,' without hesitation.

'How did I do?' she asked, afterwards, as we sat at my desk drinking coffee.

I said that I didn't know, but a few moments later my phone rang. It was the

PC who masterminds our ID parades, to say that she'd scored one hundred per cent.

'You passed,' I told her.

In the afternoon we drove up to the Lakes and booked into a B&B in Troutbeck. Next morning, bolstered by full English breakfast, toast and tea, we set out to do the Kentmere round. The sun was shining as we breakfasted, but had gone when we parked the car outside the church in Kentmere village. We waited until the service was under way then put our boots on and set off up the track towards Garburn Pass and the summit of Ill Bell. I looked up from my exertions and saw that the tops were lost in the clouds that lay across them like dead sheep. The rain started shortly afterwards and we donned our foul weather clothing. I helped Sonia pull her hood up and fastened the studs on her collar. Droplets were trickling down her cheeks and she looked terrific. I gave her a grin and pointed upwards. The top of Ill Bell is rocky, with several cairns dotted about it, but today the sky was as grey as the granite under our feet. The views down towards Windermere and the Kentmere reservoir are as good as any in the Lakes, but not when the rain is coming horizontal and the clouds are rolling across the landscape like smoke.

'Ill Bell,' I shouted at her, making myself

heard above the rattling of our waterproofs, the drumming of the rain and the rush of the wind.

'How high?' she asked.

'Not sure.' I was trying not to get the map wet. 'About two and a half thousand, I think.'

'Higher than Ingleborough?'

'Oh yes. Are you warm enough?'

'I'm fine. Let's go.'

I followed her, down a dip and then up again, keeping to the high ground. A crow came gliding across in front of me and hung stationary where the hillside fell away, balanced on the updraught. I watched it until it tipped a wing and sailed off to vanish into the mist.

The next summit was Froswick. I checked the course on the compass and we headed upwards on the long drag towards Thornthwaite Crag, where we needed to make a right turn. Miss that and we'd find ourselves in Scotland. A few thousand pairs of boots had made the path fairly distinct, and the Romans came this way, so we soon found the tall spire of stones that marked the peak. Then it was downhill into Nan Bield Pass.

Walking in bad weather, when you have the proper clothing, can be fun, but eventually the charm wears off. I was thinking about work, wondering what was happening with the cigarette butt, and if Dave had made any progress with the telephone call. I had a feeling that, come Monday morning, events would take control and the Executioner case would take another direction. Hopefully, one that led to a conviction, but there was a good chance that the suffering wasn't over, yet. At the pass we had hot coffee from the flask, drinking it standing up, and shared some chocolate. A party of walkers as colourful as a flock of parrots loomed out of the mist and we exchanged greetings made more jovial by the shared hardship. They were all carrying walking poles and their breath came out in intermittent clouds from within the hoods of their waterproofs.

'What do you think?' I asked Sonia as we watched them snake away.

'It's a bit miserable, isn't it?' she declared, although she was grinning as she said it.

'We're about half way,' I told her. 'Six miles. We can either go upwards and onwards to complete the circuit, or dive down the valley back to Kentmere. That's about another two, two and a half miles. If you're happy I suggest we abandon it.'

So we did. An hour later we were stripping off our wet gear and pulling fleeces on. The vicar hadn't wheel-clamped the car or left a terse note about worshippers only, so we drove off towards the M6. We had a late lunch at Tebay Services, which was way above motorway standards, and Sonia snoozed for the rest of the journey home, leaving me alone with my thoughts. I didn't come up with anything profound.

Leicester University lab found DNA on the cigarette butt found in Doc Bones' house and spent the weekend amplifying the sample until there was enough to work with. Monday morning they did the electrophoresis thing and produced a band pattern that would identify the smoker more accurately than his passport, driving licence and any number of utility bills. His mother might not recognise him, but we would.

There was a note in my diary to say I was expected at the firing range later in the day for some extra-curricular practice. I thought about cancelling, then decided not to. Dave and Maggie came back from the briefing with nothing to report, other than they were still waiting for the experts to produce the goods. I looked at the list of weekend crimes and passed it on to Jeff. Norman Easterby appeared before a magistrate and was remanded in custody, which was good news.

Dave gave me a thumbs up from his desk, his phone clamped to his ear. He made notes, then came to see me.

'Action at last,' he reported. 'Both calls about Doc Bones were made from the same mobile phone. It was purchased from T-

Mobile in Stantown and is one of those pay-as-you-go tariffs, which means the owner is not registered anywhere. And would you believe it, he didn't take out the extended warranty. Here's the number.' He passed me a slip of paper with an 07 eleven digit number on it. 'So far, it's been used to make the two calls, that's all.'

'Can we track it down?' I asked.

'Only if it's left switched on.'

'And it's not.'

'No.'

'So what's happening?'

'The Met scientific work with a company that traces them. They do it for anyone who registers. It's mainly company people, but you can register your kids' numbers with them if you want, and they'll keep you informed of their movements. And it works with any phone, including the cheepos. They're listening out for us, full time. If he switches on, we'll have him. It's accurate to five metres.'

'Would you want to know where your kids are?'

'I think I'd rather not.'

'Has anyone tried ringing it?'

'No. We're thinking about it. We need a good story if they answer.'

I rang Les Isles and we discussed the possibilities of dialling the number. I liked the idea at first, because it meant that we were doing something rather than wait for the Executioner to make a move, but Les talked me out of it. If we rang him and he answered, our chances of keeping him on the line while a trace was made were nil. He'd realise we were onto him and throw the phone in the river.

The exertions in the Lake District had left me hungry and aching slightly. We'd eaten at odd times, and now I was feeling the cost. My blood sugar level was in turmoil. I went over the road and ordered an egg and bacon sandwich. Great on the taste buds, hell on the arteries. I was at my usual corner table, chatting to the waitress when Dave came steaming in, his big face red with exertion or excitement. He sat down opposite me and the waitress saw he wanted to talk and wandered off.

'They've got a match,' he told me in a stage whisper, leaning across the table. My sandwich arrived and I cut it in half.

'What? On the DNA?' I said.

'That's right.'

'Great. Anybody we know?' I pushed the plate into the middle of the table and nodded towards it. Dave took half of my breakfast and bit into it.

'Yeah,' he mumbled. 'Terry Hyson.'

'Terry Hyson,' I echoed. 'Of Angie's sex shop fame?'

'That's right.'

'I don't believe it.'

'It's a match.'

'They're saying Terry Hyson is the Executioner?'

'Not necessarily, but they've proved that he smoked the cigarette. DNA doesn't lie, Chas, or so we're told. It's accurate to one in fifty quadzillion.'

'So what's happening?'

'They're getting an FSG together to lift him.'

The firearms support group don't do that full time. They are normal serving officers with specialist training. When needed they are called from their other duties to don the protective gear and go to where the action is, a bit like lifeboat men. 'C'mon,' I said. 'We're nearer than they are.'

We stuffed the remains of the sandwich into our mouths as we dashed across the road. 'Can you remember where he lives?' I asked Dave as we strode into the nick car park.

'The street, not the number.'

'That should do. I'll drive.'

We were there in ten minutes, and there was no sign of the FSG.

'How are you getting on with Eddie, these days?' I asked.

'Eddie the Lip?'

'Who else?'

'OK.'

'OK? That's an improvement.'

'Watch this space,' he growled.

Before I could ask for clarification I saw a white Transit van in my rear-view mirror, crawling along, looking for clues to where Terry Hyson lived, like his house number.

'Silly buggers,' Dave said, twisting in his seat to watch them approach. The normal technique is to come squealing round the corner, leap out, burst the door down and arrest their man before he can sit up in bed and blink the sleep from his eyes. I got out and stood in the road, waiting for them.

'I could arrest you for kerb crawling,' I told the driver, but he wasn't amused. Les Isles was in his car, right behind the van.

'Hi, Chas,' he said. 'Couldn't you stay away? Why don't these houses have numbers on them?'

'It's done to cause maximum confusion. What do we want?'

'Forty-seven.'

I pointed. 'Down there, on the left. Probably about where that car is parked.'

I told Les about Terry Hyson, about Angie's sex shop and about his latest refusal to be cautioned. I said he had no history of violence and under no account was he to be shot. We needed him alive and kicking. He repeated the mantra: DNA doesn't lie. I offered to knock at Terry's door, said I was sure he'd come quietly, but Les would have none of it. Eventually he agreed on a softly-softly approach and we processed in convoy towards number 47.

The wife of the man with shiny shoes opened her mouth wide and contorted herself in front of the bathroom window, holding her husband's shaving mirror so she could examine her teeth. Something had broken whilst she was eating her breakfast apple – *a Cox's, not one of those dreadful Golden Delicious* – and it looked as if she'd lost a filling. She went downstairs and found the number of her dentist in the diary and dialled the surgery while holding the diary open with her elbow. It was engaged.

She uncoiled the flex from her vacuum and started her chores. Mondays, Wednesdays and Fridays she hoovered the carpets throughout, Monday and Tuesday she washed and ironed, Wednesdays she dusted, Friday it was the glass. Her husband was a stickler for cleanliness, but she agreed that if you kept on top of the work it was more easily done. She wasn't scared of him, but was careful not to displease him. He'd never been violent towards her, apart from that one time, long ago. If anything, after tears all round, it had brought them closer, but he did have a biting sarcasm and could destroy her self-esteem with a carefully barbed comment about the state of the cooker or

339

the rings of talcum powder on her dressing table. She moved the low coffee table to one side and pushed the vac into the far corner of the room. Since he put the new cable on, several weeks ago, she could do most of the downstairs without having to move to a different socket.

Her tongue kept moving to the raw edge of the tooth, and soon it was sore. She'd have an ulcer there tomorrow, she thought. The dentist was still engaged. She held the diary open with her elbow again, waited a few more seconds and kept trying. There was a notepad next to the telephone, and a ballpoint pen. It was awkward holding the diary open while dialling, so she tried writing the number on the pad, but the pen wouldn't work. She tried it on the back of her hand and it wrote just fine, but when she tried on the paper it dried up again. She made an exasperated tutting noise and wrote the number on the pale skin of the back of her hand.

Twenty minutes later she'd finished downstairs. The dentist was still engaged so she cleaned the staircase using the long wand and lugged the vac upstairs to start in the master bedroom. The landing followed, then the spare bedroom and the third one, which had been converted into an office. Her husband worked in here, and although it wasn't out of bounds to her, he'd made it clear that he didn't want her meddling with his papers.

Her remit was to vac the carpet, dust the desk and clean the monitor screen. That's all, and she knew better than to overstep the mark.

The work only took her a couple of minutes. When it was done she seated herself in her husband's leather chair and relaxed. It was a pleasant room, and although the curtains were closed the morning sun shone through them and flooded the place with light. The computer was switched off, but she ran her fingers across the keyboard and imagined she was doing some high-powered work, or making a calculation that would put an end to world poverty. She'd never used a computer. Her husband had always poohpoohed the idea of her learning, just like he'd trodden on all her other aspirations. There was only need for one of them to do these things, he'd told her. Her role was the most important. Her role was to run the household. Unfortunately, running the household didn't include managing their finances or making any decisions about how they lived from day to day.

She pulled open the drawer to the left of the kneehole, idly, almost disinterested, and noted the contents. Paperclips, staples, notelets, PrittStick, Scotch tape, an assortment of pens and pencils. The usual items found in any office. She closed the drawer and pulled open the one to her right.

There was a newspaper stuffed into this one. It was the *Sunday Times* from the previous day. She pulled it out and read the headlines. Inside, there was an article about a man who'd murdered his ex-girlfriend after being released from jail for assaulting her on an earlier occasion. He'd already served a term for the manslaughter of a previous girlfriend. There was a box carefully drawn around the article with an orange highlighter, which is what had drawn her attention to it. She carefully folded the paper exactly as she'd found it and had started to place it back in the drawer when she saw the mobile phone.

It wasn't her husband's fancy one, with the built-in camera and Internet access. This was a basic model like hers. She lifted it out of the drawer but the display was dead. Then she noticed that the little cover at the back was not in place. She found it in the drawer, with the phone's battery and SIM card lying next to it. She knew about phones and SIM cards because she'd damaged her phone once and they'd transferred the card to a new phone so she didn't have to change her number. Her husband insisted that she take it with her at all times. Presumably this one was faulty and he'd been trying to fix it.

The side of her face had started to hurt because her tongue kept returning to the jagged edge of her broken tooth. She winced with pain and tried to hold her tongue away from the problem. Without thinking about what she was doing she fitted the SIM card into its socket, clicked the battery in place and re-fitted the back cover. She held down the button with the red phone on it and Eureka! It worked. The display sprang into life. It showed the TMobile logo, in colour, and a few seconds later came up with the message: *Please confirm switch on.* She pressed the OK button and the screen told her to wait.

'Well that's that repaired,' she said out loud with a giggle, and immediately regretted it because the raw side of her tongue caught the sharp edge of the tooth and a stab of pain shot through her jaw. She was prising off the cover again, to remove the evidence of her snooping, but the discomfort persuaded her to have another attempt at the dentist. The number was still written on the back of her hand. She typed it into the phone, puckering her eyes to read the figures on the tiny keyboard, and pressed the button with the green telephone on it, same as she would do with her own. This time she was rewarded by the ringing tone, and a few seconds later one of the receptionists answered.

'Oh, good morning,' the wife of the man with shiny shoes said with obvious relief. 'Will it be possible for me to arrange for some emergency treatment?'

Chapter Twelve

Terry Hyson was in bed with Angie. When he didn't answer to several hammers on the door they put the ram against it and burst in. It's what they like doing. Terry was upstairs, pulling his jeans on. She was sitting up in bed with the mascara running down her cheeks like the tailings from a coalmine, and her hair looking as if it had just gone through the spin cycle. Monday was her day off. From hairdressing, that is.

Heckley nick was nearest so that's where we took him. The duty solicitor was already there. The super was going on holiday later in the week and he wanted the case sewn up before he went, so he'd jumped a few fences before he reached them. Terry was cautioned and told his PACE rights. He was given a mug of tea and his clothes taken from him. The clock was running and Les was impatient. I said I knew Terry, had dealt with him before and he trusted me. I felt that he might be more open with an officer he knew and trusted than with a stranger. 'Fair enough,' Les said, 'We'll interview him together.'

'Where were you on the evening of May

the ninth?' Les opened with.

Terry looked bewildered. An hour ago he'd been relaxing in a post-coital glow and the next thing he knew he was wearing paper overalls, sitting in interview room number one at Heckley nick with the Neal recorder running and a high window casting a patch of sunshine on him.

Terry blinked in disbelief. 'No idea,' he said.

'It was a Sunday, if that helps.'

'No. It doesn't.'

'What about the evening of Friday the twenty-eighth?'

'I don't know.'

'Or the morning of Wednesday, the sixteenth of June?'

'I've no idea. What do you think I am? I was probably at home. I go to the pub. Go clubbing at the weekend. Stay at home. That's all.'

The brief sat forward. 'Superintendent,' he began. 'What my client is trying to say is that he leads a lifestyle that doesn't demand that he keep a record of his movements. He doesn't keep a diary.'

Les said, 'In that case perhaps you should point out to your client that he has some very serious charges hanging over him and it might be to his advantage to remember where he was on those dates.'

I nodded my approval. Well said, I thought.

'How well did you know Jermaine Lapetite?' Les demanded.

'Superintendent!' the brief interjected before Terry could reply. 'You're jumping to conclusions. I can't allow that.'

'I'll put it another way, then. Did you know Jermaine Lapetite, Terry?'

'No. Never heard of him.'

'I don't believe you.'

'Well I didn't.'

'What about John Williamson, known as Doctor Bones?'

'Doctor Bones?' Terry repeated, his voice high with incredulity. 'I've never heard of anybody called Doctor Bones.'

Les kept it up for over an hour, getting nowhere. I watched the patch of sunshine move across the desk, and the tapes in the recorder implacably noting every word. Soon we'll be doing this on CDs, I thought, when tapes are no longer available. We wouldn't have to turn them over every forty-five minutes, but with a bit of luck I'd be gone by then. I wondered what Sonia had planned for the evening, then remembered I had a date at the shooting range. I needed to tell her.

'What were you doing at 14, Canalside Gardens on June the sixteenth?' Les was asking. The brief didn't bother to object, this time.

Terry didn't answer immediately. He was

growing tired and upset. His hands were on the table top, the fingernails bitten down and ingrained grease highlighting the creases in his skin. I remembered that he dabbled with cars.

'I don't know where Canalside Gardens is,' he replied, slowly and deliberately. 'And I've never been there.'

'How do you know you've never been there if you don't know where it is?'

'I don't know. Why don't you believe me?'

'Because we have proof you were there, Terry. Proof. One hundred per cent. So why don't you come clean and make it easy for yourself? You're in deep trouble, and the more you lie, the deeper it gets. C'mon, Terry. What were you doing there?'

The brief had been listening but when he realised Les was wasting his time he sat back and relaxed. Now he leaned forward again, saying, 'Might I ask the nature of this so-called proof, Superintendent?'

Les said, 'A cigarette butt was found upstairs at 14, Canalside Gardens on the day of the murder. DNA was found on it and the genetic fingerprint sent to the data bank. It was found to match samples taken from your client when he was arrested on a previous occasion.'

Terry sat up as if electrified. 'Well that proves it, dunnit!' he proclaimed. 'That proves it wasn't me. I don't smoke. I gave it up, just over seventeen and a half months ago. Christmas, 2002, it was. I haven't smoked since, so it can't have been me, can it?'

The brief smiled and made a gesture that implied nothing but made it look as if he still was on the case. I hadn't spoken, so far, but decided it was about time I earned my corn.

'That's not quite true, Terry,' I said. 'When you were in here, in this very interview room, last month, about the vandalising of Angie's sign, I offered you a cigarette and you smoked it.'

He glared at me and a muscle twitched in his neck. For a moment I thought we had him, then he said, 'You gave it me. It was the first fag I'd had in over a year. I smoked it and stubbed it in this ashtray.' He swiped the back of his hand against the tin lid that served as an ashtray and it rattled onto the floor. 'That's the only fag I've had. I swear it.' Enlightenment struck him. 'It was you,' he snarled, straight at me and rising to his feet. 'It was you, wasn't it? You planted it. You set me up, you bastard. You fucking bastard. You set me up.'

I leaned back and flicked the panic strip with a knuckle.

In a few seconds the desk sergeant arrived. 'Take Mr Hyson to his room, please,' I told him. "We've finished for now.'

When they'd gone Les said, 'Well, so much for having someone you know and trust in on the interview.'

As I passed through the foyer Dave came in carrying a sandwich bag. 'Have you brought me one?' I asked.

'No. I thought you'd eaten.'

'You ate half of it for me.'

'Fair enough. I'll share. I've just been shopping.'

'What for?'

'A pair of those sandals with the Velcro straps. Apparently it's going to be a long hot summer and Shirl said I needed some for our holidays.'

'I've got some. They're good.'

'I know. I've seen you in them. How did the interview go?'

'I'll tell you in my office. What make did you get?'

'Berghaus. What are yours?'

'Brashers, I think. Put the kettle on.'

He made two teas and brought the sandwich into my office. It was cheese and pickle and we cut it in half with the office knife. I retrieved two KitKats from my drawer.

'So how did it go?' he asked again, using the knife to spread the Branston more evenly in his half of the sandwich.

I said, 'Did you know that they do Branston with small chunks, now, specially for sandwiches?'

'So I've heard, but I prefer it crunchy.'

'I thought you would. How did the interview go?' I couldn't help a smile. 'I think Mr Isles will be displeased with my performance.' I told Dave about the cigarette I'd given Terry Hyson in the interview room a month ago, and about his claim that he'd stopped smoking and that it was the only one he'd had in three years. He'd left the stub in the ashtray in the interview room.

'And he's claiming that you planted it at the doc's house?'

'That's right.'

'Did you?'

'Of course not.'

'It certainly looked like a plant.'

'It did, didn't it?'

'Do you believe Hyson?'

'I don't believe he's the Executioner,' I said.

'So who planted the fag end? Who has access to the interview rooms?'

'All of us.'

We finished the sandwich and Dave dusted the crumbs off my desk. He crumpled the wrapper into a ball and tossed it into my waste paper bin. 'I'll ring the Met about the phone calls,' he said. 'Thanks for the KitKat, I'll have it later.'

As he opened the door I said, 'Oh, a word of warning about those sandals.'

He stopped and half-closed the door again. 'Yeah?'

'Umm, be careful if you walk through any long grass in them late at night.'

'Why's that?'

'Well, last time I did it, when I arrived home I had two hedgehogs stuck to the Velcro.'

I ate my KitKat right then, with my feet on the cold radiator. Pigeons were cooing on the ledge under my window and the sky was unbroken blue. I went back in time, twenty-four days according to my diary, to the day I'd talked to Terry Hyson about Angie's sex shop. That was a warm day, too. He'd been wearing a Lacoste T-shirt, with a V-neck. When the T-shirt market was saturated and sales had collapsed, they invented the one with a V-neck, paid a few celebrities to wear them and started all over again. I remembered what we said, visualised that first, long, satisfying draw he took and the plume of blue smoke he sent spiralling up towards the extraction fan.

'You owe me one,' I told him. I often say it. Most of our decent information comes from informers. Then we walked together towards the foyer. He thanked me, and smoke was drifting out of his nostrils as he said it. I could see the smoke, almost smell it. He'd had two cigarettes while he was in the nick. There'd been two in the packet, and he was smoking the second one as he left the police station. I was sure of it. Anybody could have followed him, but I was thinking the unbelievable.

I spent the afternoon going through the list of names that our geographic scan had thrown up. We'd widened the search from half a mile radius to a mile. That's a lot of people. Every male on the electoral roll aged between eighteen and fifty-five was fed into the police national computer and a file created for everyone with a criminal record. Then they were sorted according to the nature of their offences, with violence gaining extra brownie points, and the number of offences. The only people we'd interviewed in the course of the investigation who were discovered in the trawl were Terry Hyson and Donovan Bender, who'd robbed a bank while armed with a carrot. Statistically, it was one of them, but according to statistics the universe is uninhabited. According to statistics, your chances of winning the lottery are the same whether you buy a ticket or not. I typed link words into the computer, like *child abuse, decapitation, racial,* and it produced the relevant files, but there was nothing enlightening there. Then I started working my way through them looking for a series of crimes that might be considered a learning curve. The offences had occurred indoors, which meant that our man may have started his criminal career as a burglar. He knew about electrics and roof joists, but not much about anatomy. He was strong. He drove a white van. He knew about mobile phones. He knew about forensic science. He knew an awful lot about forensic science. He knew that it was possible to find DNA on a cigarette butt.

I rang High Adventure, where Sonia worked, but they told me that she'd slipped out for a few minutes. There was a hesitant tap on the glass of my door and I saw a female silhouette standing there, shorter and less slim than Sonia.

'Come in,' I said, and the door opened. It was one of the civilian secretaries that I'd noticed a few times but never spoken to.

'Mr Priest?' she enquired.

'That's me,' I confirmed with a grin. I thought about adding that everybody called me Charlie, but decided it sounded a bit cheesy, so I didn't. 'What can I do for you?'

'A message for you. He said your phone was permanently engaged.'

'Oh,' I said. 'I've only been on it for about ten seconds.' She handed me a sheet of A4 with three lines of typing on it. They read:

Mr Priest
See you at 5. Bring a gun, please.
PC Lord, Firearms Instructor

'Right, thank you,' I said, and she left, giving her bottom an exaggerated wiggle as she walked away. I could have invited her to have a coffee and a biscuit before descending back to the depths of the pool, but her perfume was a bit strong and besides, I'm not in the market. I read the note again, threw it in the bin and dialled Gilbert.

'It's Charlie,' I said when he answered. 'I told you that I was applying for my firearms authorisation.'

'You did. You must be mad,' he told me.

'It's only for the sake of morale,' I replied. 'I've little intention of ever carrying a gun in anger. I'm going to the range for some practice. Can you authorise a Glock 17 for me, please?'

'From here?' he said. 'I thought they had their own guns.'

'So did I, but I've received a message telling me to take one. All theirs must be out on a job, or something.'

'Fair enough. I'll make it out and ring Arthur. Don't shoot yourself in the foot.'

The troops were filtering back and the office grew noisy with their chatter. Nobody had any revelations to make. A couple of ounces of cannabis had been found, plus some stolen property, but nothing relating to the Executioner had come to light. They'd been investigating the names on the list in a process we call Trace, Interview,

354

Eliminate, or TIE. I suppose it's politically incorrect, but I prefer to call it TIN, for Trace, Interview and Nail the bugger.

It was Dave who saved the day. 'It's me, Chas,' he said when I answered the phone. 'We've got him! We've got him!'

'Calm down, sunshine,' I said, hardly able to contain myself. 'Tell me all about it.'

'I'm down in the incident room. The telephone people – they messed up, to start with. Somebody made a call from the mobile, but they didn't manage to scan it for location. Something went wrong. They're blaming the computer.'

'Oh God, that's all we need. Go on.'

'But they got the number it rang.'

'You mean we know the number that somebody tried to contact on the Executioner's mobile?'

'That's it.'

'Great. Fantastic. Have you identified them, yet?'

''Course I have. It's a dentist in Heckley. I'm going there now to see who's rung them today. This could be what we're looking for. I'll wait for you.'

'A dentist?'

'That's what I said.'

'Damn,' I said. 'I've arranged to be at the shooting range at five.'

'This is more important than banging off a few rounds.'

'I know.' It would have waited until morning, but this was Dave's show and he was rarin' to go. He'd worked harder on the case than anybody, come up with more useful suggestions than the rest of us put together. And he'd opened the door of the microwave. I said, 'Do you realise how many people they'll have on their books, Dave?'

'Yeah, about ten thousand.'

'Right. Look. You get round there – I can tell you're itching to – and concentrate on that call. It may have been anything. See if anybody remembers it. Then tell them we want a complete list of all their patients, soon as pos. With luck it may have been one of them making an appointment. Don't spend all night on it. We'll give it everything we've got in the morning. And ring me later.'

It was a quarter past four. I went downstairs with a spring in my steps. It was all starting to fall in place.

'You want a gun,' Arthur at the front desk told me.

'Yes, please.'

'What is it? The neighbour's cat?'

'Kids riding their bikes on the pavement,' I said. 'It's the only language they understand.'

He found two big keys – one in a drawer, one hanging on a hook – and led the way along the corridor past the cells and inter-

356

view rooms towards the armoury.

'Going for some practice?' he asked, as he unlocked the heavy door and swung it open.

'That's right.'

He lifted the counter flap and let himself inside. I stood outside.

'Glock 17, I believe.'

'Yep.'

'You don't have to, y'know, Charlie.'

'It's OK, Arthur,' I said. 'I've had the sermons. It's no big deal.'

'Fair enough.' He took a pistol from a rack and pushed it across the counter. 'Ever used one of these?'

'No. Tell me about it.'

'OK. Designed by Herr Glock, who had never made a gun before, for the German police. He set out to make a better gun and won the contract. Nine millimetre, plastic frame, metal barrel and other bits. The magazine holds seventeen bullets but we only put fifteen in.'

'Yes, I know. Tell me about the sights.'

He held the gun so I could see them. 'Line the white dots up and you're away. Any questions?'

'Yes. Where's the safety catch?'

'It's built into the trigger, or, in other words, there isn't one. A safety catch is to prevent the gun firing if accidentally dropped. It isn't there to switch the gun on and off. The trigger pull is long and heavy –

it'll only fire when you mean it to.'

'Cheers,' I said, putting the weapon in my jacket pocket. 'Got any bullets?'

He plonked the gun's magazine on the counter and produced a new box of fifty 9mm soft-nosed bullets. They're nasty, real nasty. They mushroom on impact and all their energy is dissipated in the first thing they hit. There's little chance of them going straight through the intended target and hitting someone else. Arthur lifted the lid off and they sat there, brass, copper and lead, glowing like jewels. Beautiful, deadly jewels. His fingers flipped a bullet up and he clicked it into the magazine with the ease of an expert, followed by another and another, until his phone rang and broke the sequence.

'Put fifteen in,' he said, pushing the magazine towards me and turning to answer the phone, 'and sign the book.'

'How many have you put in?' I asked his retreating back, but his reply was drowned by the next ring of the phone. The bullets in the box didn't flip up for me like they did for him, and I couldn't hook my fingernails under them, so I tipped them onto the counter and started pressing them, one by one, into the magazine.

It felt strange, walking down the corridor with my jacket weighed down by the gun in one pocket and the magazine in the other. I placed the box of the remaining bullets on the passenger seat and pulled my seat belt on. It was rush hour, and I was loaded for bear, so keep out of my way. The Yardies are right about that: carrying a gun definitely gives you an edge.

You reach the range by driving through the grounds of the hotel, round their one-way system and over the speed bumps and the golf cart crossings. The speed limit is ten miles per hour, which is well meant but completely unrealistic. The grass had that permanently newly mown look and smell and the trees were at their best. I've never played golf, but if it was an excuse to be out in the fresh air in these surroundings I could see the attraction. Pity about the trousers. Approaching the hotel I took a right turn onto an un-signposted track that led towards the long, low building of the shooting range.

There were two cars parked outside, a BMW and a racy Ford Escort. I picked up the box of bullets and swung my legs out onto the tarmac. The outer door of the range opened and let me into a sort of airlock, but the steel inner door was locked. I pressed the buzzer and a voice said, 'Hello.'

'Charlie Priest,' I said into the microphone.

A moment later I heard the clunk of a well-oiled bolt and the door swung inwards. Superintendent Mark Stanwick was standing there, a big friendly smile on his face.

'Hello Charlie,' he greeted me. 'We thought you weren't coming.'

'Traffic,' I explained. 'I didn't realise you would be here, Mr Stanwick.'

He closed the door behind me and I heard the bolt slide home. 'Oh, I like to keep my hand in, you know. Did you bring a gun, eh?'

I patted my pocket. 'Right here.' He didn't tell me to call him Mark.

'Good, good. I was in the Met shooting team. Black powder, mainly. Loaded my own cartridges. Had a Colt revolver until they changed the law. Damian said you were coming tonight, so I asked him if I could join you. You don't mind, do you?'

'Of course not. Where is he?'

'He's gone for a sandwich. Apparently he has something going with one of the chefs and she feeds him. Lucky devil, eh. He said I had to show you this and we'd to have some practice until he got back.' A long rifle was lying on the counter, with a telescopic sight and extended bipod legs at the front. He traced his fingers along its length as lovingly as if it were the stocking-clad leg of a Pretty Polly model.

'Practice?' I said. 'Did we ought to?'

'It's OK, Charlie,' he replied. 'I'll look after you.'

The range is long and low. Fifty metres

360

long, but you'd swear it was nearer twice that length. It goes on forever, the far end dimly lit and diffused with smoke. The lighting is concealed behind the roof girders for protection and there is the constant hum of a powerful air extraction system. The walls and ceiling are cushioned with sound insulating material and will withstand a close-range hit from most of the weapons currently available.

'So what is it?' I asked, eyeing the long gun. There's a counter at this end of the range, with a small office and control room behind the counter. The lights weren't on in the control room.

'It's a sniper rifle, by Accuracy International. Only .243 calibre, but state of the art. Damian said I've to give you the demonstration.'

'The demonstration? That sounds intriguing.' I took the Glock and its magazine from my pockets and placed them on the counter next to the box of bullets. I removed my jacket and laid it on there with them. My mobile phone was in my shirt pocket, so I lifted that out and sat it on my jacket. Another Glock, presumably for Stanwick, was at the far end of the counter. Several pairs of safety spectacles and ear defenders were there, too, in a cardboard box, so I chose a pair of each and pulled them on. Stanwick came from behind the counter carrying a Castrol GTX five litre plastic container and walked about halfway down the range with it.

'You putting these on?' I said, offering him a set of glasses and ear muffs as he came back. My voice sounded hollow through the ear defenders.

He waved a hand dismissively. 'No, that's OK. You've never seen anything like this, Charlie,' he went on, his eyes gleaming. He picked up the sniper rifle, rotated his shoulders a couple of times and knelt on the floor, gently placing the long gun on the concrete. He lined it up with the oil drum and laid full length, the butt of the gun pulled into his right shoulder, squinting into the telescopic sight.

The container was filled with water. There was a crack, deafeningly loud even with the muffs on, and the Castrol container exploded. Water flew up to the roof and halfway towards us, and the container leapt into the air. Stanwick rose to his feet and grinned.

The drum was ripped open and turned inside out. Most of the water had flown towards the gun, not away from it.

'What do you think of that?' Stanwick asked, as proud as a granddad at the school sports.

'Amazing,' I confessed. I picked up the mangled container and examined it. 'What happened to the bullet?' There was a grey film on the plastic, with tiny flecks of copper like gold dust in a prospector's pan.

'That's it,' Stanwick said, wiping the leaden smear with a finger and showing his fingertip to me. 'It's gone.'

'And why did most of the water fly that way?' I gestured towards the rifle, standing there propped up on its bipod legs, pointing towards us.

'The shock wave,' he explained. 'The bullet is travelling at over twice the speed of sound. It leaves a great vacuum in its wake.' He spoke like one newly converted, the enthusiasm lighting up his face. Fire power impressed him. It terrifies me.

'Right,' he declared. 'The show's over. Let's have some practice. I've set up a couple of targets.' I'd seen the two effigies hanging from the wires that ran the length of the range. Last time I was here they were outlines of a Capone-like figure, but these were of a young, slim guy with a lock of hair falling across his brow. It could almost have been Elvis. Something clicked in my brain. Elvis, aka the King. That was the in-joke that I hadn't understood, in the office all those weeks ago. They hung in the gloom about fifteen yards down the range. The King and his twin brother.

'I'll just move this out of the way, eh.' Stanwick picked up the sniper rifle and moved it forward a few feet. I'd have put it on the counter, but decided he was probably right: it was safer on the floor, where we could see it.

'OK, Charlie,' he said. 'Let's see you put a pattern of five between his eyes.'

'Five?' I queried. I was taught to shoot in groups of two or three.

'That's right. If you're going to kill someone you might as well do it properly.'

I clicked the magazine into place and raised the gun two-handed. The sights on the Glock are three white dots: two on the rear sight, one on the front. You focus on the front dot, place it over the target, and bring the two dots on the rear sight in line with it on either side. Like this:

o o o

Then you pull the trigger.

I was slow. The gun boomed in my ears and jerked upwards. I dragged the dots back in line and kept firing, the ejected cartridge cases brushing my cheek as they flew out. Bang ... bang ... bang ... bang ... bang.

Elvis had five bullet holes in his face. I lowered the gun, more than satisfied with my handiwork.

'Pretty good,' Stanwick told me. I thought so, too. He raised his gun and banged off his five in about half the time it took me. He was slightly more accurate, too, but not much.

'You win that one,' I conceded.

'Practice, Charlie. That's all it is. It's you to nominate, my turn to fire first.'

'Um, his sternum,' I said.

He rattled five into the cardboard cut-out, all as near on target as would make no difference. I lifted my gun and put five into my Elvis slightly more smartly than the first five. He wouldn't have come back for more.

'You're getting better,' Stanwick told me. 'We'll make a marksman of you yet. Your turn to go first. Let's see you put the last five into his heart, finish him off.'

I was taking a few deep breaths, calming myself, letting the adrenaline level settle down, when I heard a mobile phone ringing. 'That sounds like mine,' I said, turning towards the counter. I'd recognise it any-where. Dave's son set it up for me, so it plays the first stanza of 'Like a Rolling Stone'.

'Let it ring,' Stanwick said.

'I'm expecting a call,' I told him. I picked the phone up at about *Throw the bums a dime* and spoke my name into it.

'It's me, Chas,' I heard Dave say, breath-less with excitement. 'I've cracked it. I've cracked it.'

'Go on,' I said.

'I'm outside the dentists. It's on Brighouse Road, near the magistrates' court. They offered to run their entire list off for me, after I'd convinced them how important it was, and I sat down to wait. I was looking through today's appointments when I noticed a name. You'll never guess who.'

'So tell me.'

'A lady called Dorothea Stanwick. She rang in and made an appointment for emergency treatment at exactly the right time this morning. I've checked her address and it's Mark Stanwick's wife. Superintendent Stanwick. He's on the books, too, but the appointment was for her. She rang on the same phone that the Executioner uses, Charlie. It's him. It must be. I was wrong. I'd have gambled it was ... well, you know who, but I was wrong, and it all fits.'

I turned and looked at Stanwick. He gave me a half-hearted, impatient smile and I rolled my eyes as if annoyed with the caller. Stanwick was holding his Glock down by his side.

I was pressing the phone to the side of my face so no stray sound waves could escape from it, and said, 'OK, no problem. What time's the kick-off?'

'What?' Dave demanded.

'Eight? I'll be there. Do I have to bring my own whistle?'

'What are you talking about?'

'See you there, then.'

'Oh my God,' Dave was saying. 'Oh my

God. Are you at the range?'

'Yes.'

'He's with you, isn't he?'

'Yes.'

'Oh Christ! Have you got a gun?'

'Yes.'

'Shoot him, Charlie! For Christ's sake shoot him. Now, while I'm listening. I'll take the blame. Shoot him!'

'I'll see you there, then,' I said, and broke the connection.

'Your pal Dave?' Stanwick asked as I pulled the ear defenders back in place.

'Yes. His son's playing in a five-a-side competition at the sports centre and they need a referee. Dave coaches them; I help out now and again.'

'Sounds fun, and highly commendable, being engaged with the community. Your turn to shoot first, I believe. Let's see you put the last five in his heart.'

I took my place at the line and raised the gun. The middle o swam about, hovering around the target. When I thought it was as steady as I could hold it I brought the two outer o's in line with it and pulled the trigger.

Four times.

The echo died down and the smoke drifted away. I stood there, gun aloft, and lined the dots up again. The fifth shot hit plumb dead centre. If Elvis wasn't dead before, he was now.

'Your turn,' I said.

Sparks flew from the end of the barrel as the gun kicked. Stanwick stood for a moment, as if frozen, and slowly turned to face me, the gun still held aloft. I felt an icy dampness creep up my legs and clutch my loins.

'Hey,' I said. 'This is dangerous. Put the gun down, Mark.'

'Superintendent to you, *Inspector*,' he hissed.

'What's all this about?'

'It's about you and me, Priest. That's what it's about.' The gun wasn't wavering, and I knew that the central spot was somewhere between my eyes.

'I don't understand.'

'Oh, yes, you do. You've blighted my career, right from the start. Old Mother Twanky. You couldn't resist going to the press, could you? "There's no such thing as spontaneous human combustion", you told them, ridiculing what I'd said. I was first officer on the job. It was my case, and you took it over and belittled me.'

'That was a long time ago.' I wondered what Dave would do. He ought to organise the FSG and surround the place, but he was just as likely to come blustering in all by himself. It was a worry I could do without. And Damian. Where was Damian?

'I've followed your career,' he went on.

'Mr One Hundred Per Cent, they call you. Detective Inspector Priest, scourge of the murderers. Well now you'll go to the grave with three unsolved cases on your record.'

'Where's Damian?' I demanded. 'What have you done with Damian?'

'Damian had an accident, like you are going to do.'

'You've killed him,' I hissed. 'Just like that? You've killed him to suit your pathetic mind game?'

'Not quite. The official line will be that he killed himself. There was a tragic accident and you were shot. He was showing you the sniper rifle and it went off. He couldn't face the disgrace it would bring upon him, so he took his own life. There'll be no blame on you. They'll give you a big send-off. Coffin bearers, best uniforms, the works.' He laughed silently at the thought, his shoulders shaking but his expression not changing,

'So why did you kill Alfred Armitage?' I asked. I reckoned it would take at least half an hour for an FSG to get here. They might drag a couple of ARVs off the motorway and send them, but they weren't trained for a shoot-out. Their job was to contain a situation until the real gunslingers arrived. Still, I thought, they'd be most welcome. Right then, Osama Bin Laden would have been most welcome. Stanwick still had the Glock pointing at me, with four bullets in it. My arms were down by my sides, and I was still holding my weapon.

'Alfred was a strange case, don't you agree? An unfortunate man. As far as I'm concerned it was Terrence Paul Hutchinson that I killed, aka the Midnight Strangler.'

'That's ridiculous,' I protested.

'Not to the parents of his victims,' Stanwick claimed. 'Not to them. They'd lived their lives in anguish for what had happened to their children. All that pain. All that bitterness. I helped them get over it. I brought some comfort into their lives. As far as they knew, it was the Strangler who'd been killed, and good riddance to him.'

'So why the pantomime with the electric flex?' I asked.

'Simple. I thought even you would realise that. It had to be in the papers, with photographs, so they knew the deed had been done. Same with that black piece of shit. A nice touch, don't you think, hanging him over the toilet?'

'And what about the doc?' I asked. 'What about John Williamson?'

'Same again. To get in the papers, so the world would know that acting detective inspector Priest, scourge of the murderers, wasn't as clever as we all thought he was.'

'But why the doc? What had he done to deserve that?'

'Yes, it does seem odd, doesn't it? Let's say

370

it was just an indulgence of mine. I chose the doc to hurt you, Priest. To jolt your complacency, you and that celebrity woman of yours. What's she called: *La* fucking *Gazelle?* You like skinny women, do you? They turn you on, do they?'

'You're mad!' I told him, spitting the words out like they were poisonous. 'You're stark raving mad. You're crazier than anyone I've ever had the pleasure of arresting.'

'Don't say that!' he yelled at me. The gun was wavering wildly but he brought it under control. 'Don't ever call me that again.'

'You're as mad as a fucking hatt–'

He fired and my head exploded. I clutched my left hand over my ear and the protectors had gone. He'd hit one side and sent them and the safety spectacles spinning off. I looked at my hand and there was blood on it.

I was thinking forensic, now. His story was a good one, but that was one bullet that didn't fit the screenplay. I could feel blood running down my neck and under my shirt. That wasn't in the script, either. I said, 'You'll never get away with this.' I wanted to tell him about Dave's phone call, but it might have put Dave in danger. It was pathetic, but the best I could do, so I said it again, 'You'll never get away with it.'

He bent down and picked up the sniper rifle. 'It's got to be this one, I'm afraid,' he told me. 'And a body shot. I'd be happy to shoot you in the head, but one in your guts will look more like an accident, don't you think. You shouldn't take more than a minute or so to die.'

He slid the bolt to rack the next cartridge into the chamber. It's the sickliest sound on earth when you know it's for you. I lifted my Glock and pointed it at his head.

'Put the gun down, Stanwick,' I said.

This time he laughed out loud. 'Sorry, Charlie, but three fives are fifteen. Your gun's empty.'

I placed the dot on the front sight right between his eyes. The eyes of the Executioner. A definition came into my mind: *Executioner: noun, one authorised to kill on behalf of the state.* Murderers kill for gain, or because they are mad, or for a variety of other reasons. Stanwick thought he was doing society's dirty work, at least to begin with. Until the madness took complete control. Up to that point he thought that he, Mark Stanwick, was the state's executioner.

But he was wrong.

I brought the outer dots up until all three were in a line, like Orion's belt across his forehead. Stanwick's shoulders stiffened with renewed purpose and he levelled the rifle at my stomach.

The explosion sounded like two express trains colliding head-on in my skull. Stanwick's head snapped back and he kept right on going. His feet didn't move or stagger to keep him upright because there was nothing sending signals to them. There was a brief flash of a white triangle under his chin as he went over backwards and a wet thud as he hit the floor.

I lowered the Glock and saw the effigy of Elvis swaying slightly. He had a new, bigger hole through his head, surrounded by bits of brain, bone and blood that were already running down and dripping onto the concrete. I looked down at the man who wanted to kill me and noticed that even the soles of his shoes were polished. That's an arrestable offence in itself.

'Seventeen,' I said. 'I lost count. I put seventeen in.'

Chapter Thirteen

Sonia ran in a 5,000 metres track race at Birmingham the following weekend. She'd joined Oldfield Athletic Club and taken part in an inter-club league event. It was a good field, with a couple of invited competitors sharpening themselves for the Athens Olympics and others hoping for a last chance to catch the selectors' eyes. I went with her and we travelled down on the Friday. I was suspended from duty, so having time off wasn't a problem.

The wind was blustery for the race, and it caused problems for Sonia, her tall frame being knocked about by it. She finished mid-field, but was happy with her time. She said she didn't have the depth of training to do much better, but it would come. When we arrived home there was an email on my computer for her from her contact in South Africa. It said that Cape Town University was still looking for an athletics coach for their women's team, and she had to get her application in.

'What do you think?' she asked, showing me the copy she'd made.

'Like it says,' I told her. 'Get your application in.'

Dorothea Stanwick didn't need any encouragement to spill the beans on her husband. What clinched it for me was when Dave told me she admitted that Stanwick had stopped at the bus station on their way home from the Rotary spring ball to make a phone call, saying that his mobile battery was flat and refusing to use hers. That was the triple-nine telling us to go to Lapetite's address. He also, she said, had asked for his clothes to be washed that day, and they were covered in white dust, 'like plaster of Paris'.

We – well, they – found scrapbooks in his

den, containing cuttings of major cases going back over twenty years. The Midnight Strangler and Lapetite were in there, their stories bordered with highlighter pen. Somebody called William John Hardcastle had been singled out, too, but we found him alive and kicking. Dave went to see him and he remembered a caller who came to his door a few weeks earlier, but Dave didn't tell him how lucky he was. They also found cuttings from the *Gazette* about Sonia and me.

After I'd shot him I carefully laid my gun, with its one remaining bullet, on the concrete and went looking for Damian. He was curled up on the floor in the control room with a bullet through his head. I went outside and sat on the ground for several minutes, where the golfers couldn't see me, and wondered what sort of a world I was living in. When all this is over, I vowed, I'll be out of it. I rang HQ and set the wheels in motion.

Before the SOCOs and the new SIO went in I carefully explained the sequence of events. I showed them my ear, which had stopped bleeding; told them where the bullet would be; explained about the demo with the sniper rifle; told them that the bullet intended for me was already in its breech. I drove my own car back to Heckley where the doc looked at my ear and the photographer captured it for posterity. The doc stuck a plaster on it and said I'd survive. I made a statement, sitting in one of the interview rooms, and one or two of the troops popped their heads round the door to show their concern and say well done. I wasn't allowed up into my office.

It was nearly ten when I arrived home, and Sonia was eating what had been intended as our evening meal. There was a cloth on the table, the wine was breathing and the candles were burned halfway down.

'I'm sorry I'm late,' I said, standing in the doorway, turned sideways, my bloody shirt and ear away from her.

'Couldn't you find a telephone?'

'No.'

'Your dinner's ruined.'

'I'm not hungry. What's the occasion?'

'None,' she replied.

'You could have fooled me.'

'I waited for you.'

'I've been busy.'

'Too busy to phone?'

'Yes. I said I'm sorry. So why the candles? It's not your birthday.'

'I wanted it to be special. Looks like I wasted my time, doesn't it? I've sent off my application for the job in South Africa, that's all.'

'Have you?' I said, then, 'It's a great opportunity for you. It's the right thing for you to do.' We were silent for a while, until I

376

said, 'I'm off for a shower,' and turned to go upstairs. She didn't say, 'What sort of a day have you had?'

'Oh, you know,' I'd have replied. 'I only killed one man today. I pointed a gun at his head and pulled the trigger. It wasn't in the heat of the moment, like the last one. I had plenty of time to consider what I was doing. It was him or me, so I decided to blow his brains out. Now I'm suspended until some-one I don't know, who wasn't there, decides that I had no alternative and therefore am not a murderer.' That's what I would have said, if she'd asked, but she didn't ask.

And she didn't ask if I'd like to go to South Africa with her, either.

A cosh of exactly the right size was found behind a loose plank in Stanwick's shed; the bullet that killed Damian and the one that nicked my ear were matched to the Glock with Stanwick's fingerprints all over it; and his prints were on the sniper rifle, too. A young Sikh assistant in the T-Mobile phone shop in Stantown picked out Stanwick's mug shot from the album we showed him. Eventually bits of trace evidence sealed the case, but right from the beginning I was in the clear.

At one time I would have been told to stay at home until an enquiry board studied the facts, which might take two years, and reinstated me, but not now. Now they find you a job where you can't do too much damage while you wait for the clampers to free the wheels of justice. Three weeks after the shooting I was back at work.

The inspector in charge of the area's case-building unit was off sick after a suspected heart attack, so I was asked to temporarily take over. The units are a new initiative, employing civilian staff to release proper policemen from the mountain of paperwork that every incident generates. They do exactly what it says on the packet: take statements; gather all the relevant document-ation; plug any loopholes they might find and present the case to the prosecution ser-vice. Many of the staff are ex-police officers, the gender ratio is about 50:50 and the heart attack wasn't stress-induced, so I wasn't complaining.

Sonia was officially offered the job in South Africa, and spent her time shopping for tropical gear. She finished third in a 10K race in Milton Keynes in her best time since her comeback. I took her down and we made a weekend of it, visiting Whipsnade Zoo on the Saturday. Sonia had suddenly developed an interest in wild animals, particularly big cats. She flew out of Heathrow on the first day of August and I watched the giant plane climb into the sunrise until I was at risk of permanent damage to my eyes. Then it was the long drive home to Heckley.

The inquest on Stanwick ruled that he was lawfully killed. Later, Alfred Armitage, Jermaine Lapetite and poor old Doc Bones were judged to have been unlawfully killed by a person known to the court. The case was passed to the prosecution service and filed away under NFA.

Dorothea Stanwick made a brave recovery and sold her story to the *Sunday Echo*. They trumpeted it on the front page under the banner: *I Was The Executioner's Sex Slave*. It probably wasn't what she expected, but the £50,000 they paid her will have deflected much of the embarrassment. £150,000 if you believe the local rumours.

Enthused by the Olympic Games and scared by medical stories about cholesterol levels, some of the troops started jogging regularly. After a while I joined them. When the weather was good we ran through the woods and round the golf course, on the route I used to take with Sonia. Afterwards we would call in the clubhouse for a well-deserved shandy or six.

Once or twice I saw Dorothea there. She was with a local councillor whose lifestyle was disproportionate to the modest business he ran. Not many fish and chip shop owners drive round in Porsche Boxsters. I wondered whether he was attracted by Dorothea's homely good looks, or the £150,000, or the

Sex Slave bit. I hoped she wasn't heading for another calamity in her life.

Sonia had emailed me to say she arrived OK, and a few days later I received a long one from her telling me all about it. The facilities were terrific she said, and the climate wonderful. She was staying in a rented bungalow with three others near a place called Simonstown, which was handy for the beach. They trained in the evening and then sat on the stoop sipping wine as the sun went down behind Table Mountain. She didn't enlarge upon her housemates.

I told her about the inquests, about the jogging, and how following Jeff Caton up the hill wasn't as nice as chasing her. She told me that she'd been on a trip to a game park. I told her that the weather had deteriorated. And that was about it.

I didn't apply for the case building unit job and it was given to a female inspector from Huddersfield. I gave her a day of my time and moved back to Heckley nick, kicking young Caton out from behind my desk.

The following Friday evening the phone rang at home. I was looking through a seed catalogue that came in the post, with Radio Three's *Late Junction* playing softly in the background. The pictures of flowers barely registered because my mind was elsewhere, thinking about the case and the people who'd been affected by it. We see people at their worst and at their best in this job. Two by two they came to me, like the animals in the Bible story: Stanwick and Lapetite; Dave and Maggie, working their butts off to solve the case; Doc Bones and Julie Bousfield, who never hurt a fly between them; Midnight and Gazelle. I shook my head to clear it and picked up the phone. It was the duty inspector, wondering if I could do his shift for him. Was I back at work? Something had cropped up in his personal life and he needed to go away for a couple of days. The duty inspector is there to investigate any suspicious deaths there might be, overnight, anywhere in the division.

'You don't mind, do you, Charlie?' he said.

'No, not at all,' I told him. Of course I didn't mind. It's what I do.

Chapter Fourteen

News item
Western Cape Times

Cape Town, 6th December 2004
Athletics, Cape Province champion-
ships:

Miss Sonia Thornton unexpectedly stepped off the track with one lap to go while holding an unassailable lead during the Ladies' 5,000 metres final at Green Point stadium on Saturday. It is believed she suffered a recurrence of the knee injury that kept her out of the 1996 Olympic games. The race was won for the third year in succession by Miss Eunice Mboto. A spokesperson for Miss Thornton said the injury would not prevent her completing her one-year contract as coach to the UCT athletics team.

The publishers hope that this book has given you enjoyable reading. Large Print Books are especially designed to be as easy to see and hold as possible. If you wish a complete list of our books please ask at your local library or write directly to:

Magna Large Print Books
Magna House, Long Preston,
Skipton, North Yorkshire.
BD23 4ND

This Large Print Book, for people
who cannot read normal print,
is published under the auspices of

THE ULVERSCROFT FOUNDATION

... we hope you have enjoyed this book.
Please think for a moment about those
who have worse eyesight than you ...
and are unable to even read or enjoy
Large Print without great difficulty.

You can help them by sending a
donation, large or small, to:

**The Ulverscroft Foundation,
1, The Green, Bradgate Road,
Anstey, Leicestershire, LE7 7FU,
England.**
or request a copy of our brochure for
more details.

The Foundation will use all donations
to assist those people who are visually
impaired and need special attention
with medical research, diagnosis
and treatment.

Thank you very much for your help.